PEPPERMINT STICK

BOSTON BUCKS

CATHRYN FOX

COPYRIGHT

ISBN Ebook: 978-1-998943-99-9

ISBN Print:978-1-998943-98-2

JAYLYNN

S nowberry Falls, Vermont

Two weeks before Christmas:

Ho. Ho. Holy crap.

I blink once. Twice. Nope, not a figment of my hot toddy fueled imagination. That's definitely Penn Radford—NHL heartbreaker and tabloid scandal magnet—standing at the front desk of the Snowberry Inn, arguing over a room that doesn't exist.

Should I be surprised to see him? Maybe not. We both grew up here, even if he hasn't been back for the holidays in years. Maybe after getting suspended for decking the mall Santa—yes, he *actually* punched St. Nick—he's home licking his wounds.

But the real question is, why isn't he staying with his Aunt Elaine? Sure, she's a little out there (read: owns three ferrets and claims they're clairvoyant), but she's also the kind soul who raised him when his teenage mom left him on her doorstep.

How do I know all this you ask? Oh, because this is Snowberry Falls, Vermont, where everyone knows everyone's business, and if they don't, they make it up.

Penn shifts, the snow melting on his heavy leather jacket. It lets out a low squeak as he leans toward Belinda, softening his features as he dials up the charm. Classic. I watch him tune his smile, and aim it straight at Belinda. Her face flushes as her lashes lower. She's either eaten too many candy canes and is about to go into a sugar-induced coma, or is…falling for his charm.

Honestly, men like Penn think the world owes them extra whipped cream just for showing up. Cocky, smoking hot, treat me like I'm a joke…ugh, let's just say been there. Done that. Got the emotional baggage to prove it.

A huff crawls out of my throat before I can reel it in, and wouldn't you know it, his gaze snaps to mine. And damn. Those clear blue eyes lock on, and just like that, two thoughts hit me faster than a snowball to the face.

1. I could help fix his image.
2. He could help fix my career.

Okay, three thoughts. Because there's also my ex to consider. He's coming home for the holiday with his new fiancée—a well-known influencer who doesn't even need makeup to be beautiful. No, I'm not jealous. Much. Wouldn't it be awesome to show my ex that I'm not the same girl he humiliated in high school? That I grew up to be more than the bubbly head of the Winter Spirit committee? That I was going places, making something of myself?

At least for a little while I was...

Nevertheless, as a wild, glittery, slightly unhinged idea takes hold, I set my drink down, the mug landing with a quiet thunk on the table in front of the crackling fire. I rise, my heart pounding like a drumline at the Santa parade, as I smooth my flannel "Sleigh, All Day" pajama top, and square my shoulders.

Do you really think this can work, Jaylynn?

Yes, because A, he's desperate, and B, I have a plan.

A half-baked, peppermint-scented plan.

But a plan, nonetheless.

I walk toward Penn—who, and I hate to admit it, looks like a walking GQ holiday edition—as he turns his focus back in on Belinda.

"I'm sorry, there's nothing I can do for you," she tells him. "We're completely full for the holidays. We had a cancellation earlier, but it was just rebooked ten minutes ago. If only you'd been here sooner."

"You don't have, like... a floor I could sleep on? A closet? Hell, I'd take a sleigh in the parking lot as long as it doesn't meow."

"Meow?" Belinda asks as I too try to puzzle that out.

He shakes his head and sneezes into his sleeve. "It's a long story."

I hear the strain in his voice, the tiredness, and for a moment I feel sorry for him. Until I remember that horrible day I was humiliated back in high school, and he, like the rest of my graduating class, stood by and watched. Oh, and yeah, he punched a mall Santa back in Boston.

Who the heck punches Santa? A Christmas Grinch, that's who.

"You just allergic or are you afraid of cats?"

Penn turns to me, and up close, holy holly, those blue eyes could melt a snowbank. No wonder the guy has a bunny harem. "Allergic yes, and I wouldn't say afraid...more like traumatized."

I cock my head. "I sense a story."

He opens his mouth like he's about to tell me, then Belinda pipes in softly, "Is everything okay with your Aunt Elaine? I ran into her last week at the pet store and she seemed..." Belinda gives Penn a wobbly, almost sympathetic smile as she tries to come up with the right word, Finally, she settles with, "The same."

Meaning—still out of her festive little mind.

He exhales sharply, and there it is, that flicker of something unspoken. A heaviness behind the laugh. Something's going on at home, something deeper than his aunt just being her usual... unconventional self. And just like that, my heart does that annoying pinch again.

Because for all Penn's swagger and smirking charm, he's never had it easy. No real family to speak of, outside of Aunt Elaine, the 'uncles' she's hooked up with, and her merry band of feral ferrets. And no one should be alone during the holidays. Not even a guy who once stood by while I was publicly annihilated at the tree lighting.

Still. Doesn't everyone deserve to feel like they belong?

I have a few loved ones I could lend him. Temporarily. Or

maybe permanently. Uncle Jack has been a bit too touchy feely lately.

"Let's just say," he starts flatly, "Elaine turned my old bedroom into a cat sanctuary. I was there for five minutes. Got mauled, bitten, and I think…" He lowers his voice, eyes darting around as if the walls might be listening, "…I think one is possessed."

"Possessed?" Belinda chokes back a laugh, biting her lip as if she's trying to stay professional.

Penn's throat works around the word like it doesn't sit right. "I think Muffin—"

"Muffin?" I blurt, grinning. There's just something about this broad-shouldered NHL enforcer whispering about a cat named Muffin that breaks me. "Are we still talking about a cat here?"

"Yeah. The tabby." He stares at me like *I'm* the odd one, which is rich coming from a guy who thinks a rescue cat is possessed.

"Anyway," he continues, and leans in like we're trading ghost stories around the campfire, "I think it's possessed by the spirit of Aunt Elaine's late husband, Earl."

He mock-shudders, and the seriousness in his voice just makes it funnier.

"Oh?" I arch a brow. "Tell me, is Muffin wearing flannel now?"

His eyes narrow, all humor gone from those baby blues. Maybe I'm tired. Or maybe it's his scent—clean, cold air and cedar—or the way the firelight flickers across his cheekbones, but I stare back, unable to look away, even if 'crazy' clearly runs in his family.

"No. But he's been watching curling reruns. The only person I ever knew who liked curling was Earl."

"Well then, obviously, it's Earl." I nod solemnly.

Just then, Penn's head snaps toward a darkened hallway. "What was that?" he whispers.

I follow his gaze and search the hall. "I didn't see anything."

"You don't think Muffin followed me here, do you?"

"I mean, I didn't notice a flannel-wearing cat tailing you through the door."

The phone rings behind us, and Belinda turns to answer it, leaving us staring at one another.

"I told you it wasn't wearing flannel..." he mutters, shaking his head like *I'm* the one being ridiculous. Yeah, I'm the ridiculous one. He thinks a cat is possessed by his late uncle Earl. Then, his voice softens. "You remember Earl, don't you?"

I nod, my throat tightening a little. "Elaine's sixth and final husband. He came into the picture around your junior year, right?"

"Yeah. He hated me."

"I remember that." What I don't say is how I remember Penn coming to school with stress in his eyes and extra weight on his shoulders. How I knew Earl never thought the money Elaine spent on Penn's hockey had any value. It only had worth when it came in the form of a six-pack.

"So, with the cats and the ghost of Earl judging my life choices through Muffin's eyes... I can't stay there."

"Poor thing," I murmur. My tone is light, teasing. But something inside me aches a little. I spread my arms wide, gesturing to the cozy chaos of the inn, where guests in scarves and puffy coats bustle past, mugs of cocoa in hand. "And now you're homeless. During the most magical time of year." I arch a brow. "What *would* Santa say?"

He grits his teeth and eyes me carefully, like he's scanning for signs. Trying to gauge whether *the incident* made it all the way to Snowberry Falls.

Spoiler—it did.

The twitch in his jaw tells me he knows it too.

"Clearly," he mutters, "You've heard that the last Santa I saw ended up face-down on a pile of reindeer and lollipops while a crowd of traumatized kids screamed in horror. So yeah... I'm not exactly eager to hear what jolly old St. Nick has to say to me right now."

I press a hand to my chest. "Ah, yes. The punch heard 'round the North Pole. Penn Radford. AKA Radman, the madman. The Enforcer. The man, the myth, the mitts."

He cocks his head, something sparking behind his guarded expression. "Let me guess... big fan of viral scandals?"

"Not exactly." I frown and glance down, that familiar ache back in my stomach. "Been the headline of one myself."

That quiets him.

For a second, we're both just standing in the warm flicker of firelight and peppermint-scented shame. I steal a glance at him, the sting of old wounds and public meltdowns binding us in unexpected solidarity.

Maybe he had his reasons for decking Santa.

Just like I have mine—for what I'm about to do.

I tilt my head and against all reason, pride, or lingering common sense, I blurt it out. "I've got a room."

He blinks. "Great. Congratulations. Couldn't be happier for you."

"No, I mean." I point to the floor. "I have a room here. At the inn. The peppermint-themed honeymoon suite." I clear my throat. "It's got a heart-shaped hot tub. Peppermint floaties. Mints on the pillows. A terrifying elf doll in the corner that definitely watches you sleep."

He stares at me, brow furrowed. "And you're telling me this because... you want a medal or something?"

"A medal would be nice. Maybe a parade. Later, though. Tonight, I'm too tired for that, but I'm willing to share."

Something shifts in his expression. Surprise. Softness. Like no one's offered him kindness in a while and he's not sure how to take it.

"You'd do that for me?" His voice is quieter now, edged with disbelief. Like he doesn't fully trust it.

I hold up a finger. "One condition."

His gaze sharpens. "Of course, there's a catch," he mutters. "There's always a catch."

"You pretend to be my boyfriend. Just while I run the town's Christmas festival. Maybe we could go so far as to say you're my fiancé," I add with a shrug. "We'll gauge the level of desperation as we go."

His eyes narrow, suspicion giving way to curiosity. "Why?"

I hesitate. Then I say it all in one breath. "My high school humiliation, Dylan Hayes, is back in town with a sparkly ring and a gorgeous fiancée. I'll be damned if I let him think I'm still that awkward girl who wore light-up snowflake tights to the winter formal and was never going anywhere in life, or ever getting out of Snowberry Falls." I thought Dylan and I were a solid team until the mayor's daughter came along. A girl, he assumed, that would be a better fit for him going into politics. That didn't work out so well for him.

Penn blinks once. Then his lips twitch. "You wore light-up tights?"

"They were festive."

He laughs. Not mockingly. It's the surprised kind of laugh—rough, a little reluctant—like he didn't expect me to amuse him. Or catch him off guard.

"They had bulbs?"

I shake my head. Of course, he wouldn't remember anything about my light up pants. Guys like him—and like my ex—rarely notice anyone unless there's a mirror involved. He was probably too busy admiring his reflection in a Christmas bulb to clock my illuminated fashion choices.

"Focus," I snap.

He smirks. "So let me get this straight. You're offering me a place to sleep, in a bed shaped like a candy cane, probably, if I pretend to date you? Like we're characters in a bad holiday rom-com?"

"Technically, it's shaped like a sleigh," I correct, lifting my chin. "But yes. That's the deal."

"Do I get a script, or is this improv?"

"Oh, it's improv." I smile sweetly. "Just follow my lead. Smile a lot. And maybe the only thing you 'deck' over the next two weeks is the halls."

He gives a low chuckle. "I... I guess I can do that."

"No guessing, Penn. Besides, this isn't just about me." I poke his chest for emphasis—big mistake. He's solid and warm and right there, for a second, I completely forget what this conversation is about.

His eyes flick down to where my finger lingers. "Not just about you?" he repeats, brow raised, waiting for me to enlighten him.

I pull my hand back like I've touched a live wire. "Right. It's not just about me. I'm helping you too."

"Oh, sure." He nods, playing along. "Helping me get a good night's sleep in a room without a possessed cat, but a terrifying elf doll. Very generous of you."

"No," I explain, voice firmer. "I'm helping you clean up your image."

That gets his attention. His eyes sharpen, light up in that way people's eyes do when they see something they didn't expect. "You think you can do that?"

"You want to stay on the Bucks, don't you? Secure your position. I mean, it wasn't all that long ago that you got called up, right?"

He rubs a hand across his face, suddenly looking every bit the exhausted man behind the jersey. "Right. I almost forgot your dad was my AHL coach."

"Okay, so a fiancée will look good on you. Make you seem stable."

"I'm stable," he defends and I arch a brow that has Santa written all over it. "I mean, sort of."

"We're doing this, then?"

"I...guess. So, it's our secret. We tell no one it's fake?"

"No one."

"I should probably tell Elaine. She's trustworthy. I just don't want her getting excited, you know." A pained look comes over him. "It's not like anyone really takes anything she says seriously, anyway."

That sadness on his face hurts my soul. He used to get teased terribly about his crazy aunt, until he grew three sizes in two months. The bullying stopped then and there.

"Okay," I agree and extend my hand like we're sealing a dubious business deal. "Welcome to probably the worst idea I've had since tequila on New Year's, 2019."

He slides his palm against mine, rough and warm. "Are you sure it wasn't the turkey disaster of 2024?"

"Oh my god," I practically shriek. "You know about that?"

The second that question is out of my mouth, I cringe. Of course, he knows about it. Everyone knows. It was on every major news network, followed by a week of memes, GIFs, and late-night comedy segments titled #GobbleGate.

"Like you said," he answers softly, "You too know a little something about going viral." He pauses, voice dipping lower. "I only saw the highlight clips. What exactly happened, and are you...okay?" His tone is so sincere, so unexpectedly gentle, it disarms me. There's no mockery in his eyes, no smugness. Just quiet understanding.

I exhale slowly, my shoulders dropping. "I used to work at a boutique PR firm in Boston. Brightside Creative. We did big campaigns. I was on the rise—smart, ambitious, and trusted with a big holiday campaign for a high-profile client. A gourmet grocery chain launching their new farm-to-table product line. I wore actual heels to work."

He smirks and glances down. "I like your reindeer slippers."

I lift one foot. "I must say, I am rocking them. But seriously, the Thanksgiving event. A stunt, really. I pitched a 'celebrity turkey trot'. Influencers racing in turkey costumes to raise awareness for a gourmet grocery brand's holiday line. It was supposed to be festive. Wholesome. Shareable."

Penn raises an eyebrow. "Let me guess. One of the turkeys turned on the others."

I groan. "Worse. One tripped on a fake wishbone centerpiece and crashed into a cranberry sauce display. Took out a ring light, two cameras, and an elderly blogger named Spicy-Granny74. The video hit two million views in an hour. #TurkeyTrotFail. #GobbleGate. I was on BuzzFeed. Buzz-Feed, Penn."

Penn's lips twitch. "Was SpicyGranny74 okay?"

"She started her own podcast, so yeah she's the winner here. As for me, the grocery chain pulled their campaign, Bright-side fired me, and no one in Boston PR will touch me with a ten-foot selfie stick." I try to laugh it off, but my voice cracks on the last word.

Penn squares his shoulders. "And this festival gig you got here is your redemption arc?"

"It's my Hail Mary. If I don't pull this off, I'm done. Not just in PR. In, like...life."

"Banished from the real world," he murmurs quietly. The words sting, but not because they're cruel. Because they're true. For both of us. I nod, slowly.

"So yeah, and I guess #Turkey Gate or #GobbleGate or whatever you want to call it probably was my biggest mistake."

That... and believing my ex and I were going to take on the world together. He had his sights set on law school, mayor and then governor. I had mine on a PR degree and plans to run his campaign, craft the image, shape the story. We were going to be a power couple—glossy and invincible.

Until I—and every local news crew in Snowberry Falls—caught him with his tongue down the mayor's daughter's throat behind the gingerbread float during the tree lighting ceremony.

God, I was such a fool.

When I don't answer right away, still lost in the murky tide of what-ifs and used-to-bes, his hand brushes mine. Light, almost hesitant.

"I'm sorry, Jaylynn," he says softly.

I swallow the lump rising in my throat. "If I can pull off the Christmas festival without a hitch, maybe a real firm will look at me again. Maybe the world will stop seeing me as the girl who crashed a parade and lost everything in front of a news van."

He nods, quiet for a beat. Then, "So... you're seriously okay sharing a bed with a guy who's practically a stranger?"

I arch a brow. "Not really. But I trust you're smart enough not to try anything stupid."

He lifts a hand in mock surrender. "I'm just trying to survive the cat-ocalypse. I don't have the energy to seduce anyone tonight."

I almost laugh. "Cat-ocalypse, huh? That's child's play compared to the room I'm about to show you."

He grabs his bag with mild suspicion. "Should I be afraid?"

"Yes," I say, and I mean it. "Deeply."

We make our way down the hall, passing garland-draped banisters and twinkling lights. I wave to Belinda at the front desk, who gives me a long, curious look.

"Why are you staying at the inn anyway?" he asks. "Isn't your house just down the hill?"

I sigh. "It's overrun with relatives. Kids. And..." I lower my voice. "God forbid... cats."

As if summoned by the word itself, Penn sneezes violently. I stifle a laugh as he casts a suspicious glance behind him, like he half-expects to see Muffin creeping out of a shadow in flannel pajamas.

"I'm kidding. There are no cats. But the biggest reason is I'm in charge of the festival and I want to be close to the action, so I can, you know, make sure nothing explodes." That earns me a tiny grin.

Finally, we reach the end of the hallway. From my back pocket, I pull out the oversized peppermint-striped key and slide it into the lock. "You ready?" I ask.

"It can't be worse than the cat sanctuary," he mutters.

"Oh, I don't know about that." I push the door open and step aside, watching his reaction as he walks into the full force of peppermint madness.

His eyes go wide. He actually stumbles back a step. "Ho...ho...holy... shit."

"Exactly," I say, lips twitching.

We both take in the scene—candy-cane-striped wallpaper, red and white heart-shaped pillows, a sleigh bed draped in peppermint swirl sheets, a heart-shaped hot tub, with marshmallow bath bombs, and peppermint floaties. And yes, in the corner, an elf doll with eyes that seem to follow you. I shiver.

"This," Penn says slowly, "This...this is peppermint-ageddon."

I bite my lip. "Nightmare Before Christmas has nothing on us."

2

PENN

"Are you okay?" Jaylynn asks, her voice tinged with concern, and maybe amusement. I try to drag my eyes away from the candy-cane stripes coating every square inch of the room, but it's like a train wreck in gingerbread form. I *want* to look away. Really. I do. I just... can't.

"It's not *that* bad, is it?" she asks, eyes wide and hopeful.

I glance at the elf wallpaper border. The blinking string lights wrapped around the mirror. The peppermint-stick sleigh bed.

She huffs out a laugh. "What am I even saying? Of course, it's that bad."

"No, it's good," I say quickly, forcing a smile as I shake off the mild Christmas-induced panic attack. "It's great. Festive. Cozy. Better than sleeping outside... or sharing a room with that herd of cats."

"Clowder," she murmurs.

"What?"

"A gathering of cats is called a is called a clowder of cats." I stare at her and she shakes her head. "Never mind." She grins and spins a slow circle in the middle of the room, arms out like a deranged holiday cruise director. "Welcome to the Peppermint Palace."

I chuckle, unzipping my coat as I look around again. "They really go all out for Christmas here, huh?"

"Bad news," she says with a wink. "This room looks like this year-round."

I freeze mid-sleeve. "But why?"

"Some people are Christmas obsessed."

"You're serious, aren't you?"

She pats a pillow shaped like a snowman's head. "I wish that wasn't true."

I groan. "Jaxon's family still owns this place, right?"

"Yep."

Jaxon Sheffield. Small-town hockey royalty and now my teammate. He grew up right here in Snowberry Falls. He was older than me, so we never really ran in the same circles, but I know he's a solid guy. Talented player. Always polite, even when I was just the new kid sweating through rookie camp.

I haven't really bonded with the team much since getting called up, and I'm not sure how they feel about me after the mall incident. One rogue Santa stunt and now my position is on thin ice. Literally.

"This town probably still thinks Buddy the Elf was a documentary," I mumble.

Jaylynn smirks. "Heads up. Jaxon gets back tomorrow. His room is right across the hall."

I shift my duffel onto the peppermint-striped bench and try not to notice the way Jaylynn's flannel pajama pants hug her curves as she fluffs the snowflake pillows. But the twitch in my groin says otherwise. Apparently, *he* didn't get the memo about professionalism and boundaries.

Down, buddy. Now is so not the time.

It's not that I haven't noticed her before. Believe me, you'd have to be blind not to. But back in high school, she was untouchable. Gorgeous. Smart. Off-limits in every way. Dating Dylan since freshman year, practically wearing his class ring *and* his last name. Not to mention, her dad was my coach. Which meant she might as well have worn a neon sign that read—DO NOT TOUCH UNLESS YOU WANT TO SKATE SUICIDES UNTIL YOU DIE.

But her dad isn't your coach anymore, dude.

Still. Doesn't matter.

Because this? This whole fake-engagement-for-the-sake-of-PR thing? It's about cleaning up my image, not complicating it with off-limit girls in flannel pajamas who unknowingly make my life harder—*in every way*—every time she bends over.

I snap my gaze toward the ceiling, pretending to admire the giant glittering wreath hanging from the light fixture.

It's fine. Totally fine. All good.

Just one bed. One plan. One professional, platonic arrangement.

Totally chill.

And really, maybe she's playing this game with me to make her ex jealous because she might want him back. I've seen plenty of that kind of drama and manipulation in the hockey world.

My gaze trails back to Jaylynn, who just bent to pick up a peppermint-shaped pillow. I peel off my coat, suddenly boiling, even though the room is barely heated.

Yeah. Chill.

Right.

Except definitely *not*, if she keeps bending over like that.

Fuck me.

I move my duffel bag to the bed, and when Jaylynn moves toward me, a shrill, *BZZZZZ* screams from above.

"Holy—" I clutch my chest like I've just seen my playoff hopes flash before my eyes. "Is that a fire alarm?"

Jaylynn nearly doubles over laughing. "Nope," she says, pointing upward like it's the most normal thing in the world. "That would be the mistletoe alarm."

I blink. "I'm sorry, the what now?"

"No idea how it works," she says with a shrug, stepping back from me. The moment she moves, the alarm cuts out with an abrupt *click*. She glances up, then down at the space between us. "Maybe it's a pressure sensor or something? Like if we get close, the alarm is an indication that we should, you know...kiss."

"Wow." I stare up at the offending sprig of mistletoe dangling from a ribbon like it's mocking me. "That's not festive. That's disturbing."

She smirks. "Welcome to the peppermint honeymoon suite and I really do hope it's a weight thing that sets that off and no one from the lobby is watching."

I chuckle, even as my pulse tries to catch up from the surprise buzzer. "This whole room is a booby trap. Next thing you know, Cupid's going to pop out of the mini fridge."

She laughs, then trails off, her gaze dropping to my groin area. "Though, I mean... This is the honeymoon suite and that alarm is, well, let's just say it's more likely to trigger a heart attack than a rise..."

She pauses, cheeks suddenly blooming a soft, rosy pink, and her hair tumbles forward as she ducks her head.

"More than what?" I ask, casually, but my voice comes out a little too low. A little too interested.

Abort mission. Shut it down, man. No time for jokes.

Her head snaps up, brown eyes sharp. "You *know* what I mean."

I lift a brow. "Can't say I do."

Her glare says I'm about three seconds from getting smacked with a festive pillow.

"A rise in..." She pauses and huffs out, "Let's just say *you* have one, and *I* don't."

I stare at her, wanting to push this just a little bit. I don't know why. Maybe it's because she looks so damn cute when her cheeks flush. "A gallbladder? You think that is causing a rise in gallbladder attacks? I remember when you had to have yours out in high school.”

She lets out the most dramatic sigh known to mankind.

“Yes, Penn,” she says, tone pure sarcasm. “Exactly. That mistletoe alarm is more likely to cause a rise in gallbladder attacks than anything else. Nailed it.”

I laugh, full on now, and she rolls her eyes so hard I’m surprised she doesn’t pull something.

She points at the bed. “Anyway. Which side do you want?”

I eye the mountain of heart-shaped pillows with suspicion. “Whichever you don’t. This is your room, your rules.”

She flops backward onto the mattress. “I usually sleep in the middle. Starfish style. Limbs everywhere.” She throws her arms and legs out dramatically, kicking up a few peppermint pillows in the process. Unfortunately, physics decides to get involved, and the motion makes her breasts bounce beneath her flannel top.

Goddammit, she’s about to cause a gallbladder attack. I clear my throat and focus intensely on the wreath hanging over the bed as I try to think of an intelligent response. “Starfish. Right. Limbs.”

Brilliant. Shakespeare over here.

“So uh, you take the middle then.”

A peppermint pillow smacks me square in the chest. “I’m *joking*, enforcer,” she says, sitting up. “Relax. You can have the side farthest from the creepy elf. I’m generous like that.”

We both glance toward the corner of the room, where the peppermint suite's unofficial mascot sits perched like a holiday demon. A three-foot felt elf, with googly eyes, a smirk like it knows all your secrets, and the unsettling energy of something that's definitely witnessed crimes—or was responsible for them.

I point. "Okay, no. Nope. That thing *moved*, Jaylynn. I swear to God, it *moved*."

She just plants a hand on her hip like she fully expected this. "Yeah, he does that sometimes. I think it's the festive energy."

"Festive energy?" I repeat, staring it down. "That elf is *possessed*. We're going to need an exorcist."

She shrugs and pulls back the covers like we're not sharing a room straight out of a twisted gingerbread-themed horror movie. "He only moves when provoked."

"That is *not* comforting." I unzip my duffel bag warily, half expecting the elf to blink. "So, uh... what's the sleepwear situation here?"

She tugs at the hem of her flannel pajama top and climbs under the covers, nestling into a stack of peppermint pillows like this is completely normal behavior. "Practical and adorable. 'Sleigh, Girl, Sleigh.' I'm a whole Christmas vibe."

I can't stop myself. "Does it sparkle when the lights go out?"

She glares at me like I just insulted Santa—or decked him again. "Funny."

I do a full scan of her body. Strictly for analysis and not because I'm wondering what's under all that flannel.

Okay, *maybe* a little because of that. "You won't overheat in those?"

She narrows her eyes. "Why? What exactly are you planning to wear?"

"I'm a hot sleeper." I pause. "I usually sleep... uh, nude."

She recoils, her face twisting like she'd just eaten something offensive. "Are you serious?"

Wow. Okay. That reaction stings a little. It's not like I'm some Quasimodo-looking troll. Sure, I'm not Mr. Yearbook Poster Boy like her ex, but I've got abs. Shoulders. A jawline. I'm not exactly unfortunate looking.

Simply not her type, man.

Good. She's not mine either.

...Much.

"Yes, I'm serious. But for your comfort and safety, I have these." I hold up a soft, well-worn T-shirt and a pair of sweatpants. "These work?"

"Works for me," she says with a shrug, but I don't miss the flicker of something behind her eyes.

God, these are going to cook me alive. "No promises if I strip them off in my sleep."

She gives me the driest look known to man. "Charming."

I glance around. "Is there a thermostat in here? Maybe I can cool it down a little so I don't melt into a puddle."

"You're not Frosty the Snowman." She wraps her arms around herself. "Besides, I wouldn't do that if I were you."

"Why not?"

She points at the elf, then gestures vaguely to the other side of the room. "Because the last time I cranked the heat up, I woke up and he was sitting over there. Watching me."

I pause. "Wait—you're saying the elf *moved* because you adjusted the thermostat?"

She nods slowly, deadly serious. "I think it pissed him off. He likes a very specific climate."

Okay, she *has* to be joking. Right?

...Right?

I look back at the elf. His eyes are still locked in like he's trying to decide which of my limbs to gnaw off first.

"If that thing moves tonight, I'm grabbing my bag and getting the hell out."

"To where?" she says, pulling the blanket up to her chin with an infuriating smirk. "You've got nowhere to go, Radman. You're stuck here." She wiggles her toes under the comforter. "Just like me."

I glance at the closet, then back at the elf, still sitting there like it's seconds from pouncing. "Okay, no. That thing is not staying out here with us. Absolutely not." Before Jaylynn can object, I march across the room, snatch up the creepy little menace, and open the closet door. "Time for bed, Santa's minion." I drop it inside, shut the door, and give the knob a twist for good measure. When I turn back to the bed, Jaylynn's staring at me like I just triggered a curse.

Her mouth hangs open slightly, eyes huge. She's clutching the blankets like she's in a horror movie, pulling them all the way up to her neck.

"What?" I ask.

She gives a slow, ominous shake of her head. "You shouldn't have done that, Radman," she whispers, voice full of doom.

My stomach dips. "Shit. He's actually possessed, isn't he?"

She doesn't answer. Just grabs a mint off the nightstand and holds it out like a priest brandishing a crucifix. "You have to put this under your pillow. *Now.*"

I stare at it. "There's... mint protocol?"

"Uh-huh." She nods, dead serious. "You mess with the elf, you sleep with the mint. It's the rule."

I snort a laugh, but my fingers still close around the wrapped candy. "This is absolutely ridiculous."

She levels me with a look. "I put one under my pillow the night he moved. I think it's the only reason I survived."

My laugh dies halfway out of my throat. I glance at the closet. Then slide the mint under my pillow. *Just in case.* "It won't melt?" I ask.

"Not in this freezer of a room." She flops back and grins smugly. "Honestly, I thought you hockey guys loved weird superstitions."

"Some do," I say, noncommittal.

But the truth settles heavier in my chest than I'd like. I used to have a whole routine. Gummy bears—red only. Right skate first. Same song before every game. Didn't matter if it worked, it felt like control. Back when I played for the Providence Grizzlies, I did everything by the book—everything I was told. I stayed disciplined, stayed physical, played rough. Waited for my shot.

And watched other guys get the call-up.

Over. And over.

Eventually, I stopped believing the rituals mattered. Or maybe I just stopped letting myself hope.

It wasn't until Jaylynn's dad—Coach Quinn—called me into his office one day to tell me I was getting a shot with the Bucks. I still remember that day. Jaylynn had been there, all smiles and wide eyes. She looked proud of me. Like it actually meant something.

The Bucks wanted me as their enforcer. So, that's what I do. It's what the fans want. What the team expects. Better to stay in that role than try something more and fail in front of everyone.

Jaylynn nudges me out of the thought spiral. "Wait a second," she says, pointing. "You used to eat red gummy bears before every game. I saw you do it back in high school. And even when you were playing for the Grizzlies. You always had that same little pouch."

I blink, caught off guard that she remembers. "Yeah, well... I grew out of it."

She tilts her head like she doesn't believe me, but I don't give her time to ask more.

"Is it okay if I take a shower?" I nod toward the closed bathroom door.

"Sure," she says casually, then adds, "As long as you're not afraid of the peppermint shower hose."

I blink. "Jesus Christ."

She just smirks. "May your water pressure be merry and bright."

I grab my bag and head for the bathroom. The second I step inside, I immediately regret it. My eyes start to water as a riot of red and green assaults my retinas. Candy cane stripes. Snowflake decals. A reindeer shower curtain staring at me like it knows I locked its friend in the closet. Honestly, it's like someone let Buddy the Elf loose with a glue gun and zero adult supervision.

I turn on the water, strip out of my clothes, and crawl under the spray, enjoying the warmth soaking through my skin. I stay there longer than necessary. Letting the water hit me like it could somehow rinse away the last few weeks. The headlines. The commentary. The hit. *The Santa incident.*

God, I decked Santa.

And yeah, I'd do it again. The guy was a drunk mall stand-in who told a five-year-old there was no such thing as magic, and pulled his beard down to show her even Santa was fake. Fucking asshole deserved it.

But now I'm suspended. Reputational roadkill. The guy who took down St. Nick in front of a crowd and a hundred camera phones.

And yet... that punch landed me here. In this ridiculous peppermint nightmare. With Jaylynn.

Jaylynn Quinn. *My girlfriend.* Fake, sure, but still. Kind of wild.

I snort out a laugh and lean my head against the tile. I have no idea if we can actually pull this off. But if pretending to date her gets me a warm bed, a hot shower, and maybe—maybe—a clean image that secures my spot on the Bucks, then I'll play the part.

Even if I don't plan to touch her. Unless, of course, she asks me to.

Fuck.

But truth is, I want to see her get back on her feet too. Jaylynn's always been kind—even in high school, when kindness wasn't exactly trending. We didn't run in the same circles, but she never treated me like I didn't belong. And her dad is the reason I got called up—eventually.

He didn't move me up when I thought I was ready. Maybe he didn't think I had NHL-level value. Or maybe he just knew what the league *really* wanted from me. But he always treated me with respect. That counted for something.

I shut off the water, towel off, and pull on my T-shirt and sweats. Quietly, I crack the door open, not wanting to wake Jaylynn if she's asleep.

The room's dark now, lit only by moonlight slanting through the frosted window. The elf closet remains mercifully closed. I pad across the room and pull back the blanket—

"What the—"

I leap back like I've been electrocuted, nearly knocking over the bedside lamp. My heart slams into my ribs as I catch a flash of red staring up at me from the sheets.

It's the elf.

Lying. In. The. Bed.

I suck in a breath, one hand pressed to my chest. "Oh, hell no—"

Then I hear it. A snort.

Jaylynn.

She's trembling under the covers, trying—and failing—to stifle her laughter. Her whole body shakes as a giggle bubbles up and finally breaks free.

"You should've seen your face," she wheezes.

I stare at the elf, now curled under the blanket like it's ready for a bedtime story, then look back at her, deadpan.

"I miss the cats."

3

___

JAYLYNN

___

When I feel Penn stir beside me, I roll onto my side, rest my cheek on my hand, and chirp, *"Good morning, lover,"* in a sing-song voice so high-pitched it could shatter glass—or at least any illusion of me being cool. Even I wince.

Penn groans and flops onto his back, cracking one eye open like he's halfway convinced he's in a dream, or a very weird hostage situation. The second eye joins the party. He narrows them at me, suspicious, like I've just licked his toothbrush or declared myself Queen of Peppermintville. His gaze drifts over my face slowly, methodically, like he's trying to solve a puzzle.

"Lover?" he murmurs and scrubs a hand through his messy hair, voice rough with sleep when he adds, "Did we...?"

I snort so hard I nearly give myself a headache. "Oh, hell no." I throw an arm over my eyes, mostly to hide the fact that I had, in fact, fallen asleep thinking about him. Specifically, how big he is, how warm he is, how not-terrible it would've been to curl up against that wall of muscle like a human-sized teddy bear. But I can't let him know that. I've got pride. Dignity. Standards. Also, I'm not about to become another notch in Penn Radford's bedpost, or, more accurately, another bunny in his harem.

"Jeez," he says, feigning offense. "Why don't you tell me what you really think?" He's still smoothing back his hair, which, annoyingly, looks good even in bedhead form. And those biceps? Rude. Honestly rude.

"I thought I just did," I mutter, looking anywhere but his arms. Or his eyes. Or his mouth.

He arches an eyebrow. "Then why did you call me lover?"

"Just trying it out," I say, casual as a cucumber in a gin and tonic. "Seeing how it sounded on my tongue."

"And?"

I pretend to ponder, tapping my chin. "It was okay. I think we're going to be able to fool everyone."

"Great." He rolls toward me, and the bed dips beneath his weight. Suddenly I'm sliding toward him, our bodies colliding. His arm shoots out instinctively and wraps around me, catching me against his side like we've done this a hundred times before. And I freeze.

Like full-body stiff board freeze.

"Relax," he mutters, his breath tickling my ear. "I know I'm repulsive to you, Jaylynn, but if you flinch every time I touch you, we're going to blow our cover."

Blow.

Oh no. Nope. We're not going there. I do not have the maturity of a twelve-year-old boy. Much.

I clear my throat and force myself to lean into it. Act natural. That's what lovers do, right? Touch and…exist comfortably in shared beds.

"I think we're going to have to work on that if we want to pull this off," he mumbles.

"What are you suggesting?" I ask, careful to keep my tone level. Or as level as it can be when I'm being spooned by the human equivalent of a hockey-playing Greek god.

He smiles at me. Or wait, is that a smirk? Why is he smirking like he knows something I don't?

"I know this is platonic, and I want it that way," he says, all calm and rational. His indifference shouldn't stab me in the heart, but suddenly I'm wondering why I'm so easily overlooked by a guy with a reputation for having *a* type. Which is all types. It shouldn't sting. I don't even want him. Not really. Not outside this fake-fiancé thing we've got going on. So why does my ego feel like it just got dunked in the snow?

Ridiculous.

"Good. I want it that way too," I say, lifting my chin forcefully. Maybe too forcefully, because now he's giving me that look. The one that says, *I know a lie when I hear one.*

"I think we need to practice," he says slowly, like he's testing the waters.

I narrow my eyes. "Practice what?"

His smirk widens. "Being…touchy."

My voice jumps an octave. "Touchy?"

"Yeah. You know. PDA. Public hand-holding. Snuggling. Pretending we can't keep our hands off each other. That kind of thing."

My brain short-circuits. "Are you suggesting we run drills? Like... fake kissing warm-ups? Do I need a helmet?"

He laughs. "I was going to start with something simple," he says, totally unfazed. "Can I put my hand on your arm?"

I blink. "You're asking if you can touch my arm?"

He shrugs. "Consent is sexy."

Damn him. He's right.

I glance down at my arm, then back at him. "Fine. You may... touch my arm."

He reaches over and lays his hand gently against my forearm. It's warm. Firm. Weirdly intimate for something so tame.

We stare at each other. "Well?" I ask, voice a bit breathless. "Are we convincing?"

He quirks a brow. "I don't know. I think we need more data."

"Oh God."

"Purely scientific," he adds.

I think he's enjoying this. I should be terrified. And maybe, just maybe, not so excited.

"I suppose that's not the worst idea," I say slowly.

"No." Penn grins lazy. "And we've already established our worst ideas now, haven't we?"

Oh, we *have*.

Unfortunately, my brain decides to show me a fast-forward highlight reel of said terrible ideas. Turkey Gate, humiliating PR disasters, and my ex with his tongue down some girl's throat at the Snowberry Falls Christmas lighting. So yeah. Not exactly the playlist I want running in my head while lying in bed next to my fake fiancé with the body of a Norse god and a grin that should be illegal in all holiday zones.

"Can I touch you somewhere a little more intimate?"

"As long as it's not one of the bases."

That makes him chuckle. "Baseball...cute." His hand moves slowly—*deliberately*—to my hip, which is exposed because my shirt has risen, and my pants have slipped. The second his skin meets mine, a full-body shiver rolls through me and goosebumps explode across my skin like popcorn in a hot pan.

"You cold?" he asks, brow raised, because of course he notices everything. Like a sexy human lie detector with bedhead.

"Yes," I lie. "This room is freezing."

Girl. No. You're toast. And not the dry, whole-wheat kind.

He starts rubbing his hand up and down my side to create friction, as if I'm not already combusting from the inside out. I swear, there's a needy little pressure point low in my belly that's about to start applauding him. Wildly. With jazz hands.

"Warm?" he asks, all innocent like.

Oh, if he only knew.

"Yes," I squeak, voice tight and two octaves higher than usual.

Penn chuckles. "So, you're not about to bolt to the bathroom and puke up a peppermint stick from the horror of me touching you?"

I roll my eyes. "It's still early. There's plenty of time for post-traumatic peppermint shock."

He smirks. "How about you touch me now?"

And *there* it is.

I try to act casual. Like this is no big deal. Like I'm not internally combusting at the mere idea of touching him. "I suppose I should," I concede, and he tugs the blankets down a little to give me access.

I reach out—hesitantly—and lay my hand flat on his chest. Which is...bare.

Bare chest.

Bare.

Chest.

Skin.

Heat.

Muscles that were clearly forged in the gym or by Thor himself.

"Where's your shirt?" I croak out, like my vocal cords have gone on strike.

He blinks sleepily. "Shit. Must've ditched it in my sleep."

Casual. Chill. Just another night of spontaneous shirt-shedding. And then—*dear baby elves*—he lifts the blankets, and I get a glimpse of a whole lot of nothing.

As in...nothing underneath.

Like…pant-less. Commando. Stark freaking *North Pole* naked.

"Uh—" I squeak, and he shifts slightly. His abs ripple under my palm like a well-oiled snow plow. My brain blue-screens. My hand is still on him. Still touching actual, real-life, naked Penn Radford.

And I don't hate it.

"It's not looking good, Jay," he says, voice low, almost teasing.

Yeah, well, I'd like to be the judge of that.

Wait, what the hell am I saying? I need to get away from this man. Immediately. Before I do something extremely un-platonic and end up on his harem list.

I try to roll away, but gravity, and Penn's stupidly strong, stupidly shirtless body, has other plans. The bed dips under his weight and sucks me back in. I huff. I grunt. It's not graceful. Meanwhile, he's under the blankets, rummaging around like one of his aunt's ferrets trying to find a snack.

"Found them," he says, voice muffled.

A moment later, his head pops out from the blankets. He twists and contorts himself into some kind of yoga-laced gymnastics move. A final kick sends the covers flying, and he sits up triumphantly.

"Decent."

Well, decent-adjacent.

"Good," I mutter, grabbing my robe and marching toward the hot tub. But then his voice floats after me, laced with suspicion and entirely too much amusement.

"Wait…" he calls. "You didn't take them off me in the middle of the night and do unspeakable things to me while I slept, did you?"

I spin around, one eyebrow raised. "Oh please. If I was going to do unspeakable things, you'd *know*."

Wait, what?

His slow, wolfish grin spreads, and I realize too late what I've just said.

"Noted," he says, and settles back against the pillows with a satisfied smirk.

This man is going to be the death of me. And I'm not entirely sure I mind.

"But hey listen. I can only speak for myself. What he did is between him and Santa." I nod toward the corner, where the elf sits staring at Penn. Penn squints in the direction I'm pointing, and immediately startles.

"How the fuck did he get out of the closet?"

I press my lips together to stifle a laugh. "Maybe you didn't shut the door tight enough after you stuffed him in there the second time."

He narrows his eyes at me. "Did you—" He stops himself, shakes his head like he's afraid of the answer. "Never mind. I don't want to talk about that thing anymore."

"Wise choice." I smirk and move toward the hot tub. Lifting the cover, I dip my fingers in and sigh. "Ohhh, that's so nice."

Penn's watching me now with the same intensity he probably reserves for breakaways and playoff games. "You getting in?" he asks.

"I didn't think to bring a bathing suit," I say, wiggling my fingers in the water. "Besides, I've got a town council meeting in a bit. Parade stuff. Mr. Tingley's got his knickers in a festive twist."

"Over what?"

"He doesn't want us stapling antlers onto the deer."

Penn's jaw drops. "You're kidding me?"

"Nope." I straighten up, trying to look serious. "He's a real pain in the candy cane sometimes."

"Jaylynn..." He points an accusatory finger at me. "You're seriously not stapling antlers to live deer, are you?"

I grin. "No. You're kind of gullible, you know that?"

He groans. "That's actually one of the *nicer* things people have called me lately."

That... makes my heart squeeze in a way I wasn't expecting. I tilt my head. "What's on your agenda today?"

He shrugs, stretching like he has all the time in the world—and a torso that should be framed in an art gallery. "Not much. I want to go see Elaine, but I'll probably have to stop by the pharmacy first. Stock up on allergy meds."

I chuckle. "You should come to the council meeting. Volunteer work will look good on you."

I'd look good on you.

Whoa. Okay, brain. Dial it back. Not an immature twelve-year-old boy, remember?

He raises an eyebrow. "I could do that. What time?"

"Just after lunch."

"Perfect." He adjusts his position and leans against the head-board, arms crossed, looking every bit like the sexy distraction I absolutely do not need right now. "What exactly goes on at these meetings? You're not going to rope me into playing Santa, are you?"

"I'm surprised you don't want to."

"Why would I want to play Santa?"

I don't bother saying I know his type all too well. Brute. Attention seeker.

"Did you think I'd want to punch myself in the face or something?"

I chuckle. "The honor of playing Santa goes to douchebag deluxe, Dylan Hayes."

His expression hardens. "Dylan Hayes... as in Mayor Dylan Hayes. Your ex?"

"The one and only." Dylan was never nice to Penn. He liked to make fun of the guy on the outskirts of town. But Penn always kept to himself, focusing on school and hockey, and not social events, so I wasn't even sure he knew Dylan and I were a thing in high school. Apparently, he did.

"Now I'm not sure if I can keep my promise to only deck the halls," he murmurs and cracks his knuckles.

"Penn," I warn, even though the visual of him taking Dylan down a notch is rather appealing.

"Fine." Penn's eyes narrow, the hard as nails enforcer coming out in him. But nothing about this man scares me.

"Unfortunately for me, I'm playing Mrs. Claus and I have to be on the float with him." I mock shiver. "It's probably going to take extreme discipline not to push him off. I'll have to keep reminding myself we're there for the kids."

"Why isn't Mayor Banks, Snowberry's actual mayor, playing Santa."

I snort out a laugh. "Cause he's eighty-six, Penn."

"Right, okay, will Dylan be at the meeting?"

"Yup."

A slow smile spreads across his face, but there's something steely behind it—like he's gearing up for a faceoff. "Then I'm definitely going to be there." There's a sharpness in his tone that tells me this isn't just about volunteer work. Not anymore. While he might not have stepped in back when Dylan publicly humiliated me at the Christmas lighting ceremony, it looks like he's finally ready to take a stand.

And this time, he's standing beside *me*.

I find that oddly endearing.

"Just no hitting," I reinforce.

"Right. Will his fiancée be there, too?" Penn asks, and I swear I can hear the distaste already curling in his voice.

"Oh, Peppermint Barbie goes wherever he goes," I reply sweetly. No, I'm not going to admit I've checked her socials a time or two or a thousand. I don't do it because I want to know what Dylan is up to. As an influencer, she's quite charming and good at what she does.

Penn throws his head back and laughs—a real, full-bodied laugh that echoes off the walls as he repeats, "Peppermint Barbie." His laugh bubbles up in my chest and pulls a smile from me before I can stop it. Okay... maybe this fake relationship thing is going to be more fun than I thought. Dangerous for my sanity, maybe. But fun.

"Sloane's her real name."

"Of course, it is," he responds.

"Her handle is @dreamgirl."

He scoffs. "Probably a nightmare."

I grin at him. "Transferred animosity, I like it."

He gives me a playful wink that sends shivers down my spine. "I am always going to side with the girl who let me in her bed."

"Maybe I can talk her into playing Mrs. Claus. That'd be great for her socials. Unless you actually do play Santa, and then I won't have to be near Dylan."

"Nope, sorry. Not a gig I want."

A little surprised by that—not that I ever thought Dylan would give it up—because it would be really good for his image, I pull the hot tub cover closed with a satisfying thud, then cross to the window. I tug back the striped peppermint curtains and blink in surprise.

"It's snowing." Tiny flakes drift lazily past the glass, soft and sparkly, like powdered sugar falling from the sky. I hug myself, warmed by the sight, and maybe a little by the company.

Behind me, the bed creaks. I glance over my shoulder. Barefoot, half-naked, and all six-foot-something of sinful temptation, pads across the room and comes to a stop directly behind me. The heat coming off his body blankets me. Then he leans over me, just enough that I feel the warmth of his breath at the shell of my ear.

"Pretty," he murmurs, his voice so low and velvety I nearly melt. "Maybe we can go skiing later." He moves back, leaving cold where there was heat.

"That could be fun," I say, hoping I sound casual and not like my heart is suddenly doing triple axels. "We'll see if there's time. These meetings can drag on."

"There's always tomorrow."

"Tomorrow night I have a big family dinner, and when I say I, I mean we, since we're a couple and all."

"Uh, how is your father going to take all this? Isn't there some coach/daughter hands off rule?"

"I'm an adult, Penn. I can date, or get engaged to, whoever I want. Besides, he's not your coach anymore."

"Right," he says, almost like he's not too sure that's not going to happen again.

"It's fine." I let the curtain fall back into place, and when I think he's stepped further away than he has, I turn, only to hit a wall.

Except... not a wall.

Penn.

Solid, hard chest, no shirt, and now two hands catching my arms as I wobble.

"Oh, sorry," I squeak.

He steadies me like it's nothing and gently pulls me closer, holding me against him for a second longer than strictly necessary.

"You good?" he asks, looking down at me with those ridiculous ocean-blue eyes that should be illegal.

"Yup," I lie, pretending my entire nervous system isn't short-circuiting.

Then he smiles.

Not just any smile. *That* smile. The one that has been messing with my brain and my hormones and possibly the space-time continuum since he walked into the inn last night, and maybe even back in high school.

"And look at that," he says, voice light, teasing. "You didn't flinch when I touched you."

I smirk, trying to recover some ground. "Good thing we practiced." With a strategic pivot, I dart around him. "I need to shower."

Smooth.

I march toward the bathroom like I didn't just trip over my own libido.

Wow. Way to play it cool, girlfriend.

I shower fast, hoping the cool water will chill whatever nonsense my hormones are cooking up, but it's no use. The heat in my body is not water-soluble. I towel off, throw on jeans and a sweater, and pad back into the bedroom only to find Penn standing beside the bed, brow furrowed, struggling to arrange decorative pillows.

"The inn has someone for that."

"I know, I just..." He trails off, his hands stilling mid-plump. "I don't like to make too much work for other people." His voice is light, but there's something tight behind it. A shadow flickers across his face, something old and quiet and worn thin. He shrinks back half a step, like he's trying to take up less space, trying to disappear into the peppermint wallpaper. Heck, I think the elf even let out a sigh of sympathy. But then Penn straightens with a crooked smile, but there's a flicker in his expression, something tight around the eyes. "I've got a lot of good deeds to knock off if I want back on the 'good' list."

"Were you ever on the 'good list', Radman?" He puckers up his face and I chuckle. "Let me help," I say, stepping in. But the second I get within range—*BZZZZZ!* The mistletoe alarm shrieks. My heart leaps into my throat. Penn's eyes dart upward. "Okay, seriously," I mutter, glaring at the ceiling. "I'm going to have that thing uninstalled. Possibly exorcised."

"Wait," Penn says, straightening. His tone shifts, thoughtful, serious, but still with that little edge of playful danger that makes my knees suspiciously wobbly. "You know... maybe it's not the worst idea."

"What's not?"

"This. Us." He gestures between us. "Kissing. Maybe we should try it. Just once. So, we're not weird if one of these buzzers in the inn catches us off guard again."

I blink. "You... you want to kiss me?"

He shrugs. "I mean, it couldn't hurt. Right?"

Hurt? Oh, it's going to hurt all right. Deep between my legs.

"Yeah," I say slowly. "I guess I don't like to half-ass anything."

"Same," he replies, his voice dropping half an octave. "If I'm in, I'm going all in."

Gulp.

He winces. "That... that came out wrong."

"No, I got it," I say quickly, waving a hand like we're cool. So cool. Antarctica cool.

"So... kissing? Yeah, okay. Let's... do that." I step forward, go up on my toes, mentally prepping for a quick, harmless peck.

But Penn apparently missed that memo.

His hands slide around my back, warm and confident, and suddenly I'm pulled flush against him like this is not a drill. His lips brush mine—soft at first, tentative—but then they shift, melt, press. And then...

His tongue.

Penn Radford's *tongue* is in my mouth.

And I...

I...like it.

A soft, helpless moan escapes me, and his response is instant. He deepens the kiss, pulling me tighter, until there's not even air between us. My hands find his bare back, instinctive and greedy, fingers skating over hard muscle and smooth skin, mapping the territory like I plan to move in.

And, uh... he's definitely not unaffected. Like, *visibly*.

Is that—?

Whoa.

My brain is doing backflips while my body is composing a thank-you letter to Santa.

I break the kiss, just barely, breath coming in hot gasps. "Penn?"

He blinks down at me, dazed, lips kiss-swollen, hands still clutching the back of my pajama top like he's not ready to let go.

"Yeah?" he murmurs.

I lift one trembling finger and point up to the ceiling. "So... is that..." I nod toward the still-buzzing mistletoe alarm. "...causing a rise?"

He glances up, then back down at me, his mouth twitching. "Uh, yeah..." A beat. "...gallbladder."

PENN

Goddamn traitorous motherfucker.

And no, I'm not talking about my gallbladder. Because while we were fake kissing—*fake*, mind you—that bastard between my legs decided to rise to the damn occasion. No chill. No loyalty. Just pure, shameless betrayal.

And... nothing about that kiss felt like practice.

Not even a little. It felt real. Like warm, sweet, slow-burning real. The kind of kiss that stays on your lips long after it ends. The kind that tastes like seconds.

But nope. Not going there. I'm not here to get tangled up with anyone, especially not someone who is equal parts sexy trouble and sugar-sweet sass. Jaylynn might have a smile that short-circuits my brain and a laugh that lives in my bones, but that doesn't mean I'm stupid enough to catch feelings.

Honestly though, how could I even dream about falling for a woman who hid an elf under my sheets and scared the living crap out of me? Jaylynn thought it was comedy gold. But that's fine—I'm already plotting my revenge. Something involving glitter. Or googly eyes. Or both.

I'm still grinning like a lunatic as I hurry up Elaine's walkway, taking the stairs two at a time, and pause outside the house. My old house. The one I grew up in and never quite fit inside. Especially after she remarried. Some of the guys tried. Some didn't. When they didn't, it meant keeping my head down and following the rules like I was walking a tightrope over broken glass.

Truth is, I wanted Aunt Elaine to have someone who made her happy. I just didn't want to be the reason that happiness cracked. So, I stayed quiet. Invisible, even. Anything to avoid being shipped off... wherever unwanted kids go.

But Earl? Earl was the worst of them all. The last of the rotating door of husbands. He showed up during my high school years, and was here when I was trying to make something of myself with the Grizzlies. The day I moved out was the first time I could breathe freely in years. The guy made this house feel like a prison with floral curtains.

Elaine tried. God, she tried. But Earl's cruelty was quiet—just out of her line of sight. The glares, the digs, the constant reminders that I wasn't wanted. That I'd never amount to anything. That Elaine only kept me around out of guilt or obligation. And when you hear that enough, especially from someone who's supposed to be family... you start to believe it.

He didn't live long enough to see me play in the NHL. Part of me wanted to rub it in. Shove my jersey in his smug face. But the truth is, I probably wouldn't have done any of that.

Because... maybe... he wasn't entirely wrong about me being

good enough. If I had been, I wouldn't have been held back so long, and deep down, I still don't feel like part of the team.

My hand lifts to knock, but the door creaks open before I touch it.

"Oh, Penn, you don't have to knock," Elaine says with a light scold and a fluttering wave of her hand.

From inside, a loud meow slices through the air, followed by a piercing wail.

Guess Muffin—AKA Earl, the reincarnated hellcat—isn't thrilled I'm back.

"Are you ready for lunch?" I ask, eyes landing on her fuzzy llama sweater and matching hat, complete with little ears flopping off the top.

I blink. "Let me guess... National Llama Day?"

She beams like she's been waiting all morning for someone to ask. "You know it!"

I chuckle, already picturing the hoof-shaped cookies I know she baked this morning. "To think, if I'd come a day later, I'd have missed this majestic celebration."

Aunt Elaine is, without question, the only person on earth who tracks National 'Whatever' Day with the same dedication most people reserve for tax season or playoff games. But hey, her weird little holiday cookies are actually kind of amazing.

"Let me just grab my coat. Come in."

"I think I'll wait out here," I say, stretching my arms and tilting my face to the sun. "It's too nice not to soak this in."

She nods and disappears inside, leaving the screen door shut and the heavy wooden one open. I'm just admiring the quiet street when—

WHAM.

Four clawed paws slam into the screen with demonic fury.

I lurch backward, catch my foot on the top stair, and go down like a sack of bricks—arms flailing, pride disintegrating— until I land flat on my back in the snow with a thud loud enough to wake the dead.

Smooth, Penn. Real smooth.

And to think I ever imagined I had the reflexes of a professional athlete.

I lie there for half a second, doing a quick inventory of bones and organs, then scramble upright, brushing snow off my jeans like it might somehow erase the embarrassment now radiating off me. Which, of course, is exactly when I hear it— the crunch of tires on snow, the low purr of a window rolling down.

No, no, no.

"Hey, Radman," comes the too-familiar voice of Dylan-freaking-Hayes. "Or should I say... *snowman?*"

I glance up and yep, there he is, the human equivalent of a wedgie, leaning out his car window with that smug, punchable grin.

"Hayes," I mutter, nodding stiffly. My gaze flicks to the girl in his passenger seat. If she caught my fall, I'll be a viral meme by dinner—but she's too busy reapplying her lip gloss to notice I exist.

Small mercies.

"Is that Dylan?" Elaine's voice drifts from the stoop as she emerges, pulling on wool mittens with little llama hooves knitted into the fingers. Of course.

"Hello, Elaine," Dylan calls, all fake cheer and empty charm. "Happy holidays."

"You too," she sings back, then waves as he drives off. "Douchebag," she mutters under her breath.

I blink. "What?"

"*Moosh*," she says innocently. "Yiddish slang. It means affection."

"Uh-huh. Since when do you speak Yiddish?"

She shrugs, completely unbothered. "I watched *Fiddler on the Roof* last night."

Sure.

I offer her my hand to help her down the steps, which, note to self, desperately need shoveling. "Does Gerald still come by to clear the driveway and stairs?"

"I told him not to bother today. It's just a light dusting. Can't hurt anything."

Tell that to my tailbone.

"Elaine, come on. Let Gerald clear it. Doesn't matter if it's a dusting or a damn blizzard," I say as I help her into the car. "I don't want you slipping and breaking a hip. Or worse."

She waves me off like I'm some nervous mother hen. "Oh, stop fussing. I can take care of myself."

Sure, but that doesn't stop the worry from creeping in more and more these days. She's still got her spark, but sometimes spark doesn't stand a chance against black ice.

I shut the door gently and hurry around to the driver's side, climbing in. She buckles up and flashes me one of those warm, crinkly smiles that have been softening the sharp edges of my life since I was six years old. My chest tightens.

I love her. Fiercely. She's the one who stepped in when no one else did. But loving her also scratches at the scar tissue left behind by the one who didn't.

My mom—Elaine's baby sister—was younger, single, totally unprepared for motherhood. She said she wasn't equipped, and maybe she wasn't. Logic says she did the right thing by handing me over to someone who could handle it. But logic doesn't do much to quiet the kid in me who always hoped she'd show up one day and say, *"Just kidding. I changed my mind."*

She never did.

"You want to hit the Jolly Bean?" I ask as we pull out of the driveway, keeping my tone light.

Elaine perks right up. "It's my favorite."

I grin. "Figured it might be."

She clutches her purse as we cruise slowly down the main road, letting her take in the town all done up in garlands and candy canes. Even I have to admit—it's charming in a way that sneaks up on you. Like one of those Hallmark movies you mock but secretly enjoy.

"You were able to get a room at the inn?" she asks.

"Yeah, no problem." I shoot her a quick smile. And I got a surprise roommate situation with Jaylynn, but Elaine doesn't need that particular update. Not yet.

"That's good. If I'd known you were coming home..."

"It's okay," I say quickly, maybe too quickly. Regret nips at my heels. Maybe I should've come back for Christmas all these years. She's the only real family I've got. But coming back has always carried a kind of ache I don't know how to handle. It's a reminder of everything I didn't get. Everything I wasn't wanted for.

Still, Elaine did what she could. She didn't sign up for motherhood, but she gave me a home, gave me love—even if it was a little unconventional.

"You did a good thing taking those cats in, Elaine," I say, half teasing, half serious.

She chuckles. "They needed me."

Yeah. I get it.

We roll into town and I pull into a spot near the square, slipping a glance at the clock. I've got an hour before the meeting. Plenty of time to grab lunch and keep pretending I'm not being haunted by memories and unresolved mommy issues.

I circle the car and help Elaine out, steadying her elbow as we walk past a Santa shaking a bell for some local cause. I fish out a twenty and drop it in the red bucket. He nods and offers a jolly "*Ho ho ho!*" like he's proud of me.

Then we push through the door of the Jolly Bean and—

Oh hell.

There she is.

Jaylynn.

In an apron. Carrying menus. Smiling at someone.

My head jerks back like I've just been smacked with a snow shovel.

No one said anything about *her* working here.

And judging by the way my pulse kicks and my stomach does a weird, traitorous flip, because maybe I'm not as prepared to fake this in public, as I thought I was.

"I... uh... you work here?"

Jaylynn shrugs like this is totally normal. "Tess called in sick. I told them I'd cover the morning rush."

Of course, she did. Because she's sweet and likes to help people out. Look what she's doing for me.

She flashes Elaine a warm smile. "Nice to see you again. Want your usual seat?"

"Of course."

Jaylynn leads us to the booth in the far corner, and my stomach tightens as we pass Dylan's table. Because naturally, he's here too—like a zit on prom night, just showing up when no one asked.

He leans back in his chair, smirk already locked and loaded. "Santa still standing out there? Or did you take him down too?"

Elaine cuts him a sharp look. "You mind your manners, young man. Or I'll call your mother."

He snorts, tries to make a llama sound, but it comes out like a goose being strangled mid-honk.

Do not hit him. Do not hit him. Do. Not. Hit. Him.

I'm repeating the mantra in my head like it's a damn spell, until I glance at Jaylynn. She's watching me with this mischievous glint in her eyes—like she knows exactly what I'm thinking.

"You don't have to serve him, do you?" I ask under my breath.

"Unfortunately, yes," she says, rising up on her toes so her voice lands just for me. "But don't worry... I do things to his coffee."

I blink at her. "Jesus. Really?"

She whistles innocently, spinning a placemat into place like she's not low-key admitting to caffeine-related vengeance.

"Remind me never to piss you off," I murmur.

Elaine points a stern finger in my direction. "Language, Penn."

"Right. Sorry, Elaine."

"I'll grab you both a coffee," Jaylynn says with a wink, already heading for the counter. "Just made a fresh pot."

I watch her go—too long, probably—then glance down at the menu as Elaine throws dagger eyes toward Dylan's table.

"Ignore him," I whisper.

Elaine snorts. "How that guy ever became mayor... If he ever takes over the position in Snowberry, I'm out of here."

"You could always come to Boston with me," I say lightly,

testing the waters. "I think you'd love it there. We could get a house."

She shrugs, noncommittal—but then pivots, sly. "Now, what's this I hear about you punching Santa?" I groan. She pounds one tiny fist into her palm like she's ready to throw down herself. "I bet he deserved it."

"He did," I admit, then sigh. "But I can't go around hitting people, Elaine."

"You can if they deserve it."

"That's not how it works."

"I'm your aunt. I raised you. If I say it's okay, it's okay."

I laugh under my breath, shaking my head. "So... if I walked over there and decked Dylan for being a mouthy jackass, that'd be fine by you?"

"Wouldn't mind." She leans in, eyes twinkling. "Heck, son. I'd clear a path for you."

Son.

The word lands with a little thud in my chest. Simple. Casual. But somehow, it hits harder than any punch.

She starts to rise, but I catch her arm before she can make a getaway. "No more hitting, okay? I've got to clean up my image if I want to keep my spot on the Bucks. Just so you know, I made a secret pact with Jaylynn."

Her face lights up like a Christmas tree. "She's a sweet one, Penn. Everyone loves her—well, except for SpicyGranny74. Though she turned out just fine. Got her own podcast now."

I blink at Aunt Elaine. Strange duck? Sure. But the woman's got her finger firmly on the social media pulse.

"All right, spill. What's this pact about?" she pushes.

She unzips her coat while I shrug off mine, settling in for the truth. I lean in a little. "I need to fix my image. So, she's helping."

"And in return?"

Her milky blue eyes lock onto mine.

I glance around at Dylan and Peppermint Barbie, busy snapping fish-lip selfies, then lower my voice. "I pretend to be her boyfriend. Maybe even fiancé. She has to pull off this festival without a hitch if she wants a real job again. I'm going to help her with that, and with Dylan back in town..."

Elaine finishes for me with a grin, "She wants to rub it in that she snagged a famous hockey player."

"Something like that," I murmur, not exactly feeling famous —or sure I'm even a hockey player for much longer.

"I like this plan," she says, genuinely pleased just as Jaylynn arrives with fresh mugs, pouring from a full carafe.

"That smells amazing," I say, grateful for the caffeine.

"Elaine, I love your mitts," Jaylynn chimes as my aunt peels them off.

Elaine beams. "I could make you a pair, you know."

"That's sweet, but I could never rock them like you do," Jaylynn smiles warmly at me, and I can't help but love how gracious she is with Elaine.

Elaine turns her attention back to us, pointing a finger between the two of us like a seasoned detective. "So... you and my boy here. Faking a relationship." She leans in, eyes twinkling with mischief. "But what I really want to know is... is the sex real?"

Ho. Ho. Holy shit.

5

JAYLYNN

If Peppermint Barbie clicks her nails on the long boardroom table one more time, I swear I'm going to stab myself in the eye with my pen. Honestly, it might be less painful. At least that injury comes with a trip to urgent care and an excuse to leave early.

"So," I say, dragging out the word with as much subtle irritation as I can pack into a single syllable. "Is that it? Did we cover everything?"

Sometimes these town meetings feel like a group therapy session nobody asked for. I mean, half of this could've been an email. But our town clerk, Mr. Ben Tingley, likes to hold them in person. Ever since Marianne passed, I think he just... needs the company. Which makes me feel like a monster for even wishing this was a Zoom call with a mute button.

"Where are we with the signs?" I ask Cassie, our spirited library trustee, who's currently wearing a cardigan covered in miniature snowmen. "They should've been here weeks ago," I add.

She huffs dramatically. "It took *far* too long for Ben to agree on the theme."

"That's because 'Peppermint Wishes and Mistletoe Kisses' is ridiculous," Ben grumbles.

"It's *romantic*," Cassie shoots back, eyes narrowed, as if daring him to challenge her Hallmark-level vision of joy.

"There's nothing romantic about couple sleigh rides, mistletoe selfie stations, or peppermint-flavored everything," he mutters.

"I'm with ya, buddy," Penn murmurs under his breath beside me, and I nearly choke on my laughter. I nudge him with my elbow, my mouth twitching. His lips curl into that slow, crooked smile that should come with a warning label.

Ben crosses his arms. "I still say 'Twelve Nights of Snowberry' would've been better."

"We'll keep that in mind for next year," I say diplomatically, mentally counting down how many more comments until I can leave and eat dinner without a headache.

"Fine," he mutters, sinking back into his chair.

"The signs are arriving today," Cassie says, adjusting her glasses with purpose. "I've already got Gerald and Gus lined up to put them up."

I glance at Mayor Banks to check for his input, but his eyes are closed, and I hear soft breathing sounds.

"I can help too," Sheriff Garrett Reynolds chimes in from the far end of the table. His tone is casual, but his eyes keep drifting toward Penn. It's either concern or mild flirtation—I haven't decided yet. Honestly, with Garrett, it could be both. He's nothing if not thorough.

"With the potholes that still need fixing," Gary Garner from Fire & Emergency says, shooting a death glare at Barry Madison, the road commissioner, "We'll need to reroute."

Barry straightens like he's been personally insulted. "If you gave us more budget money, maybe we could *actually* fix the roads," he fires back at Monica, our unflappable treasurer, who doesn't even blink.

I glance toward the exit, wondering if anyone would notice if I pulled the fire alarm just to end the meeting. Next time, I'm bringing snacks—and maybe a flask.

I pinch the bridge of my nose as a headache starts brewing behind my eyes. I flick a glance at Penn, who looks just as thrilled to be here as I am. He slouches in his chair like he's watching a mildly entertaining sitcom, while I'm reminding myself to breathe.

But I force a smile anyway. This festival has to go off without a hitch. Because I need this job. I need something real, something steady.

"And what will *you* be doing during the festival?" Dylan asks, his voice sharp, almost accusatory.

My gaze snaps to him. But he's not speaking to me. Oh no. He's locked in on Penn, like this is a showdown at the Snowberry Corral.

I open my mouth to interject. To explain that Penn will be helping me coordinate events and manage crowd control and a million other thankless tasks. But Penn doesn't need rescuing. Not from Dylan. Not from anyone.

"Kissing booth," he says smoothly. "Thought we could raise money for the hospital. If you want to be first in line, I'll save you a spot."

I choke back a laugh. Dylan blinks like someone just slapped him with a candy cane. Honestly, we've never had a kissing booth before, and while it's silly, it's not a bad idea to raise money. Especially if a hot hockey player is involved.

Peppermint Barbie, who's somehow been both scrolling her phone and absorbing every juicy detail, perks up and sets it down. "You can save *me* a spot in line," she says sweetly, fluttering her lashes in Penn's direction.

Dylan turns to her, aghast. "What?"

She gives a casual shrug and loops her arm through his. "It's for a good cause, Dylan. Don't be such a Grinch."

I nearly applaud. I might even hire her as my PR intern if she keeps this up. That image alone—*her* wrapping herself around *him* while making eyes at Penn—will do wonders on my socials. Especially with Penn being, you know, a hot NHL player and all.

Dylan sputters. "Yeah, well, I'm the mayor of Rutledge. Youngest mayor ever." He puffs up his chest, what little there is of it.

Second-hand embarrassment hits me like a rogue snowball to the face. But Penn? He's loving every second of it. He leans back, arms crossed, smirk firmly in place.

"Then maybe you should run the kissing booth," Penn says coolly. "Sounds like it's more your speed."

Dylan smooths down his lapels. "Of course, it should be me."

Penn grins, pouncing like a cat with a laser pointer. "Perfect. Then I'll take your spot on the float as Santa. Wouldn't want to steal your thunder—especially since *my fiancée* is playing Mrs. Claus. And, you know, tradition says Santa should be her..." He pauses, then flashes a wink so devastating it could probably be fined.

"...Big Daddy."

Big Daddy.

Oh. My. God.

I slap a hand over my mouth to keep the laugh from bursting out. Across the table, Dylan looks like he just swallowed a Christmas ornament. "You're... you two... are...?"

"Engaged," Penn says easily, sliding an arm around my shoulders like he's done it a thousand times. "Why do you seem so surprised?"

His warmth settles against me, and I lean in, looking up at him with stars in my eyes. Okay, sure, it's all for show. But it doesn't feel fake. Not when he's putting Dylan in his place so effortlessly. Not when he's stepping in, showing up, and playing the part, even when it doesn't benefit him.

I haven't spent much time with him, but maybe Penn Radford isn't like my ex after all. Maybe he's something better.

"We snagged the Peppermint Honeymoon Suite over at the Snowberry Inn," Penn announces with a grin. "Not married yet, but hey, good practice, right, babe?"

He looks down at me, all warmth and charm, and I somehow resist the urge to fan myself with my clipboard.

"I...you didn't tell me you were engaged," Dylan snaps, eyebrows practically leaping off his forehead.

I open my mouth to respond, but Penn beats me to it. "Why would she tell you that?" he says, tilting his head. "Actually, we haven't told anyone, and I didn't mean to let it slip. We were planning to announce it tomorrow night at her family's big dinner. You weren't invited, were you?"

Dylan stiffens. "No. I wasn't."

"Right," Penn says, not even pretending to be sorry. I watch Dylan stew in silence and realize, this man might be the *youngest* mayor of Rutledge, but Penn is playing chess while Dylan's still trying to figure out how the checker board works.

I tap my pen on the table, trying to steer the train back on its snowy tracks. "Okay, let's get back to business. Barry, do up the new parade route and email it to me. I'll forward it to all the participating businesses. Town Hall's already prepped for the craft fair this weekend, and all the kids' activities are good to go. The beer tent—sorry, *beer town hall*—will run in the evenings. Garrett and Gary are overseeing that with a small army of volunteers. I want fun, not a frat party."

"As long as Santa's not going to be there," Dylan snorts, glaring at Penn. "We don't need an incident." When he doesn't get an immediate response, his gaze flicks to me and narrows as I lean toward Penn, and I wonder if he's sensing our lie. The man knows me. We dated for a long time.

I rest my hand on Penn's thigh and slowly start rubbing, as if it's the most natural thing in the world, like I've done it a thousand times. Maybe in this fake life I can also rub other... areas. I give Dylan a sweet, closed-mouth smile as his eyes drop to my arm and narrow with suspicion, or jealousy. Honestly, it's hard to tell with him.

"For the record," I say crisply, making sure Mr. Tingley's pen is scratching away on his notepad, "Dylan will now be working the kissing booth, and Penn is officially our Santa Claus. Which means he *will* be at the beer tent. And unless

Penn plans to deck himself in the face, I think we'll all survive the night just fine."

Dylan slouches in his chair like a moody teenager who just got grounded. I know it's petty, but God help me, I'm enjoying it. Just a little.

"Oh, and the Rotary Club has agreed to make the post-parade meal," I add. "Gateway Grocery is donating turkeys."

But then Dylan's eyes narrow, his tone shifting from sulky to sly. "Turkey," he says slowly. "Maybe it's not a Santa incident we need to worry about after all."

The room goes quiet.

I put my hand over Penn's when he makes a fist and meet Dylan's gaze and glare, refusing to flinch. I picture him choking on a wishbone and briefly feel better. Then I lift my chin and straighten my spine. I will *not* let him rattle me. Not today. Not ever again.

"Right," I say, voice calm. "We've covered the carolers, live music, the ice rink, carol karaoke, kids' crafts and face painting, the ugly sweater run, and the tree lighting after the parade. Anything I've missed?"

I hope not, because if not, I have a peppermint honeymoon suite—and a fake fiancé—to get back to.

"If Penn is playing Santa now," BJ Webb says, tilting her head with open admiration, "Someone's going to have to let the suit out a bit."

All eyes shift to Penn like we're all just now seeing him for the first time. Tall. Broad shoulders. That casually muscular frame. The way he somehow makes flannel look like a fashion statement. And not even a hint of a pot belly. Just pure, unwrappable holiday thirst trap.

"He's not that much bigger," Dylan grumbles, arms crossed and ego bruised.

BJ ignores him completely, eyes still locked on Penn. She giggles like a teenager with a backstage pass. "Might need to order in more fabric."

A few nods circle the table. Someone coughs. I pretend not to hear someone mutter *"Ho-ho-holy hell."*

"Okay, is that everything?" I ask, desperate to wrap this circus up before someone offers to climb into Penn's lap and test his 'naughty or nice' list.

Silence.

"Can I have a motion to close the meeting?"

Peppermint Barbie—bless her shimmering soul—raises her hand, only for Dylan to place a firm, awkward hand on her wrist and gently lower it.

"I'll motion," he mumbles.

Barbie blinks up at him, lips pursed into a pink, glossy *O*. The filler makes forming words a little tricky, but hey—those lips are doing their best. And I'm not jealous. Not at all. I'm just...observant.

I'm sure Dylan will explain she needs to actually *be* a member to motion in a meeting. Or not. Maybe deep conversation isn't a cornerstone of their relationship.

"I'll second," Garrett Reynolds says with a shrug, and that's all I need.

I close the cover over my iPad and collect myself before addressing the room. "Thanks again, everyone. I appreciate the time and energy you put into making this festival special. If anything goes off the rails, don't hesitate to reach out. You all have my number."

"Pretty sure I don't," Dylan tosses out with a smug little grin.

Before I can respond, Penn's hand slides over mine, still resting on his thigh beneath the table. He gives it a squeeze. Steady. Protective. Possessive in a way that feels... really, *really* good.

"Fine," I mutter, rattling off my number. Dylan types it into his phone like he's just won something, and I stand with full intent to walk away from his smug little face forever. Or at least until our next meeting.

"Ready to get out of here?" I ask Penn.

He stands, leans in and nuzzles my neck, playful and warm, and even though I *know* it's all for show, it sends a jolt straight through my body. "Been dying to get you all to myself," he murmurs, loud enough for Dylan to hear, of course.

We step outside together, and the clouds have rolled in, painting the sky with deep charcoal shadows. The air smells like snow. The kind that cancels school and makes you crave hot chocolate and fuzzy socks.

"I hope it doesn't dump on us," I say, glancing up. "I don't want the weather interfering with the festival."

Penn reaches down and laces his fingers through mine.

There's no one watching.

No crowd. No cameras. No Dylan.

Just us.

And yet… he holds on.

And I don't let go.

We walk hand in hand down Main Street, where wreaths sparkle from every lamppost and the shop windows glow with warm light. The whole town looks like it's been professionally gift-wrapped, and I feel that deep, old-school kind of Christmas magic settling into my bones.

"Hungry?" I ask.

"Starving," he says. "But I've had enough peopling for one day."

I laugh. "Same. Let's order in."

"And maybe shower off the Dylan exposure."

"Definitely."

We head back to the inn, our hands still intertwined. And even though the fake engagement is barely 24 hours old, my brain's already skipping ahead to tomorrow night—family dinner. The moment when I have to tell the people who raised me that I'm engaged to Penn Radford.

"They're going to have questions," I say, chewing my lip. "We need a good back story."

Penn nods without hesitation. "We met on an app."

"During my time in Boston," I add. "Whirlwind romance. I came home, we tried long-distance, but it didn't work. But when we saw each other again at the inn…"

"I dropped to one knee. You said yes. Cue fireworks. No time for a ring."

"Boom. Sold." I glance at him. "You're disturbingly good at this."

We reach the inn just as the sky lets out a soft flurry, and Belinda, stationed behind the front desk, lifts an eyebrow as Penn and I brush past her, laughing a little too loudly, hands tangled like we can't quite keep from touching.

Inside the suite, Penn gestures toward the bathroom. "I'm going to jump in the shower real quick. I didn't even go into the house but I have cat hair all over me."

"I think I might soak in the hot tub," I reply, already peeling off my cardigan.

He pauses, hand on the doorframe. "Maybe I'll join you after I clean up?"

"Yes," I say sweetly, then smirk. "But only if Mr. Elf hasn't joined me first."

He flashes that crooked grin. "Jay. You can't do naughty things to the elf. Santa's watching. You *will* go on the naughty list."

With a wink, he disappears into the bathroom, and I flop backwards onto the bed with a groan that comes straight from my soul. I stare up at the peppermint-swirled chandelier above me, which is aggressively festive—like it's judging me for every life decision I've made that brought me to this exact moment.

Which, to be fair... is kind of a lot.

I hear the shower start and close my eyes, letting the hum of water fill the space. The idea of Penn, six-foot-plus of NHL-grade temptation, standing in that shower just a few feet away... well, it does something to my stomach. And my chest. And every inch of my overheated skin.

I invited this. *I* asked him to play boyfriend. *I* suggested we share a bed. *I* asked him to act like he's in love with me—for two full weeks—in front of everyone I know.

And he's doing it. Perfectly. Naturally. Like it's no big deal to be completely convincing as someone who's completely smitten with me.

What would it actually be like to be engaged to someone like Penn? Someone who makes people feel safe and seen. Someone who makes you laugh in the middle of a town meeting meltdown. Someone who can turn a fake engagement into something that feels dangerously close to real without even trying.

Would he wrap his arms around me when I'm overwhelmed?

Would he kiss me just because I looked tired?

Would he wait up for me when I got home late?

I shake the thought away. It's just pretend.

Totally, *completely* pretend.

I strip off everything but my bra and underwear, then lift the hot tub cover, turn on the jets, and slip into the water. Instantly, my body thanks me. Muscles I didn't even know I had start to unwind. I lean back and let my head fall to the side, the soft sound of bubbles and the distant hum of water from the shower lulling me toward a half-doze.

Then the bathroom door creaks open. My eyes flutter open just in time to see Penn walk out, toweling his hair dry. He's in a plain white T-shirt that clings to his chest and shoulders like it was designed by a sculptor with an agenda. His gray sweatpants hang low on his hips, and I'm suddenly very aware that we'll be sharing a bed again.

"Nice," he murmurs, eyeing the hot tub. He walks over and dips his fingers into the water. "Want me to order something in?"

"Yes, please," I say, trying not to sound breathless.

"What's good?"

"I'm so hungry I could eat a reindeer."

"You leave those poor reindeer alone," he says, grinning as he grabs his phone. "Pizza?"

"Nothing says holiday romance like meat lovers," I reply, leaning my head back with a sigh.

He orders while I soak. When he hangs up, I point a finger at him. "Turn around."

He lifts his hands in surrender, turning his back, and I step out, wrap a towel around me, and hustle into pajamas. Moments later, I crawl beneath the cozy sheets. I flick on the TV, and when the food arrives, Penn fills two plates and joins me.

We eat in bed—because we're monsters—and it's the best thing I've tasted all week. With the TV low in the background, he tells me about his aunt, about growing up in Boston, and how his favorite Christmas ever was the one he spent snowed in with no power and nothing but canned soup and board games. I talk about how my parents still make us wear matching pajamas for Christmas Eve.

Eventually, we brush our teeth together. I catch our reflection in the mirror—shoulders bumping, sleepy grins, toothpaste foam—and something in my chest tightens unexpectedly.

Back in bed, we end up watching a holiday romcom, some predictable but charming mess with a predictable but charming guy who realizes the love of his life was the girl next door all along. By the end of it, I'm blinking heavily, my body sinking deeper under the covers.

Penn glances over, his voice low. "You okay?"

I nod, curling on my side. "Yeah. Just tired."

He turns off the TV and lights. The room goes quiet except for the low hum of the heating vent and the gentle hush of wind outside. He slides in beside me, the mattress dipping under his weight, and even though we don't touch, I can feel him there.

Warm. Steady. Real.

And for one tiny, ridiculous second, I wonder what it would be like to fall asleep every night next to someone like Penn Radford.

From the darkness, Penn says softly, "We did good today."

"Yeah. Real good."

"I hope you're okay that I tricked Dylan into letting me play Santa."

"More than okay."

There's a shift in the mattress, and then he's closer. Not touching me, but I can feel the heat of him curling toward me. "Night, Jay."

"Night, Penn."

A pause. And then—

"Jay?"

"Yeah?"

"I really hate Dylan. And I don't hate a lot of people."

I turn toward him, the edge of my pillow muffling my smile. "You don't have to hate him for me."

"One," he says, holding up a finger I can barely see, "He's an attention-seeking douche. And two, yes I do."

There's a rustle of sheets, then his hand finds my face, brushing a piece of hair gently away. His fingers linger for a second too long, and when he pulls back, it's like the air cools. "Sorry," he murmurs. "I should've asked."

"Right," I whisper. "Because consent is sexy." I say it like a joke, but it lands somewhere serious.

His eyes flick to my mouth, and I see it—need, want, hunger.

"You're sexy," he says, quiet and almost to himself.

"What?" My voice cracks like a twelve-year-old boy.

"I didn't mean to say that out loud," he breathes. "We should —uh, we should build a pillow wall."

I blink at him. "What?"

"Last night, you starfished across the whole bed. I thought you were going to break my nose."

"Fine." I shove a bunch of pillows between us. "Great idea."

"This is excellent," he says, fluffing one. "But what are we going to do about your snoring?"

I grab a pillow and smack him in the face.

He laughs. "Easy, Jay. Santa's helper is watching, and violence is definitely naughty-list behavior."

He shifts again, lying back, and his voice turns thoughtful. "I really liked watching you work today. You're... you're good at what you do."

I exhale slowly. "If only a real firm could see that. But apparently, one turkey incident is a career death sentence."

He laughs gently. "Okay, yeah, that one's a little hard to recover from."

"It was kind of funny though. I know I'm not supposed to laugh when people fall, but when SpicyGranny74 went down...hilarious."

"Want to watch it?" he teases.

"Hell no." I grin. "We could always watch *you* decking Santa."

"Trust me, he had it coming."

"I believe you."

There's another pause, quieter this time. And I feel it again, that warmth that comes off him in waves. Not just his body, but *him*. That quiet steadiness, that deeply buried sweetness he tries so hard to hide. Honestly, I can't imagine what it must have been like for him, being given up as a baby, told it was for his own good. Even if it was... it still had to hurt. That kind of pain leaves fingerprints on a person's soul.

And somehow, he still turned into this, this good, solid man who protects, and listens, and volunteers to play Santa just to help me. I glance at the window. Snow is falling again, thick and dreamy. The whole town wrapped in a blanket of magic.

"Beautiful, huh?" he murmurs.

"Yeah," I say softly. But I'm not looking at the snow anymore.

I'm looking at him.

And for a split second, I wonder what it would be like to actually be engaged to someone like Penn Radford. To have this not be a performance. To fall asleep next to him night after night. To let him kiss me for real. To let him keep brushing my hair away like I'm something to be cherished.

My throat tightens a little.

I shift closer, just enough to feel the pillow wall bend between us.

And then I whisper, almost daring myself to say it—

"Penn?"

"Yeah?"

"I think I want to be on Santa's naughty list."

He laughs, low and warm. "Good," he says. "Because that's exactly where I want you."

6

PENN

With the snow falling outside, a hush settles over us. The darkness is broken by the faint golden glow from the decorated lampposts beyond the window. The light slices across the floor casting shadows that flicker like candlelight.

I toss the pillows aside and pull Jaylynn into my arms. She exhales a breathy laugh, the sound low and unguarded, as I shift her beneath me. Her hands glide under my shirt, her fingers warm against my skin, and I swear my heart stutters.

A small smile curves her lips. "Is this a trick? Some elaborate plan to sleep naked? Because I saw how you worked Dylan earlier."

I grin, pressing a kiss to the corner of her mouth. "Guilty. But for the record, I want both of us naked. And let's not mention his name again."

She chuckles, soft and breathy, the sound curling around me and hugging tight. I feel myself harden, responding not just to her touch, but to the way she's looking at me, like maybe this isn't just a game.

"Also," she adds, her voice dropping, "I was thinking sex might help sell our fake engagement."

"Oh, so that's why you're doing this?" I tease.

"Not exactly."

I raise an eyebrow. "Wait, you don't think we actually have to do it in front of people to convince them, right?"

She smacks my arm lightly. "No, Penn. God." Her laugh is husky now, her gaze soft. "But a little... intimacy couldn't hurt."

"Right. So, if we're going on the naughty list... we're going all in, right?"

Her grin turns wicked. "We don't half-ass anything, remember? And I think I'm really going to enjoy watching you go all in."

Jesus.

I catch her mouth in a kiss that's anything but fake. Her lips taste like peppermint and longing, and when she sighs into me, it punches the air right out of my lungs. My hand cups her cheek, my thumb brushing her softness as I kiss her deeper.

"Penn..." she breathes, her voice shaking a little. Her legs part beneath me, welcoming.

But first—clothes.

I pull back just enough to yank off my shirt. She sits up, arms lifted, offering herself to me. I strip her shirt off gently, and when her bare skin catches the soft lamplight, it feels like I'm seeing something sacred. My hands trace over her breasts, slow and light, and when her nipples peak beneath my touch, I swallow a groan.

"This won't do," I whisper.

"What won't?" she asks, voice soft, low, full of arousal.

"I need to see all of you."

I slip off the bed, switching on the lamp beside us. Warm amber light floods the room, wrapping around her curves. My sweats grow tight with need, and I push them down, stepping out of them as I wrap one hand around my shaft. She watches, her breath catching, her body answering mine without a single word.

"Now that's better," I say as I drink her in.

"I like seeing you too," she murmurs, voice low and smoky, as she crooks a finger at me, inviting me back into her warmth.

Yeah. Consent has never looked so goddamn sexy.

I raise a brow. "Something you need, babe?"

She shifts against the sheets, her eyes flicking down, unashamed. "Oh, I think you know exactly what I need."

I step closer, watching her breath hitch as her gaze lands on my cock. The room feels hotter now, like the air itself has thickened around us. I glance at the twinkling lights outside, then back at her, my voice playful.

"Could it be... a peppermint stick?"

That makes her laugh, a real one, the kind that lights up her whole face and melts something in my chest. She looks relaxed now, more herself. After everything she's been carrying, it feels good to be the one who gives her that.

My cock twitches as she licks her lips, and yeah, maybe what I'm offering is a little harder than peppermint, but the intent is all the same.

"It most definitely could be," she says, her voice thick with heat.

"Ah," I say, crawling back onto the bed, "I'll give you what you want, but right now, it's about me."

She angles her head, a spark of something sad, or maybe it's disappointment. But it's definitely a spark of something long ago in her eyes. I get it. Douche bag probably never put her first, but I'm about to show her how pleasuring her is everything I want first.

She makes a move to push herself up, but before she can retreat into that old wound, I slide my hands under her thighs and pull her toward me, settling between her legs. She moves to prop herself up, confused, but then I slide her pants down, toss them away, and lower my mouth to her sex. Her gasp steals the air from the room.

I grin against her, licking her slow from bottom to top, feeling her legs tremble as she melts beneath me.

"Penn, oh God it's... it's..."

Her words tumble out in fragments, and I lift my head just enough to say, "It's all about me, remember?"

Her head lifts, her eyes locking with mine, wide and full of something that looks a hell of a lot like disbelief, but also relief. And then I'm gone again, tongue and fingers working in sync, taking my time, learning her with every sigh and shiver. I spread her open, stroking her slowly, caring for her deeply.

"How is it…" she starts, but her voice dissolves.

"Because this…" I curl my fingers just right, brushing her inner wall as I take her clit between my lips, "…is all I've thought about since I crawled into bed with you last night."

Her hips lift off the mattress, her body arching into me. She grips the peppermint-striped sheets, knuckles white, and when I graze her with my teeth, she cries out, raw and unfiltered.

"Sleigh all day, babe," she gasps, breathless. "Sleigh all day…"

I chuckle into her, the sound muffled by her wet heat. God, she tastes like everything I've ever wanted. I add another finger, curling them deep as her body tightens around me. Her thighs quiver. Her whole body pulses. Two days ago, I thought this Christmas was going to be rough. Lonely, even.

Now?

Now I've got Jaylynn trembling beneath me, moaning like I'm her whole damn world. I glance up, needing to see her, to watch her fall apart for me. She's touching herself now, fingers cupping her breasts, and something primal surges in my chest.

Mine.

The word crashes through me like a hard hit on the ice.

Yeah, those breasts are mine tonight. And I plan to claim them. Right after she comes apart from my mouth. I shift the pace, adjusting the rhythm of my tongue and fingers as I learn her. Every gasp, every moan, every twitch of her hips becomes a kind of map, guiding me deeper into her pleasure. Her fingers dig into my hair, holding me there, and I take it as the only answer I need.

Then she shatters.

A broken moan leaves her lips as her thighs quake around me, her body pulsing with release. I don't stop. I lap her up slowly, gently, savoring every last drop like a man about to die of thirst.

"Penn…" she breathes, her voice wrecked in the best possible way.

I keep my fingers inside her as she rides out every last wave, her walls clenching around me so tight I wonder how long it's been since someone touched her like this? That thought lands with a hard thud in my chest. She deserves so much better in her life, and for the next couple of weeks—if she lets me—I'm going to give her everything she's been missing.

As her breathing begins to slow, I gently withdraw my fingers and press a kiss to her inner thigh before slowly climbing up her body. I take my time, pausing to mouth over her breasts, sucking one taut, perfect nipple between my lips. She groans, arching into me, her nails raking down my back. It stings. I want more.

I trail kisses along her flushed skin, over the curve of her collarbone, up her neck, until I reach her mouth. Then I kiss her. Deep and hungry and possessive. My cock presses against her slick heat, and for a second, I lose myself. Every part of me is tuned to her.

Then her voice, breathless, cuts through the haze.

"Condom," she murmurs.

"Shit, Jay... I didn't even think to buy any."

Her lips brush mine. "Good thing this is the honeymoon suite. They thought of everything."

I blink, brain still fogged. "Wait, what?"

She smiles, lazy and flushed. "Nightstand. I found a box in there the other night."

"Thank you, Jesus." I grin and press my forehead to hers.

She laughs. "Pretty sure he didn't put them there."

I glance toward the little menace on the shelf and smirk before I reach over and yank open the drawer, fumbling until I find the box. "You don't think Santa's minion poked holes in these, do you?" I ask, only half joking.

She props herself on her elbows, smiling softly. "It was sealed. I checked. Date's good too."

I nod, slipping one out, still half aware of the stupid elf in my peripheral vision. I examine the foil package. I've seen teammates burned before. Caught in traps they didn't see coming. Women with lies, with agendas. I've been wary, too. Always careful.

But with Jaylynn?

I don't feel that hesitation.

Maybe it's the shared trauma of going viral for the worst possible reasons. Maybe it's the way she looks at me like she sees the man beneath the hockey gear. Maybe it's because she doesn't want anything from me.

Except this.

Except tonight.

And to play the part of the man who loves her—for two weeks.

She's making it far too easy to pretend.

I push up on my knees, tearing into the condom wrapper, my pulse hammering. Seconds before I'm about to slide it on, she sits up, those small, warm palms wrapping around me. A slow, deliberate stroke that makes my head fall back.

"Fuck," I groan, threading my fingers into her hair. She blinks up at me, sweet and innocent, but blazing with need. "Jay…"

And then her mouth is on me. Warm. Wet. Heat so intense my vision blurs. I thicken in her mouth, every muscle locked to keep from losing it right then and there.

"Christ."

She eases off me just enough to speak, her lips slick. "This is all about me."

My heart stutters. I touch her chin, tilting her face toward mine. "This is what you want, babe? You want my cock in your mouth?" I don't even know how I'm managing words. She nods, eager and certain.

My thumb drags softly over her cheek as she takes me in again, deeper this time, until I'm sure I'm going to choke her. But she doesn't stop. She *wants* this, wants to swallow every inch of me like she's been starving for it.

I keep my hand on her, needing the connection as much as the friction, her mouth and hands working me until every nerve in my body is lit up, my release threatening to take me under. I pull back before I lose the fight, and she actually pouts.

"Lay back," I murmur, my voice rough as I put on the condom. "I need to be inside you."

Her eyes soften. "I want that too."

She falls onto the pillow, legs spreading in invitation, and my breath catches. I slide the condom on in record time. Settling over her, I angle my body so I don't crush her, but when she cups my face—eyes hungry, needy, open—any restraint I had shatters.

I push into her, and the sound she makes steals the air from my lungs. Her nails rake my back as her hips roll up, grinding against me, her need matching mine. She wraps around me, hot and tight, as I pull out just to drive back in harder.

When I hit deep, she opens her mouth but no sound escapes, only a sharp inhale that punches straight through me. We move together, discovering each other in a frantic, perfect rhythm. I'm on the edge, trying to hold on, when her voice breaks through the haze.

"I want to feel you come inside me."

"Babe," I growl, teeth clenched. "Not yet. It's just so fucking good."

"Yeah, I know. And I'm so happy our fake engagement comes with sex."

Sex.

Real sex.

And damn me, while everything about us is supposed to be pretend, this is the most real thing I've ever felt in...maybe ever. I thrust harder, chasing the moment, and when she clamps down around me, flooding me with heat, I can't stop. My arms lock around her, pulling her tight as I sink all the way in, my body letting go.

Goddammit, when we said we didn't half-ass anything and that if we were going in, we were going *all* in, we were only talking about sex, right?

JAYLYNN

Balancing the tray in my hands, I fumble for my key, trying not to send two plates of breakfast skidding to the Inn's floor. My body shifts, and muscles I didn't know I had tug tight and my brain instantly takes me back to last night.

Holy God, when was the last time I was touched like that? Never. Not like that. Tender and wild, deliberate and devastating. Penn unravelled me and put me back together, twice. Twice. I hate to even admit that in the past I was always left finishing the job myself.

Is all sex supposed to feel like that?

It wasn't with Dylan. Nor with that cringe-worthy college hookup. I've been basing my entire sex barometer on those two disasters, and wow... colossal mistake.

Maybe it was good because Penn and I bonded over being the unwilling stars of viral social media humiliation. Or maybe it was the ticking clock and our complete surrender to it. But when he'd said it was all about him first, I hadn't expected him to drop to his knees and slip between mine.

For a moment, I'd braced for my ex's move—take what you want, leave her cold. But no. Penn had taken pleasure in pleasuring me. Either he's one of a kind, or I'm in some peppermint fantasy.

A door opens behind me, jerking me back to reality. "Morning, Jaylynn." I shift, and the tray wobbles dangerously. Jaxon's gaze drops to it. "Oh, shit. Let me help."

Relief floods me as he takes it. "Thanks. Just let me get the door."

I slip the key in, conscious of the nightgown I'd been hoping could pass as a casual dress. I nudge the door open with my foot, hand reaching for the tray. "When did you get in?" I ask, trying for breezy, though one of his teammates is very much in my bed. Penn and I are faking a relationship, so I guess Jaxon will soon find out.

"Late last night. I'm only here for the weekend. Games right up until the twenty-second." He keeps hold of the tray. "Hey," he says, voice dipping a notch, "I'm sorry about...well, you know."

"Yeah. I know."

"Mom said you're running the festival this year."

I nod.

"It's going to be amazing." His smile is warm, reassuring. I hope he's right. I need this to go flawlessly. And when I think of Penn, somehow wrangling himself onto the float as Santa, a grin tugs at my mouth.

"I can take that," I say, trying to wrestle the tray from Jaxon without sending our breakfast airborne.

"It's fine, I'll carry it in." Before I can argue, he's balancing it effortlessly on one palm and nudging the door open. "How many people are you feeding?" he teases, then freezes mid-step. "Oh. Hey, Penn. Shit, sorry. I didn't realize."

I'm still half in the hallway when Penn's low, sleepy voice drifts out. "It's okay. Need a hand with that?"

Dear God, please don't get up. He's still naked.

"No, uh, I got it," Jaxon says quickly. I don't know why my cheeks are burning. We're consenting adults, for crying out loud.

"Didn't realize you were back in town," Jaxon says.

"Yeah. Just laying low." His voice has that edge—awkward, careful. Is it because of the Santa fiasco? Because he's naked in my bed? Or something else entirely? Why do I sense that it's something else entirely?

I push into the room. Penn's gaze locks on me. "Breakfast," I announce a little too brightly, my cheeriness about as subtle as a marching band at eight a.m.

"I'll just get out of your way." Jaxon moves past me. "See you guys later."

"Beer tent!" I blurt out like an idiot. "Be there or be square." Oh my God. Did I just channel my grandfather? From him, such a saying is charming. From me, I sound like the town weirdo.

"You bet," Jaxon says, and slips out.

The door clicks shut, and my eyes dart back to Penn. "Sorry about that." He watches me, brow knit, then pulls his knees up, resting his hands there. "Coffee," I say, because that's safe ground, and start pouring two oversized mugs.

He takes his. "Thanks, Jay."

I set the plates on the little table. "Hope you're hungry. I went overboard." I glance back. He's staring into his coffee like it holds the secrets of the universe.

"Everything okay? I know that was awkward, but... we are pretending. Jaxon is going to find out we're a couple."

He shakes his head. "Yeah, you're right."

Then he throws back the sheets and stands, stark naked, morning glory on full display.

Well. Hello.

"I'll just make a quick trip to the bathroom," he says casually, leaving me gripping my coffee like it's a lifeline.

I watch his very fine backside disappear into the bathroom, but a knot twists in my stomach. Call it intuition, but something tells me there's... something between him and Jaxon. And not the good kind of something.

I drown my pancake in syrup while I wait. When the door finally opens, he's tugging on sweats, settling across from me like nothing happened. I sip my coffee, studying him.

It's none of my business—this is all fake, after all—but the words slip out anyway. "You don't like Jaxon."

His head snaps up. "What? No. Jaxon's a great guy."

"Then why was all that..." I wave from the bed to the abandoned breakfast tray "...so awkward?"

"We just... I don't know. I haven't been on the team long."

It's not his words I read, but the weight in them. "You just don't know him well," I say, though what I'm hearing feels bigger. This isn't about Jaxon—it's about Penn. He hasn't bonded with his teammates. He's worried about losing his spot. And maybe—just maybe—he's never been the bonding type. He wasn't in high school, either.

The boy from the edge of town with the eccentric aunt, the parade of ferrets and now cats, and six husbands. Maybe he simply never learned how to fit in with the guys. A thought lodges deep in my chest. Over the holidays, I'm going to give him what he needs. Whether he likes it or not.

He bites into his pancake, eyes brightening. "These are amazing. Didn't realize how hungry I was."

Heat creeps up my neck. "We did burn a lot of energy last night."

A slow grin curves his mouth. "Yeah. We did."

My phone pings from the nightstand. "Here we go," I mutter, already bracing for disaster number twelve of the week. One glance and yep. "They need more craft paper for the kids' art fest this afternoon."

"They text you for that?"

"I'm the catch-all person." I take a much-needed sip of coffee. "I have to check in with the craft vendors and make sure they have everything before the doors open to the public anyway. Feel like shopping?"

He makes a face. "Craft fairs and shopping. Only my favorite things in the world. But yeah, sure."

"I also have to pick out the town square tree and get it set up."

"I thought you'd never ask." His tone is mock-grumpy, but there's something in his eyes—interest. Maybe even excitement.

"Have you even been tree shopping, or did you just cut down your own?" I ask.

A pained look comes over his face. "Elaine always had ferrets, and they had an aversion to trees so we never put one up." I open my mouth, to tell him I'm sorry, but he hurries out with, "We still had a nice Christmas, until..." His words fall off for a moment, and then he brightens up and asks, "When's the lighting?"

"Next weekend. Right after the parade."

He shakes his head, almost laughing. "I still can't believe I'm going to be Santa."

I chuckle. "Did I thank you for that?"

He glances down at the rumpled sheets, then back up at me. "I believe so. But that's kind of a big deal, so more thanking will definitely be needed."

I pick up a grape and flick it at him.

"Hey. That's grape assault."

"Grape assault, huh? What's the punishment for that crime?"

Before I can blink, he's on his feet, tugging me up with him, pressing me back against the hideous striped wall.

"Well," he murmurs low, his breath hot against my ear, "First, it requires me to kiss the living hell out of you. And second..."

His lips crash onto mine, deep and hungry. My legs go weak as his tongue slides inside, exploring like last night was just a warm-up, like he's been starving for more. He breaks the kiss, chest heaving, eyes dark and smoldering as they roam my face.

"Second?" I prompt breathlessly, desperate to hear the rest.

His grin is wicked enough to scare the creepy elf. "How about I just show you?"

His lips move toward mine again, slow and deliberate.

"Does it involve spanking?" I tease, bolder than I'd ever been before.

He freezes, a rough sound caught deep in his throat. "Jesus, girl. You *really* do belong on the naughty list, don't you?"

I press my hips forward, bumping against the growing hardness beneath his sweats. He captures my hands and puts them above my head. "Actually? I think I belong on you."

That pulls a low, guttural growl from him, wrapping around me like fire, setting me on edge until the world narrows to just us. Suddenly, one of my hands is free, and he tugs on my pajama pants with slow, possessive fingers until they brush the lace of my panties.

"Well, since I'm already on the naughty list," I breathe out. "I might as well take full advantage of it... meaning, take advantage of you."

With a quick, fierce motion, he yanks my panties down from my hips. I gasp, and before I can catch my breath, his mouth covers mine, swallowing the sound, claiming me.

No man has ever ripped my panties off before. It's raw, fierce, and insanely erotic—like a shot of adrenaline straight to my core. He pulls down his sweats just enough to free his hard, aching erection. The next thing I know, I'm weightless, lifted against the wall, my legs wrapped tight around him.

Holy God. What the hell is happening to me? I don't know, but now is definitely not the time to be questioning it.

"Penn," I whisper, mind spinning.

"Fuck, wait. Condom."

"Right," I say. But just as he's about to set me down and shatter this electric moment, I stop him. "I'm clean and protected. Nexplanon."

He's breathing hard when he replies, "I'm clean too, Jay. Tested regularly. And it's been a while."

I cock a disbelieving brow. "I read the papers."

He snorts out a disgruntled laugh. "Don't believe everything you read."

I don't know why it makes me happy to know he's not a man-whore. "Except for Thanksgiving trauma and decking Santa."

"Truth." His gaze sharpens, all humor gone from his voice when he asks, "You sure, Jay?"

"I'm sure."

And with that, he pulls me closer, sinking into me in one seamless, breathtaking motion.

"Oh, God," I groan as every muscle clenches around him. I wrap my arms tight, surrendering as he moves me against the wall, sliding me up and down his cock with effortless power.

It's wild. Crazy. Nothing like anything I've ever known, and suddenly something I want every single day. Every hour.

He pounds into me and I bite down lightly on his shoulder, eliciting a raw grunt that sends a shiver racing through my core. There's something primal in that sound, something so utterly masculine it makes me tremble. He moans, and I know, he feels it too.

With every hard thrust, my clit grinds against his pelvis, and I'm blown away by how fast he's driving me toward the edge. Is it the heat of skin on skin? The urgent pulse between us? Or just that this is Penn—unforgettable, untamed Penn?

I hold him tighter, nails digging into his flesh as he pushes me higher and higher, filling me deep, hitting my cervix with every powerful stroke. When I let go, my juices slick down his pistoning cock, and the world falls away.

"Jesus, yes," he murmurs. "Jay, you feel so damn good."

He clutches me close, mouth trailing fire along my neck as he moves—seeking more than release, more than just the physical. Then his whole body tightens, shudders, and he lets go.

I gasp, breathless. "I feel you. I feel everything."

He presses into me, slow and heavy, his warmth flooding through every inch of me. And in that moment, I know—this man just might ruin me for anyone else.

PENN

After dropping off the latest haul of arts-and-crafts supplies at the rec center, I slide back behind the wheel. The heater hums, filling the cab with a cozy warmth, and out of the corner of my eye, I catch Jaylynn buckling in. There's a soft, relaxed glow to her, like the edges of her smile are still humming from earlier... activities.

Her phone pings, and she checks the message before setting it on the center console. Must not have been an emergency as she still has that happiness about her.

"What's your favorite Christmas movie?" I ask, stealing a quick glance at her before merging onto the road that winds toward the tree lot on the edge of town. I'm not imagining it—she looks content. Loose-limbed. Sated. All the sex must be doing her good. I grin. Hell, it's been doing me good too.

"Christmas Vacation," she says without hesitation, and I can't help the smile that tugs at my mouth.

"Looks like we have something else in common."

She shifts in her seat, the faintest sparkle in her eyes. "I like the Grinch too. After your Santa encounter, and I saw you at the inn, I figured you were basically the Christmas Grinch home to ruin Snowberry."

"You don't think that anymore."

"The Grinch is stingy." Her hand slides across the seat, warm and deliberate, settling on my thigh. Boing. Instant arousal. The kind that shoots through me so fast I have to readjust my grip on the steering wheel. "But you," she adds in a lower, playful tone, "Are anything but stingy."

A big laugh bursts out of me, half to cover the way my pulse just spiked. "It's the holiday season. I feel generous."

"Oh, yes. Very generous." She chuckles, and I refocus on the road, though I can't help the occasional sidelong glance.

"Something about driving out here reminds me of that movie," I tell her. "Clark and his family going to cut their own tree."

"Well, we're not cutting one down," she says, brushing her thumb over my leg. "We're going to the lot. And didn't Clark punch that plastic Santa?"

"My favorite part," I admit.

"Like I had any doubt."

She settles back into her seat, her profile bathed in the pale winter light filtering through the windshield. Snow begins to swirl lazily from the gray sky, softening the edges of the world around us.

"Family dinner tonight, huh?" I ask.

She nods, still smiling.

"Do you think they're really going to buy this?" I slide my hand over hers, still resting on my lap, and give it a squeeze.

"I think anyone within twenty miles can feel the tension radiating off us."

"We don't have to fake that part," I murmur.

The snow thickens, dusting the road in white, and I ease my foot off the gas. "What do you want for Christmas? Other than getting your career back on track."

She tips her head, thinking. "Honestly? I've been so busy I haven't given it much thought."

"You have time now."

"Okay, let me try. One, I already have a hot guy in my bed..." Her grin tilts mischievous. "Two, that hot guy already put my high school humiliation in his place."

"Not done with that either," I say, my voice lower now, a promise hidden beneath the words.

She chuckles. "Noted."

The sound fades and silence fills the cab. I steal a glance at her, expecting the same playful glint in her eyes, but it's gone. Her gaze is distant, her smile nowhere to be found. Something about the stillness in her expression makes my chest tighten. She's not here with me—she's somewhere else, somewhere in the past. I can guess where. And I hate the thought of her alone with whatever shadows her Christmas memories hold.

"I'd like to make new Christmas memories," I say, my voice quieter than I intend.

Her eyes shift to mine. "Yeah?"

I nod. "We always had a quiet Christmas when I was growing up."

"Not me." She cocks her head. "Be careful what you wish for, Radman."

"Oh, I'm not wishing for chaos," I say with a faint smile. "I loved a quiet Christmas. Back then, Elaine and I would play cards and board games. My favorite was Trouble. Well, I shouldn't say it was my favorite because I could never seem to pop a six and get out of home." I laugh. "But it really was fun. We'd bake until the kitchen smelled like cinnamon for days. We'd make homemade gifts—ugly ones, sure—but they meant something. Those were good times." My voice thins out, the warmth of the memory colliding with something colder, heavier. Old hurt, sharp as glass, presses against my ribs.

"But those days were shattered when Earl came into the picture," she states quietly, as though reading my thoughts.

"Yeah," I murmur softly.

"You never got that time back."

"No." I keep my eyes on the road. "We didn't."

"I'm sorry, Penn."

"It's okay," I say automatically, though it isn't—not really. But if I let myself sit in that ache too long, I'll drown in it.

She shifts in her seat, her tone lighter now. "My house... let's just say it was the chaos of the Griswolds without the squirrel."

I let out a low chuckle. "I could probably rustle up a squirrel for you if you want."

"Heck no," she says, wrinkling her nose. Then her lips purse in thought. "Although, I wouldn't mind giving Uncle Jack a good scare."

My amusement dies. "Uncle Jack?"

Her gaze flicks to mine, almost defiant. "He's been a bit handsy lately."

A hot spike of anger shoots through me, and my grip tightens on the wheel. "He better not be handsy with you."

She waves it off. "I can handle him."

I don't like the way she says that. Like she's had to handle things before. "Do you do things to his coffee too?"

That earns a burst of laughter from her. "I think you're getting to know me too well."

"I'm never drinking your coffee again," I warn, though a smile tugs at my mouth.

"Don't worry, you're safe." Her gaze sharpens in mock warning. "As long as you stay on my good side."

"Noted," I say with a nod full of assurance, because I'd never do anything to upset this woman. Not intentionally, anyway.

A song drifts through the speakers, the familiar chords filling the space between us. She turns it up and hums along, her voice low and warm. I don't want to break the moment, but then she glances at me, hesitant, and I brace myself, knowing what she's going to ask.

"Do you... ever hear from your parents?"

Even though I knew it was coming, the question still hits me like a cold wind. My hands lock on the steering wheel.

"I'm sorry," she blurts out quickly. "I didn't mean to bring up bad memories. You just mentioned a quiet Christmas, and I wondered... I didn't mean to upset you."

I keep my eyes on the snowy road ahead. "I'm not upset with you, Jay." I take a breath, then another, searching for the words. "I understand now that my mother gave me to her older sister because she was young, and it was the right thing to do."

Her voice softens, like she's afraid to touch the wrong nerve. "But that wasn't easy for you."

Wow. She reads me better than anyone ever has. Maybe it's because I usually keep the gates shut tight—quiet, controlled, making it clear that my business is my business. But it's more than that. I've built this wall for so long I don't even notice it anymore.

Sure, on the ice I can be a team player. I can play my role, throw my weight, take hits for the guys. But off the ice? I'm not always confident that people actually want me around.

Why would they, when you snarl at them half the time, dude?

Yeah... true.

And if I'm being honest, I'm not all that confident on the ice either—not in the way people think. I'm the enforcer. That's my box, my brand. I've got that covered. But I hold back. I know I can do more, but no one's asking for the skilled guy. And if I show it, and it's not what they want, I could be sent down. Better to stay the guy they expect than risk showing the parts they don't.

"No, it wasn't easy," I admit quietly. "I know it was for the best, but I always wonder... was there something I could have done?"

"You were a baby, Penn," she says softly.

I shrug. I know she's right, but when you've been left—no matter the reason—there's this shadow that settles over you. A voice that whispers you weren't worth keeping. And when it comes to my dad, there's no sugar-coating it. He truly abandoned me. He's somewhere out there, fuck knows where.

I glance at her. She's watching me, eyes warm and unflinching, like she's trying to hold some of my weight for me. "I thought she'd come back, you know? My mom. I thought if I followed the rules, did everything right, became exactly what people wanted, she'd see value in me and come back. Last we heard, she was out west. But that was a long time ago."

Her throat works as she swallows, eyes glistening before she looks away. I don't want her pity—I hate pity—but with her, I don't feel the same urge to hide it. I don't know why. Maybe because she's carrying her own scars, and deep down, we're both still a little lost.

"I'm okay, Jay."

"I know," she responds, but I see something different in her eyes. "I just... feel for the little boy who grew into a man, and never got to know his parents."

I clear my throat. "Thanks."

"Do you want to see her? Your mom, I mean."

"I don't know," I admit. "But I don't think that's ever going to happen."

"Your dad?"

"He bailed too. I have no idea who he even is." I shake my head, forcing a lighter tone. "Wow, this got deep for Christmas tree shopping, huh?"

"I like that you shared it with me," she says, her hand finding my thigh again. "I'm guessing you don't really open up much."

I dodge the question. "Your two older brothers. They're not going to mess with me, are they? Stealing the heart of their younger sister, and that I might not be good enough for her."

She smirks. "Have you seen yourself? The guys don't interfere in my dating life." In a quieter voice, she adds, "Believe me, you're good enough."

Her words hit something deep inside me. "They didn't go after the douchebag who humiliated you at the tree lighting?"

"They were both away at college. They only saw it after the fact. And no, they didn't go after him."

"I would have."

She makes this little sound—half gasp, half disbelief.

"You mean if you were my brother?" she asks.

"No," I say, my voice firm now. "I mean if I'd seen the way he treated you that night, I would have torn him a new one."

Her mouth falls open. "Penn... you were there."

"What? No. I wasn't there. I've never gone to a single tree-light event growing up. Not one."

Her brow furrows. "But... I saw you. In the crowd. Just before we lit the tree up."

I stare straight ahead at the road, the memory stirring to life. "Yeah, I was there. I forgot. It was a couple days before Christmas, right? Like the twentieth or twenty-first?" She nods and I continue. "Elaine asked me to go to town to get a box of cereal. That was Flake Appreciation Day?"

"Flake Appreciation Day?" I glance sideways at her, her eyes silently asking if I'm serious.

A grin touches my lips. "Aunt Elaine," I answer in response, those two words saying everything.

She laughs, the sound bright and warm. "Right. Flake Appreciation Day means you..."

"Eat flaky cereal," I finish, grinning.

"Ah, yes, of course." She shakes her head like I'm a mystery she's slowly unraveling. "You had a very interesting upbringing, Penn."

"I did." I shrug, voice softer now. "That night, I ran to town to get cereal for dinner, and left before the ceremony even started."

She nods slowly, puzzle pieces clicking together in her eyes. "I didn't realize you never attended any of the ceremonies."

I keep my gaze steady on the road ahead. I always felt a little out of place, even in my own town. But I don't say that. The weight of the last half hour hangs between us, heavy enough for a season's worth of stories. I want to shift the mood, lighten the air.

"Yeah. I am a little disappointed I didn't get to see your light-up pants, though. You don't happen to still have them, do you?"

She shakes her head but doesn't laugh at the joke. Instead, she crinkles her nose, eyes searching mine. "You really would have decked Dylan?"

"Damn straight."

"We didn't know each other that well, though."

"Doesn't matter."

"Why would you have stood up for me?"

My chest tightens. There's a sudden pinch, like a thread pulling me closer to her. We're more alike than either of us realize. She had friends—more than I ever did—but no one stood up for her. I saw the video afterward. If I'd been there, let's just say I wouldn't have been laughing or documenting her humiliation. I swallow hard, remembering the posts, the heartbreak in her eyes.

"I would have introduced my fist to his face, because I don't tolerate people treating other people badly." Maybe it's the way I've been treated that makes me want to stand up for others. "You know I decked Santa, right? I'd have done the same to Dylan."

A new light flickers in her gaze. "You can't just hit people when you feel like it."

"Did you forget what I do for a living?" I ask, voice low and rough.

"I know, but off the ice..."

"If they deserve it, I think it's okay. Even Aunt Elaine would've approved."

"Maybe we could get her to sic her feral cats on him."

I grin. "Yeah, but I think I can handle him."

Her eyes flicker down, playfully. "But who's going to take care of you?"

I take her hand, placing it boldly over my cock. "You."

She gives my swelling dick a soft squeeze, and when I groan, she laughs—soft, genuine, and full of promise. "Can't wait." She grins. "Actually, why wait?"

With that she pops the button on my pants, slow and deliberate. But just then, her phone buzzes on the console, shattering the moment. I glance down. The caller ID makes my blood run cold.

JAYLYNN

"Looks like the party's already in full swing." I glance at Penn as we crunch up the front walk, my fingers curling tighter around the neck of the wine bottle. As we approach, the sound of music and laughter seeps through the cracks in the old front door, spilling onto the quiet street.

"Is it like this every Christmas?" he asks, voice pitched low, as if he's trying to brace himself for chaos.

I pause, my hand brushing his sleeve, before taking hold of his arm. His coat is cold beneath my touch, but the muscle underneath is warm and solid. "It is."

His steps slow. "Your dad's not going to toss me out, is he?"

"No." I laugh. Like I said, he's not your coach anymore, and I'm a grown adult."

"Right."

He scrubs at his face. Is something else bothering him? Like the fact that one day, somewhere in the near future, my dad could once again be his coach? "Are you sure you're okay? Honestly Penn, if this is going to be hard, you don't have to—"

"One," he says, eyes glinting, "I do have to, considering we're trying to pull off a fake engagement. And two, no way am I letting you walk in there after *he* wrangled himself an invitation."

A deep line cuts into Penn's forehead. Yeah, I get it. I'm not exactly thrilled either. I couldn't freaking believe it when Dylan called earlier—smug as ever—asking what kind of wine he should bring. As if this was some kind of game. As if he'd belonged at my family's table tonight. He lost that privilege ages ago. What the hell is he up to?

My stomach knots. Does he want to be here for our announcement? Does he already know we're faking?

Unease weaves through me. "I have no idea why he'd even want to come."

"Maybe he wants you back," Penn says, and the muscle in his jaw jumps.

I huff a laugh, though it's hollow. "Doubtful."

"People want what they can't have, Jay."

The way he says it, the way his gaze hooks mine in the cold, sends shivers through me. My breath puffs white in the air. "So, you're saying he sees me with a guy like you—"

"A guy like me?" His tone dips, softer now, and there's something raw in the way he's studying me, as if my answer matters more than it should.

"You know." My voice thins a little. "Big. Scary. Bucks enforcer. A guy with a great career who's going places."

"That's how you see me?"

"It's how everyone sees you." The words are out before I can reel them back. It *is* how everyone sees him—or at least how he wants them to. Tough. Untouchable. Built for impact. But there's something else I've seen, something he doesn't parade for the cameras. And I can't stop my mind from drifting back to that day I'd watched him play for the Grizzlies. It wasn't about the game—it was after the game, when the ice was empty and the roar of the crowd had faded.

It was *that* moment. That brief, unguarded space when his shoulders dropped and his stick moved in ways most people would miss—deceptive skill, quiet brilliance. The kind of magic you only spot if you've been raised on hockey tapes and post-game analysis. And I had been. I'm my father's daughter, and my father is an AHL coach.

For just a second, something shadows his face, small enough that if I hadn't been watching him so closely, I'd have missed it.

"Penn?"

He blinks, the moment shuttering. "I'm just saying... he might want you back. Guys like him will do whatever it takes to get what they want."

But his voice is lower now, threaded with something that feels like a warning.

I shove away the strange, uneasy current snaking through my blood. "Even if he did, the North Pole would have to melt before that ever happened." My steps slow on the icy walk. "Do you think he's on to us? Maybe he just wants to watch me squirm again. Maybe he's a sadist who gets off on hurting me."

"The only one who will be watching you squirm is me, and that will be in our bed," Penn says, low and deliberate, "And if he dares try to hurt you again, he'll have me to deal with."

I open my mouth, ready to remind him that punching people is *not* the way to fix his image, but he barrels on. "If he thinks he's on to us, then we'll just have to give the performance of a lifetime."

"I'm not that great of an actress," I warn. Sure, I did a summer play at the country club, and a play in high school.

"I watched you in Macbeth back in high school. You were great."

That stops me. "You...watched me?"

He shrugs like it's nothing, but I can hear the truth in his voice, how casual he wants it to sound. "Yeah, sure."

It takes me a second to regroup. Going to that play wasn't mandatory. It was optional. He didn't have to be there.

"Aunt Elaine wanted to see it."

"Right." How silly of me to briefly think it meant something. He might have kept to himself during high school, but he wasn't into me. He was the damn star on the hockey team, the guy all the girls wanted. Funny thing is, I can't actually remember him with any of them.

"What about you?" I ask, tilting my head. "How's your acting? Any secret plays I should know about?"

He lets out a short, surprised laugh, but there's a hitch in it— like I just brushed against something private.

He sobers quickly. "Secret plays? Uh...no."

I narrow my eyes. "Then what?" His reaction was too strong for that simple answer. We might be pretending now, but I suddenly want to know—when else has he put those acting skills to use? What's he hiding?

He shakes his head. "Nothing. Let's just say...I can handle this."

"If only Mom had said no to Dylan." I shake my head. "She's still friends with his parents and her motto is, it's just one more potato."

"More like one more douche bag."

As I chuckle, he takes my hand, warm and steady, his fingers sliding between mine like it's second nature. My pulse stutters. We step up to the door together. He glances at me, like he's waiting for me to knock, but when I push it open instead, he just nods.

And then, thunder down the hallway. "Aunt Lynny," Jesse barrels toward me like a pint-sized missile.

I drop the wine on the side table and throw my arms wide. "Jesse. Look at you. You're getting so big!"

"I'm seven and a half," he says proudly. Then his gaze shifts to Penn. His eyes go saucer-wide, his body locking up like he just spotted Bigfoot—or, more accurately, his sports idol.

"You know Penn?" I tease.

"Penn Radford," he whispers. "I...I..."

"Nice to meet you, Jesse." Penn dips down onto one knee so they're eye level. "Are you a Bucks fan?"

Jesse can only nod, still star struck.

"Want me to sign something?"

Another nod, and then he's gone in a blur, yelling, "Mom! Dad! Penn Radford is here!" as he disappears down the hall.

Penn chuckles, straightening, and I give him a nudge. "Well, that was quite the welcome. I knew you had that effect on women. Just didn't know it extended to grade-schoolers."

"Women, huh? That include you?"

The question hits like a body check—half joke, half something else—and before I can figure out what to say, my sister-in-law Bella and my brother Oliver appear with Jesse in tow.

"Hey, sis," Oliver greets, without actually looking at me. His attention is all for Penn. "Penn, I didn't know you'd be joining us. Welcome home. Congrats on getting called up to the Bucks."

"Thanks." Penn shakes my brother's hand, but I catch the shift in him, the faint stiffening, the less-certain posture.

"Mom said you were bringing a plus-one," Oliver adds, "We had no idea it was Penn."

Which means Dylan isn't here yet. Or worse, he is here, lurking somewhere inside, waiting to make his move and turn this night into exactly the kind of spectacle he wants.

The other two kids—Gillian and Liam—come tearing down the hall, voices shrill with excitement. They're younger than Jesse and, judging by the way they dive straight into my arms, they have no idea who Penn is.

After a round of hugs and exaggerated squeezes, I make the introductions. Gillian gives Penn a shy wave. Liam just grins at him like he's trying to figure out whether this giant in a Bucks jacket is friend or foe.

We follow the stampede into the living room, where a game of cards is in full swing. Conversation halts mid-sentence. Every head lifts—first toward me, then locking on Penn like he just stepped out of the TV and into their Christmas.

"Look who's here," Oliver says, pointing at Penn.

"Excuse me? What am I, the lump of coal no one asked for?"

He laughs, catching me in a brotherly headlock, his knuckles dragging across my scalp in an ancient sibling move I'd hoped he'd outgrown. I squeal, squirm, and pinch his side hard enough to make him yelp and let go.

"Jaylynn, darling." Mom sweeps in, pulling me into a hug before turning her attention to Penn. "I didn't know you were bringing Penn home."

"You said plus one," I remind her.

She smiles warmly at Penn. "It's so good to have you here. Will Elaine be joining us?"

"No, not tonight." His smile is polite, but there's a flicker in his eyes that makes me want to press my palm to his chest and keep the world from getting at him. "It's National Gingerbread Decorating Day, and she's busy with that."

"Well, she's always welcome if she changes her mind."

Something in his expression makes my heart pinch—a subtle shift, gone as quickly as it comes. But I recognize it. It's the look of someone who hasn't always been welcomed, who's learned to brace for indifference or worse. I replay my own history with him in my mind. No, I don't think I was ever unkind. But I also didn't go out of my way. And now that feels like a missed chance.

"Thank you, Mrs. Quinn."

"It's Judy," she says with a warm smile. A faint blush rises in Mom's cheeks. "I heard rumors...I didn't know if they were true or not."

Of course, she heard rumors. This is Snowberry Falls and news travels faster than snowplows in a blizzard.

"I just didn't realize..." She trails off as Dad gets to his feet, wrapping me in a hug before clapping Penn on the back hard enough to make him rock a little.

"Good to see you, son." I don't miss the way Penn swallows, like the word 'son' hit a soft spot. I'm guessing it did. "Been hearing good things. You've been hard-hitting..." Dad stops, a flash of embarrassment crossing his face. "...hard-hitting *player*. On the boards...on the team, I mean."

Yeah, sure he's not going to bring up the hard-hitting Penn's been doing outside of the rink—with Santa and possibly his daughter, but in different ways. Crap, now my cheeks are blushing.

"Thanks, Coach." Penn grins, then shakes his head. "I mean, Mr. Quinn."

Dad barks a laugh. "You can call me Will."

"Right. Will." Penn chuckles and then clears his throat. "I don't know why that sounds so weird."

"You'll get used to it." Dad steers him further into the room, "Come meet everyone." Uncle Jack and Aunt Maureen stand. "We're all putting together a fun, festive hockey game out on the pond tomorrow. I'm sure they'd all love it if you join us. Jaxon is home and he'll be playing too."

For a moment, I lose sight of him in the swirl of family bodies, the buzz of conversation shifting around his tall frame. I stay where I am, surrounded by Mom and Bella, when my other sister-in-law, Katy, comes hustling over. Her eyes are wide, her voice pitched in a scandalized whisper.

"You're with Penn?"

I can feel Penn's gaze from across the room, and the weight of it makes my next breath hitch, because his eyes look like they're silently asking if that's true, if what's going on between us is more than just for show. But that's silly. We're different people who want different things. I am not looking for a relationship and neither is he. We're doing this for a purpose, so here goes...

"Uh... yeah. I'm with Penn."

"Like with with...?"

"I'm not sure what 'with with' means, but if you're asking if we," I pause and shoot Mom a glance. This isn't awkward... much. "If we're ah, romantically involved, then yes." Look at that. Not a lie, which is probably why it so easily slipped from my lips. I knew sleeping together was a good idea. It makes pretending so much easier.

That, and it totally rocked my world.

As Dad drapes an arm across Penn's shoulders—just like he's done countless times on the ice—I find myself watching them. Penn moves easily among my family, greeting each person with that practiced, easy smile. But beneath it, I catch glimpses of something softer. Something almost...hungry. It hits me then. Penn could use a man like my dad in his life—outside the rink.

My brothers, Oliver and Conrad, are more the academic types. They played hockey, sure, but not at a level that ever brushed against the NHL. Not that Dad was disappointed—well, maybe a little. And maybe for the next two weeks, Penn can be the NHL-playing son Dad never had. The thought settles in me like warm hot chocolate. I think that could be very good for Penn. Maybe for Dad, too.

"Well," Katy says suddenly, looping her arm through mine and giving me a playful shake. "On that note. You have to tell us everything."

I blink back to the present and realize I've got three pairs of curious eyes—Katy's, Bella's, and Mom's—trained squarely on me.

"Look at her," Bella laughs. "She's so into Penn she hasn't even heard a word we've been saying.

"Okay, come on." Mom waves her hand. "Now that everyone is here, time for a family photo."

Across the room, Penn catches my gaze. That silent connection we've been building since we first ran into each other, since I first offered him my room—my bed—stretches between us. He's not comfortable with being in the family portrait.

"Mom," I begin. Heck, what am I supposed to say? Penn and I are pretending so he really shouldn't be in the photo? Ugh.

Mom gathers us all up, and the next thing I know the timer on the camera is set and I'm tucked in beside Penn. His arm circles my waist, steady, but as unsure of this as I am.

After a dozen or so pictures, everyone disperses, and I glance up at Penn. When he nods, I know exactly what he's thinking. It's time to make our announcement. My heart starts pounding again as something tight and uneasy coils low in my stomach.

Guilt.

Damn. This is my family. I don't want to deceive them. Not about something as big as this. Maybe we shouldn't have pushed this to an engagement. The word only slipped out yesterday because Penn was trying to put Dylan in his place... for me.

The doorbell rings.

Speaking of Dylan.

Penn's eyes narrowing slightly as he reads my expression. "You okay, Lynny?"

"Not funny." My voice is quiet, almost lost in the buzz of Dylan and Sloane's arrival.

Penn slides his arms around me again, pulling me into his warmth, and I shiver just enough for him to notice. I blink rapidly, my mind racing, my lips twisting.

"Hey," he murmurs quietly. "What's going on?"

"I just... I feel bad," I admit, tilting my face up to his. "Maybe we shouldn't say we're engaged. Just boyfriend and girlfriend. It'll make it easier when—"

The rest of my sentence is swallowed by a booming voice.

"Happy holidays!"

Every head turns as Dylan steps inside, brushing snow from his coat as Sloane trails in behind him. The smirk he sends me is all teeth and challenge, his gaze lingering far too long before he waves his finger between Penn and me and speaks again.

"Tell me I didn't miss the big announcement?"

Penn's arm tightens around my waist, his stance shifting, not just in defense, but in possession.

"Announcement?" Mom asks.

And just like that, any plans of backing out are ruined.

PENN

What the ever-loving fuck am I supposed to do now?

Jay just tried to abort our whole fake fiancé plan mid-mission, but there's Dylan—smug grin, standing there in the foyer like he's front-row for my humiliation. He's waiting for us to admit something ugly, something he can chew on later.

Yeah, no. Not happening.

"Now that we're all here…" I loop an arm around Jaylynn, dragging her closer in a way that's only partially for show. I drop a smile down at her, and catch the uneasy wobble in her lips before she covers it with a quick inhale. I give her a squeeze, a silent *I've got you*. "Don't tell me you're getting cold feet," I joke with a laugh.

"My feet are cold because it's freezing outside." Quick, clever, and exactly why she's dangerous in this game. She tilts toward me. "But not about us."

"Good." I dip my head and kiss her, slow enough for the room to go quiet, long enough for Dylan's smirk to falter. When I lift my head, she's looking at me like I've just promised her the moon.

"How about in there?" I nod toward the living room.

"Perfect," she breathes, and I guide her in. The Christmas tree dominates the corner, tall and decked with homemade ornaments and twinkling lights. I've never regretted not having a tree growing up, but this one...this one tugs at something buried deep. Excitement, maybe. Longing. Happiness.

Belonging?

Nope. Not for me. This is still pretend.

"Jaylynn and I have an announcement." My voice cuts through the hum of conversation. Her mother gasps, covering her mouth like she's reading my mind, and maybe she is. For half a second, my gut tightens with the old instinct that she's going to shut me down. That she'll see I'm just a guy who punches for a living and tell me her daughter deserves more.

But the confusion on her face gives way to something warm. Hopeful, even.

I deliberately keep my eyes off Dylan. I don't need to see his reaction to know he's about two seconds from grinding his molars to dust.

"Babe," I say, handing Jaylynn the floor.

"We're engaged," she blurts. Squeals of joy erupt like someone's just scored in overtime. "We didn't have time for a ring," she rushes on. "It was all so fast." Then she turns to me, eyes shining. "And magical."

"I didn't even know you two knew each other that well," Will says, glancing between us.

"We got close when I lived in Boston," she says. "Then the move, long distance, and—"

"And the second I saw her again at the inn," I add, pressing a hand to my chest, "The heart knew what it wanted, and my knee knew to bend."

"You got down on one knee? That's so sweet," Katy sighs, smacking Conrad's arm when he rolls his eyes.

"It was romantic," Jay says with a swoony little look that does the strangest things to my insides. I catch Dylan's careful, narrowed gaze on her, and my jaw tightens.

"We're going to pick a ring out together after the holidays," she announces. "It was all just so fast, and we need to think about Christmas first."

Sloane extends her hand. "Oh, Jaylynn, you have to go to Tiffany's. That's where mine's from."

"It's gorgeous," Jay says sincerely, examining the diamond. For a flicker of a moment, I wonder if she's picturing Dylan's ring on her hand. And from the way Dylan's eyes sharpen, yeah, that asshole is suddenly far more interested in my fiancée than he should be.

My fiancée.

Fake or not, that's a no-go.

"Dylan," I say, and his attention snaps to me.

It's not the time for it, but I find myself saying, "You play hockey, right?"

He straightens like I just challenged him for alpha status in the room. "Yeah. You don't grow up in Snowberry without playing. I'm a goalie."

I might not be able to put him through the boards here, but at the rink? Oh, I can. Sure, it'll feed the stereotype that I'm just the enforcer, but watching him bounce off the glass might just be worth it. Although, we're playing on a pond. Maybe I'll shove him into a snowbank.

Everyone is looking at me, no doubt wondering about the strange shift in conversation but I couldn't help myself. "Great, we're having a fun game with the kids tomorrow."

"I'll be there," he assures me as Judy pulls Jay in for a hug, then drags me into it too, squeezing me with a warmth I don't know how to process.

"Congratulations," she says, eyes bright with a dreamlike essence. "We could use a wedding in Snowberry," she says. "The country club is a perfect venue. That's where your dad and I got married, and your brothers."

"Thanks, Mom. No plans yet," Jay says quickly. "Not sure if we'd get married here in Snowberry Falls."

"Just putting it out there," Judy replies with a glint in her eye like she's already planning a country club wedding. "I'm looking forward to helping no matter what you decide."

And there's that guilt again, right between my ribs. Damn.

"We might actually have a winter wedding," I add, just to help Jaylynn out, and gasps of outrage fill the room.

Alrighty then.

"I think this wonderful announcement calls for champagne," Will announces.

Good, because suddenly I could use a drink. Or ten.

Wait, did he say wonderful, or am I hearing things?

"Or coffee," Jaylynn says, glancing at Dylan. "I know how much you love my coffee," she adds sweetly, as everyone looks at her with the same confusion as they just looked at me when I mentioned the hockey game. But I know what she's up to. I bite back a smile as she grins at me. We really are on the same page here and there's a part of me that likes having secrets with her.

"Come help me, son," Will says firmly, and my insides tighten. Dammit. Is this going to be a lecture about being a good man, a good husband... maybe even a father? Honestly, I could use a good lecture, because when it comes down to it, what the hell do I know about any of those things? I don't even know my damn father.

As we walk, I scramble for something to say, but Will fills the silence. "How's Elaine?"

Great. We're going there—the unconventional way I was raised—and maybe that's enough for him to want his daughter far away from me.

"She's doing well," I say. "I'd love for her to move to Boston, be closer. I worry about her."

He gives me a warm, fatherly smile. "Soon enough she'll be family." My pulse kicks harder. Jesus, what the hell are Jaylynn and I doing? How can we deceive these nice people? He winks. "But just so you know, we all keep an eye on her anyway."

My heart jumps. "You do?"

"Don't be so surprised, son. This is a small town. We look out for our own."

"That's… really nice, Coach. Uh, I mean, Will." When I really think about it, he's right. It is a small town, and during my high school and Providence Grizzlies years, he did look out for me. But suddenly that gives me pause. Was he responsible for the hamper baskets that miraculously landed on our steps at Christmas? What about the new skates he 'found' at an estate sale, two towns over? New skates that were exactly my size.

Why has it taken me so damn long to put that together?

You're dense, obviously.

"You'll both come for Christmas dinner." A statement, not a question. With a nod, he walks behind the bar, opening the fridge to pull out a bottle of champagne.

"I can ask her. We usually have a quiet Christmas at her place, but… cats," I add with a cringe.

"Yes, yes. I heard she turned one of the rooms into a cat sanctuary."

"My room," I clarify.

Another wink. "Not like you needed it. Not with you staying in the peppermint room."

Holy crap, this man is tuned in. Despite being a grown man and Jaylynn and I both being consenting adults, heat creeps up my neck.

Then… he turns serious.

I brace.

"Penn," he says, setting the champagne on the counter, "You were always a good kid. Grew into a good man. I've always liked you."

I wait for the *but*.

Instead, he reaches for the crystal glasses hanging overhead, sets two on the counter, pops the cork with a quiet *pop*, and pours a splash into each. He slides one toward me. We clink. Sip.

"Do you have any idea why I waited so long to send you up?"

"No," I say quickly. But in the back of my mind, I always knew. I clear my throat. "I wasn't good enough," I finally admit. What I don't say is how hard I worked to be what they wanted and how difficult it was to always be the guy left behind. That I was—am—too afraid to do more. If I do exactly what is expected of me, play the game they want me to play, then I won't be sent back. My value lies in what's expected of me.

Will's gaze doesn't budge. "You were good enough a long time ago. But knowing it yourself? That's the difference. There's doing the job... and then there's believing you can do more than the job."

A knot tightens in my chest. "I've always done what was asked of me."

"You've always fought for your team. That's true." His tone softens. "I was waiting for you to fight for you."

I blink at him. "Fight for me?"

He leans in just slightly, voice low. "She saw it before any of us." The way he says it—measured, deliberate—settles somewhere deep, but I can't quite untangle the meaning.

I'm about to ask him what the hell he's talking about when Judy sweeps over like a snowstorm. "Champagne!" she calls, breaking the moment as she pulls down more glasses

Will's face shifts back to proud dad mode, but his words... Yeah, those stay lodged under my skin, louder than the holiday cheer bouncing off the walls.

A hand slides around my waist, and I glance left to find Jaylynn moving in close. Her eyes meet mine, the silent question there. *Are you okay?*

Am I okay?

Hell if I know.

For a guy who spends most of his life alone, this is... a lot. But I don't hate it. The lying, though. Yeah, that part still itches under my skin.

I tug her closer and press a kiss to her forehead, right before Dylan "accidentally" bumps me, nearly spilling my champagne.

"Oh, sorry," he says, with all the sincerity of a cat knocking a glass off a counter.

Once everyone has a drink, Will raises his. "To Jaylynn and Penn."

"To Jaylynn and Penn," Uncle Jack parrots, then leans toward Jay like he's about to kiss her. I slide in between them like a human Zamboni. She gives me a *I can handle this* look, but as long as she's with me, she doesn't have to. And tomorrow, at the game? I'll be handling—man-handling —the douchebag who's standing too close to my girl as he ignores his.

Chatter fills the room, and Dylan's watching us again. I bend and kiss my fiancée, my silent way of telling him to fuck right off.

Judy and Katy sweep in with trays of hors d'oeuvres, and while everyone eats, Jaylynn slips her hand into mine and tugs me away.

As she leads me up the stairs, I grin. "Are we going to your bedroom?"

"Yes."

"Is it still a shrine, and filled with all your old stuffed animals?"

"Yes again."

I lower my voice. "Are we going to do it?"

She grins at me. "Would you like to?"

"Yes."

She laughs. "As much as I'd like that too, no. My aunt and uncle are staying in my room."

"Then why are we sneaking away?"

"I didn't pack enough clothes. I need to grab some more."

"Sexy ones?"

"Do you ever stop?"

"Do you want me to?"

"No, fiancé. I don't."

We step into her childhood bedroom and I glance around. "Nice."

"Not much has changed," she says, dropping onto the bed with a frown. "It's like they kept it exactly the same because they knew I'd be a failure in Boston."

"Babe, no," I murmur, dropping to my knees in front of her. I push her knees apart, sliding into the space between. Her lashes flutter as I cup her face. "You made a mistake. It happens. You'll get back on your feet. I know you will."

She gives a half-shrug, not fully buying it.

"You're killing it with the festival." I brush my thumb over her face, as I admire everything about her. "Running it like the boss bitch you are."

"Boss bitch?" she laughs.

"I don't know what I'm saying." I hang my head in shame. "Me, being here between your legs like this? The blood flow situation is... compromised."

Her fingers thread through my hair. "We fooled them, huh?" she murmurs.

I nod in agreement, and taking note of the guilt threading its way through my body, I exhale and say, "We did." My thoughts go to Dylan, the main reason we're doing this. "I love how fast your announcement wiped the smug look off that asshole's face."

"Yeah, I liked that too," she says quietly.

"I like your family, Jay."

"Me too." She tilts her head. "Wait, Dad didn't lecture you, did he?"

He did. Or... something. I'm not sure yet. I need to sit with his words.

She saw it before any of us.

Who the hell is *she?*

"Can't remember," I lie, angling toward her lips. "No blood, remember?"

"Right," she breathes, and I kiss her like I mean it. Maybe... I do.

When I pull back, she smirks. "You said you were confident I'd get back on my feet. While I believe you, maybe I'd like to *not* be on them right now."

I stand and walk to the door.

"Where are you going?" she asks, then gasps when I shut it and twist the lock.

"To get you, my sweet fiancée..." I take two steps and give her shoulder a gentle shove. As she falls onto the bed, I say, "...off your feet."

"But..." She pauses and points. "Downstairs."

I chuckle, and pop the button on her jeans. "Yeah, that's exactly where I'm going, babe."

JAYLYNN

Penn comes back to our table at the inn, a plate full of crispy bacon. I arch a brow and he gives me a warning look as he points a finger at me. "Don't tell Coach."

I cock my head. "Oh, and what do I get for keeping your secret?"

"Something very special," he tells me with a playful wink as I reach over and steal a piece of bacon.

"Something more special than clogged arteries, and a future bypass?" I ask, and he laughs. "Don't worry. Your secret is safe with me."

"What secret?" Jaxon asks, as he steps up to us. He glances at Penn's plate, cringes, and then tries to hide his own when he says, "Dude, that stuff is going to make you sluggish today."

"You're one to talk," I shoot back, protecting Penn as I point at the plate he's trying to hide.

He hangs his head. "Yeah, okay. Busted."

"Join us," I say.

His brow lifts. "Yeah?"

Penn waves his hand, but that nervousness is back. "Sure."

Jaxon pulls out a chair and sits and I take another big drink of my coffee. A young boy at the table next to us turns, his eyes wide as he sees the two NHL players sitting together. I gesture with a nod. "You guys have a fan."

They glance at the boy, and his parents try to turn him, but the guys give him a wave. "You playing today?" Jaxon asks Penn.

"Not that you need an enforcer for a friendly holiday game with kids," he jokes with a laugh.

"Actually," Jaxon says. "Why don't you take left wing?"

"Left wing? You want me on the same line as you?" he responds, and reaches for his coffee.

"Actually, yeah," he responds casually. "But why don't you play against me? It'll be fun."

"Yeah, sure. I guess. If Coach wants me there." He takes a sip of his coffee, as more people enter the inn's guest dining area.

"Grab a beer tonight?" Jaxon asks.

Penn nods, looking unsure when he answers. "Uh, yeah sure."

"Beer tent!" I once again blurt out like an idiot.

"How about we show up for one drink, then sneak out and hit up Freemans and play some pool?" He shakes his head and glances around, then he leans in. "I love my parents, and this inn, and Christmas, but a guy can only take so much peppermint."

"Preach," I shoot back and we all laugh. Just then, said parents walk into the dining room.

"Jaxon," his mom Fiona says, coming up behind him. He stands and gives her a hug and I note the uncomfortable way Penn shifts. "I can't believe you have to leave tomorrow. You just got here."

"I know. But I'll be back. Nothing is keeping me from Christmas dinner." He hugs his dad, and that's when Penn shifts even more.

"Penn, it's so good to have you staying with us," his dad Donovan says. "You and Elaine are welcome to join us for Christmas dinner."

"Thank you," Penn says. "That's very kind, but we'll be having dinner with family." He smiles at me and I reach across and put my hand over his.

"Ah, so it's true," Donovan says as Jaxon's gaze goes back and forth between us. "Wedding bells in the future."

Jaxon's brow crinkles. "You mean...you two..."

"We're engaged," I blurt out, and Jaxon sits back, a strange expression on his face. Sure, Jaxon caught us in bed together, but an engagement is a whole other thing.

"I actually didn't even know you two knew each other all that well," he mumbles.

That clearly seems to be the consensus. "Oh, it's a long story." I give a dismissive wave. "But yes, we're engaged. No big plans yet. Mom is set on the country club of course, but we could have a winter wedding." All eyes are on me, and for some reason I can't seem to stop babbling. I glance at Penn, needing him to come to my rescue.

"We have lots of time to make plans." He gives me a slow, easy smile that helps calm me. "Right now, you have a festival to run."

"Are you two enjoying the peppermint honeymoon suite?" his mom asks.

"It's perfect."

She grins. "What do you think of the mistletoe alarm?"

I pause. Do I tell her the truth?

Penn links his fingers through mine. "We think it's fun."

"Oh, good," she says and claps her hands. "Okay, we'll leave you for breakfast. We'll see you guys at the game this afternoon."

Jaxon sits back down, quieter now as he studies us. "Jaylynn," he finally says. I lift my brow and he continues. "Are you moving back to Boston?"

"I…well…right now. The festival."

"We're just taking things slow," Penn says.

Jaxon snorts out a laugh. "Doesn't look that way to me." He shakes his head. "Sorry, I'm not judging. In fact," he begins, and wipes his mouth with his napkin. "Did you know our team's media relations officer is moving?"

"What no." I sit up a bit straighter, my heart jumping, but I try to calm myself. Honestly, I can't let myself get too excited about anything. I've got nothing but rejection after rejection since #GobbleGate.

"Yeah, I just heard about it before I came home." He glances at Jaxon. "You know Deanna, right? Married to Mackenzie?"

Mackenzie is on the fourth line like me. I didn't know he was married to the PR officer, though. But I mostly keep to myself so there's a lot I don't know. "Yeah," is all I say.

"Mac is going to Pittsburgh. She's going with him. The position is going to be open. Maybe you should apply. I'll put in a good word for you."

"Are you serious?" Honestly, it's a dream job.

Calm down, girlfriend. After all the rejections, you know better than getting too excited.

"Totally serious. Penn could put a good word in for you too."

"Uh, after the incident, I'm not sure my word is worth much."

"Yeah, well." He grins at me before tuning his focus to Penn. "If anyone can clean up your image, it's Jay." He makes a fist, turns back to me, and gently nudges my chin.

OMG, does he know we're pretending? Wait, no that's crazy. He can't. Right? Even if he did, no big deal. He needs Penn's image cleaned up for the team and he clearly cares about me. Our families do go way back.

"Thanks for the vote of confidence." My phone pings, and I reach for it. I read a message from Garrett. "Shoot, Garrett was supposed to go to the country club to get the star for the town's life-size nativity set. Apparently, it somehow got boxed up with the club's float last year. He's tied up. I'm going to have to go."

"Right now?" Penn frowns. "You're not staying for the game?"

"I can go after the game."

"Snow is coming later tonight," Jaxon informs me. "A good eight inches."

Eight inches.

Gulp.

Penn sets his mug down. "I'll take you. I have the SUV. If we're getting pounded with eight inches, it's safer."

Pounded.

Do they have any idea what they're saying? Wait, are they messing with me? I eye them. They don't seem to be. Yeah, okay. Sure. I have the maturity of a twelve-year-old boy, but still...can we stop talking about getting pounded by eight inches already.

"I'm sure we can get there and back before too much falls."

"That would be great, Penn." I set my utensils on my plate and stand. "Right now I have to hit up Main Street and get voting boxes out for the displays."

"Sounds fun," Jaxon grumbles.

I pause. "That means you want to help Penn and me out," I tease.

His phone pings. "Actually, if you need help, sure, but—" His face drops when he looks at his phone, and then his head lifts, to see his ex-fiancée walking into the room. When she starts toward him, I suck in a breath and hold it. Those two have history, and not the good kind.

"We've got it covered," I blurt out. Penn looks bewildered by our reactions and I wave him up. "Come on. I need your help to carry...um, the ballot boxes."

He gives me an odd look and stands. When he does, Jaxon's ex slides into his seat, and I can feel the tension in the room growing. Penn grabs his plate and I snatch up mine. We set them in the bin and leave the dining area.

"What's going on?"

"Have you been living in a cave?" I ask him.

"Not that I know of. I mean, Elaine's place is on the outskirts, and I haven't been back in a while."

"That was Jaxon's ex." I point to the dining area as we walk past reception toward the hall to our room, passing the blazing fire and the sparkling tree. As soon as we reach the threshold of the hall, an alarm goes off and I nearly jump out of my shoes.

"What the—"

Jaxon's mother claps her hands, and new guests coming inside turn to see us, no doubt wondering why I'm in the middle of a cardiac arrest.

"Mistletoe alarm," Penn informs me and points overhead.

"Ooh, it works." Fiona grins from ear to ear.

"I think we might need to turn the volume down," Donovan says as he cringes.

You think?

"Okay you two lovebirds, you know what that means." Fiona points up as all eyes turn our way.

"Just go with it," Penn says and pulls me into his arms. I lift my face to his and he dips his head, his lips closing over mine, and for a second, I lose myself in him, forget that we have an audience watching us. Honestly, I could stay in his arms, lips locked like this all day.

Donovan clears his throat and when I inch back, heat moves into my face.

"That was fun," I joke. I turn to Fiona who is beaming at us. The woman truly loves Christmas. I mean, I do too, but the mistletoe alarms are overkill. A cold breeze rushes in and when the door opens and the second Fiona turns her attention to her guests, I grab Penn's hand and hurry down the hallway.

Once inside our room, I head to the bathroom and brush my teeth, and when I come back out, Penn is staring out the window. "You okay?" I step up to him and place my hand on his back.

"I am." He turns to me, and pulls me against him. The movement is so natural and easy, it's like we've been together for years. "Should I be worried about Jaxon?"

"He's a big boy. He can work things out."

"Maybe I shouldn't have bailed. What happened between them, anyway?"

"It's kind of sad really. They were engaged—"

"Jaxon was engaged?"

I cock my head and study his face. "You really don't know much about him, do you?"

"Not really."

"You're teammates. Aren't teammates supposed to play and party together?"

A measure of sadness falls over him. "I haven't been with the team long."

"Do the guys not invite you out?"

"They do."

"You don't go."

He looks over my head, his thoughts miles away. "I'm a team player," he murmurs almost to himself. "I'm a bit of a loner outside the rink."

I pull him against me, hold him tight. "There's nothing wrong with being a loner, Penn. But it seemed to me that Jaxon was trying."

"Yeah. I just…" he exhales. "This is going to sound strange."

"Hey, we're engaged," I tell him playfully. "You can tell me anything."

"I don't think I'm really good at bonding. I don't know why. Maybe it's because…"

I don't want to say anything to upset him, but add, "You didn't have a lot of stability in your life, or a father figure?"

His throat makes a sound as he swallows. "Yeah, maybe."

"You're part of the team, Penn. As much a part as Jaxon and any of the other guys are. I know you're new and—"

"What if I get sent back down?"

There it is. One of the biggest reasons he's afraid to bond with the guys.

"You're good at what you do. Dad wouldn't have sent you up if you weren't."

"He said something weird to me last night."

"Oh?"

"He said something about believing I can do more...believing in myself." He struggles, like he's trying to find Dad's exact words.

"Maybe he just means you could be more...on the ice?"

"I do my job," he shoots back almost defensively. "I do what I'm supposed to. If I..." He lets his words fall off again, like we're broaching a subject that's just too painful to voice.

"Have you tried doing more?" I ask very carefully, not wanting to upset him. "What was that Jaxon said about you playing winger with him? Have you ever thought about what else you can do on the ice?"

"He only meant for this game," he says.

I think about what he said about his mom. That he thought she'd come back if he did everything right, became what people wanted. Then maybe she'd see his value—keep him. He's afraid to put himself out there. To try something different. Because if he's not good enough, he won't be valued, and he'll be sent down...left behind.

My heart aches for the little boy who was dropped on his aunt's doorstep. "What if he didn't?" I ask, knowing his fears of trying and failing. "What if Jaxon sees something else in you?"

12

PENN

The pond gleams beneath the low winter sun, its edges banked with freshly shoveled snow. A dozen kids wobble across the ice, sticks flailing, cheeks flushed with excitement. Jaxon and I were supposed to be on opposite lines, but the kids had other plans. Twelve against two, no goalie—Dylan didn't show up. Totally fair.

Coach blows his whistle. "All right, let's play by the rules I taught you."

I glance at Jaxon and grin. "There are rules?"

He gives me a shove and laughs, the sound carrying across the ice.

"Remember, it doesn't matter who wins or loses, it's about having fun," Coach reminds us.

Fun. Jeez. When's the last time I played hockey just for fun?

At center ice, Jaxon squares off against a girl half his size. Coach drops the puck, and she whacks it straight to me. A cheer rises as the entire team swarms. Kids fly at me from every direction, and I want to skate, but hesitate. What if I knock one over?

"Go, Penn!" Jaylynn's voice rings from the sidelines. She bounces with the others, one mittened hand raised, the other wrapped around a steaming cup of hot chocolate. That smile, that wave, yeah, it distracts me. One second is all it takes for a kid—Jeremy, I think—to steal the puck and pass it off. Another kid buries it in our empty net.

Not legal. But whatever.

The crowd erupts. Jaxon shakes his head at me. "Dude!"

I just grin. "We'll get the next one." Their laughter and stick-banging is infectious. When I was a kid I was too serious on the ice, but right now? This is pure Christmas magic.

The puck drops again. A five-year-old shoots straight through Jaxon's legs, cackling as he goes. Jaxon makes a half-hearted chase, but I intercept before he can catch up. Another wild stick clatters against my shins. I glance at Jaxon, send him the puck, and it lands tape-to-tape—perfect.

The kids scatter like bowling pins. Jaxon dangles the puck with ease until a pint-sized defender plows right into him. He gives up the puck, and the little guy spins in gleeful circles, snow spraying everywhere. I lunge for the puck at the same time Jaxon does, and we collide mid-slide, tumbling into a spray of cold white.

The onlookers roar as tiny Emily snatches the puck. Her name echoes in a chorus of cheers as she carries it down the ice and passes it off—goal.

Jaxon grins as he pushes to his feet and holds his hand out to me. His glove is warm as he hauls me up. "All part of the plan."

Coach skates over, still laughing, and tosses the puck to another kid. "Show 'em how it's done." The boy takes off, trips over a stray stick, and sends the puck flying toward Jaxon. He swerves, the puck ricocheting off a snowbank and bouncing back to me.

I line up a shot, but a flying snowball—definitely Coach's doing—smacks me in the back. I stumble, and the puck slides right past me, straight into our own net.

The kids erupt into cheers while Jaxon and I freeze, staring at each other.

"I can't believe you scored on our own net," he laughs, shaking his head. "We're doomed. Absolutely doomed."

The whistle blows again. Coach claps his hands. "Well done, kids. Quick hot chocolate break, then we add snowball penalties and extra pucks."

I groan and strip off my gloves. "You hear that? Snowball penalties. I'm never surviving this."

Jaxon leans in with a smirk. "Oh, come on. Snowball penalties are the best. And let's be real. You probably deserve a couple to the head after what you did to Santa."

I shove him playfully. "You're lucky I'm too tired to fight you right now."

"Seriously," he says, softer now, "I've never seen you have this much fun."

I shrug. "Kids are fun."

He bumps his shoulder against mine. "Yeah. And you showed them what you've got."

I groan. "By scoring on my own net?"

We fall quiet as we skate toward the edge of the pond. Just before stepping off, Jaxon turns to me, his expression shifting. "It's going to be okay, Penn. We all make mistakes. Suspensions happen. And honestly, I'm sure Santa deserved it."

"He did," I admit. "But still. I risked my career."

"Would you do it again?"

I let out a humorless laugh. "Probably."

"Good." His grin flickers back, but there's something steady underneath it. "You didn't mess anything up. Once Jaylynn cleans up your image, you'll be fine. I'm looking forward to playing with you again."

"Yeah?"

"When you get back. Let's run some practices. You and me. Winger to winger."

"I'm not—"

"Not yet," he cuts me off, skating toward the table piled with donuts and hot chocolate.

I trail after him, grabbing a cup of my own. Across the way, Jaylynn catches my eye, grinning as I lift my drink in a small salute. Warmth slides through me despite the cold. After a quick drink and a donut, we're back on the ice, getting our asses handed to us—and I wouldn't have it any other way. When the little ones score again, making it double digits to zero, Coach blows his whistle. Good thing too. The kids are flagging, and who knows, we might have actually found a scoring chance.

"Great game," Jaxon says, clapping me on the back. "See you tonight."

"Tonight," I answer. "Beer and pool."

Jaxon's a really great guy. Easy to be around. Honestly, I'd love to play on the same line as him sometime. As he heads toward one of the benches to take off his skates, I notice the woman from the dining area this morning standing there, waiting for him. I can see him tense, and I'm about to head over when Jaylynn calls me to her.

The sky has grayed since we started playing, and I know she's anxious to get to the country club before the snow starts falling. I skate over, and she must sense my distraction. She glances around and frowns when she sees Jaxon.

"He doesn't look happy," I say, stating the obvious.

She crinkles her nose like she's debating whether to intervene or not when suddenly another woman walks up to them and slides her arm through Jaxon's.

"Whoa," Jaylynn breathes.

"What?"

"That's Rowyn Perry. She and Jaxon are great friends. The two go way back. She helped him out and did a real journalist story on Rip Hart's wife, Charly...AKA Indie Rhodes."

I scrub my face with a hand. "You're really tuned in, aren't you?" I drop onto the bench and start unlacing my skates.

She laughs. "I'm out of work. I have to find something to do with my time."

"I actually heard about what went down with Rip's wife. Charly seems really nice." Not that I've had a conversation with her. I watch Jaxon and Rowyn for a moment. "Looks like she's coming to Jaxon's rescue this time."

Rowyn laughs and places her hand on Jaxon's chest, like she's claiming him as her own. "Yeah, she knows what Theresa did to him," Jaylynn whispers, practically snarling.

Apparently, everyone knows but me. I open my mouth to ask, then it clicks. "Rowyn's a reporter, huh?"

"Yeah. From here, but lives in Boston." Jaylynn sighs, no doubt remembering her own thriving career there. "Do you remember her?"

"Not really."

"She's back home to cover the festivities."

I finish unlacing my skates. "That could be good for both of us."

Jaylynn seems a mile away. "That's the plan." She refocuses and checks the time. "Okay, hurry up. I want to beat the snow."

I slip into my boots. As we make our way to the SUV, she says, "Playing with the kids is good for your image. I saw Rowyn taking pictures." She grins as we reach the car. I hit the fob to unlock it. "That was actually a lot of fun, Penn. The kids love it," she says. Her cheeks are pink, her little nose red, and the way she smiles at me makes my chest tighten. I want to kiss the hell out of her.

"That was chaos," I tell her, then nod. "But yeah, definitely fun."

"You and Jaxon...slayed." She laughs. Hard.

"Ah, so that's what made it fun for you? Watching us get slayed?"

"A little. Maybe I should get you a sweatshirt that says *Slayed All Day*. Spell it SLAYED instead of SLEIGHED."

"I get it. No need to spell it out. Honestly, I had no idea you were a comedic genius." I shake my head, laughing at how happy she seems. "Honestly, we were doomed from the start. Those tots and your dad had it in for us. We never stood a chance."

She laughs again as I open her door, and she slides into the passenger seat and buckles in. "Jesse is going to be bragging all night about scoring on you."

I throw my hands up. "We didn't have a goalie."

"Aww, is the NHL player butt-hurt he lost?"

"It's just..." I stop and laugh. "It's not like I could knock any of them into the boards. They were kids."

"There were no boards. Where was Dylan, anyway?"

"Beats me."

"Maybe he was too afraid you'd emasculate him." She shrugs, then adds with a smirk, "He probably snuck off to our room to plot something sinister with that damn elf."

I give a mock shiver. "Probably." I walk around the SUV and slide into the driver's seat. "Where to?"

"We have to set out the ballot boxes and get our ugly sweaters for tonight's event."

I groan. "Whose idea was that?"

"Mine, of course." She pokes me in the ribs. "And you'd better like it."

"Best idea I've ever heard," I lie with a grin.

I back out of the lot and chuckle quietly to myself.

"What's funny?" she asks, arching a brow.

"Just thinking about how much fun Jaxon and I had. I mean, I know it was just a silly game, but...we actually had fun playing together."

She grins, the light catching her eyes. "Yup. Maybe you ought to try it more often back in Boston."

"It's not that easy, Jay." I scrub my face. "He mentioned something about that, but Coach would never put me on the first line." Or even the second. He doesn't have a clue what else I can do.

Then show him, dude.

But what if...

Enough with the what-ifs.

"You're really considering the PR job?" I ask, partly because I want to change the subject, and partly because it's an amazing opportunity for her. And yes, I'm a selfish jerk who kind of likes being around her.

"I am. But I don't want to get too excited." She points. "Turn here."

I follow her direction and see Stowe's department store ahead. I don't see any decorations, so she can't be dropping off ballots. "What are we doing here?"

"This is where we're going to get some ugly sweaters for tonight."

I ease into a parking spot, and before I can cut the engine, she's already halfway into the store. I follow, and find her rifling through racks of sweaters with a grin. She holds one up. I shake my head.

"Nope. Not going to do it."

She laughs, the sound bouncing off the walls, and I feel a tug in my chest. Part amusement, part something I can't quite name. She's playful, teasing, and yet there's a warmth in her I can't ignore.

"Come on, it's perfect.

"You can't be serious."

"I like the candy cane."

"Yeah, but it says, 'It's not going to lick itself'."

"Okay...maybe that's not the one." A glint lights her eyes as she drapes it over her arm. "Or...you can just wear it in private."

"What are you getting?" I ask, eyeing her over the rack.

She holds up a sweater that reads, *Dear Santa, Can I Have Your Naughty List?*

"Seems like you," I tease.

She playfully whacks my arm. "I'm only on that list because of you."

I grin. "I don't know about that. You seemed like a willing participant, and if I remember correctly, you were the one who told me you wanted to be on it."

She rolls her eyes and laughs. "Right. Okay, so my Yelp rating is 10/10. Would do again."

I chuckle, shaking my head. Jesus, she's funny...sweet...smart.

And somehow, she's got this way of making my chest tighten without even trying.

"How about this one for you? Seems fitting," she says, holding up another ridiculous sweater.

Before I can even protest, she strides to the counter to pay for them all. I shake my head, watching her, a little breathless. But seriously, what is with her taste in ugly sweaters? I don't know, but I can only hope that last one is for wearing in private too...

13

JAYLYNN

Unease prickles through my body as we continue down the long road leading to the country club, its grand silhouette tucked on the outskirts of town. The towering pines bend beneath the weight of heavy snow, branches groaning under the burden. The SUV fishtails slightly, tires struggling for grip on the slick road, and I clutch at the door handle like it's a lifeline.

"Maybe this wasn't such a great idea." My voice comes out tighter than I intend, and I tug at my seatbelt until it bites against my shoulder.

Penn squints through the windshield as fat flakes slap against the glass. "Didn't think it was going to come down this early."

"Weather forecasters." I huff. "They promise eight inches and deliver twelve."

As soon as the words are out, Penn's mouth quirks, his brow arching in that delicious way that makes my ovaries clench.

"That's what she said."

"Oh my God." Heat flares in my cheeks. I smack his arm and he winces, dramatically, not because I actually hurt him.

"Careful," he says, grinning. "I'm delicate."

"Right. Delicate as a bulldozer."

He flicks the wipers to high and cranks the heat, the SUV rattling in protest. "Do you want to turn back?"

I shake my head as the winding road curves and the massive country club comes into view, a hulking shadow against the storm. "We're here now. Let's just get in, grab what we need, and get out."

The parking lot is buried under an unbroken blanket of white, so Penn just pulls up in front of the columned entrance and kills the ignition. Snow lashes sideways against the glass.

He leans forward, peering through the storm. "Want me to run in and get it?"

"Do you even know where it's stored?"

"Nope. Never been inside."

The words hang there, heavier than they should be. A reminder that even though he grew up in this town, the country club wasn't his world. He belonged, but never really belonged. Everyone looks out for his aunt, sure, but they're both outsiders, always orbiting the town without being fully in it. My chest squeezes. I want to fix that for him, to anchor him here, to make sure he feels welcomed. Wanted.

Loved.

I blink hard. No. Not loved. Liked. Just...liked.

Penn's gaze slides over me, lingering on my coat and my ankle boots, the ones that are already a poor match for a light dusting, never mind a full-on snowstorm. I tug my mittens on in self-defence.

"Let me come around and get you," he says firmly. "If I lose you out here, we won't find you again until spring."

Despite the storm, despite the nerves clawing at me, I nod. I watch through the fogging glass as he circles the SUV, shoulders hunched against a brutal gust of wind. The storm batters at him, but he moves with purpose, solid and steady, the kind of man who doesn't back down from weather, or anything else.

And as he wrenches the door open and holds out his hand, something tightens deep inside me. Something warm, solid, safe. Something that makes the storm feel a little less terrifying. Even in the middle of nowhere, in the middle of chaos, he makes me feel safe.

I slip my hand into his outstretched one. A second later, his arm is firm around my waist, guiding me against the biting wind. Big, fluffy snowflakes the size of cotton balls, attack my face, sticking to my lashes until I'm blinking through a snowstorm of eyeballs. We half run, half stumble to the front door, laughing and swearing under our breath.

Shivering, I dig around in my purse until my fingers find the cold jangle of the oversized key ring. My hands shake so badly the keys rattle like sleigh bells. Penn takes them gently from me, his big hand brushing mine, and slides the right one into the lock with ease. The double doors groan open, and he ushers me inside.

The silence hits first.

"Spooky," I whisper, hugging my arms around myself. My

voice echoes in the cavernous foyer. "I've never been here alone. Or in the dark."

"Do the lights even work?"

"They should. Maintenance comes once a week."

Sure enough, with a decisive flick, the chandelier blazes to life. Dozens of glittering crystals spill light across the grand entrance, scattering shadows across the polished floor. We both pause, cataloguing the scene like intruders who've stumbled into a palace.

The long check-in counter looms to one side, while the mahogany bar stretches along the right wall, its brass foot rails gleaming faintly even in the low light. The shelves behind it are lined with silent bottles of liquor, glinting like forgotten treasure. Some kind of wedding garlands, still strung from the summer season, drape across the mantelpieces, their ribbon tails stirring in the draft.

On the far wall, the trophy case gleams with polished victories—golf cups, tennis plates, and shiny sailing prizes. Old photographs line the walls, black-tie galas, proud tournament winners, glowing brides and grooms on manicured lawns.

"This is where your mom wants you to get married, huh?" Penn's voice is casual, almost too casual. He lifts a shoulder. "Seems like a nice place."

"It is," I say softly. For a moment, memories rush back—my brothers' weddings, the laughter, the dancing, the champagne corks popping. My smile fades almost as quickly as it came. Dylan and I had once talked about standing in this very place as husband and wife. Now the thought feels like a bruise I'd rather not poke.

Penn must sense the shift, because instead of pressing, he rubs his bare hands together, blowing on them dramatically. "It's freezing in here. If I get frostbite, you're carrying me out."

I let out a laugh, the sound bouncing in the vaulted space. My gaze flicks to the leather chairs positioned before the massive stone fireplace, a cozy tableau begging for a fire. For a split second, I imagine curling up there, the storm raging beyond the windows, the world shut out. But we're on a mission, and the storm outside is only getting worse.

"Where's the star?" he asks.

"From what I was told, it was packed away with last year's parade decorations. Which means..." I shrug, unknowingly. "Storage room?"

"Which is where?"

I turn in a slow circle, lips pursed. The grandeur of the club suddenly feels like a labyrinth. "Uh...let's start with the basement storage?"

He cocks a brow, amused. "You don't actually know where the basement is, do you?"

"Not...exactly."

His hand finds mine again, warm and sure. "Then let's go find ourselves a door."

We head down a long corridor lined with portraits of stern-looking board members. Penn pushes open a door at random, and we peek inside. The room is smaller, more intimate, cloaked in heavy curtains that smell faintly of cigar smoke. An antique chessboard waits in the corner, and faded leather chairs are gathered around a low table.

"I think the board of directors use this one," I murmur.

Penn points to the polished game table, his mouth quirking. "Poker night. Guaranteed."

"Probably. Let's keep looking." Penn nods, and we continue down the long, quiet hall. My heels click on the polished floor, echoing in the emptiness. "Why does it feel like we're doing something illegal?" I murmur, glancing over my shoulder.

"I don't know... but it does." His hand tightens around mine, warm and reassuring as we check a few more doors.

At the end of the hallway, we come to glass doors. Before Penn can push them open, I whisper, "The ballroom."

"Maybe they store stuff in here," he says, a mischievous glint in his eyes.

He opens the doors and we step inside. The space stretches endlessly before us—a parquet dance floor that gleams under the soft chandeliers, the walls lined with sconces that throw gentle pools of light. He spots a door near the small stage. "Let's look there."

Our shoes click across the floor as we approach the stage, usually home to bands and speeches and sometimes summer camp productions. Penn tries the closet door. Locked.

I point to his coat pocket. "Check the keys."

He digs through the ring, testing several before one finally clicks. Inside, we find boxes of old costumes, tattered dress clothes from summer plays, and stray pieces of décor.

"No star." I sigh, shoulders slumping. I pace the room, eyes scanning the elegant archway that leads to the formal dining room. Sunlight—or in this case, snow light—would usually pour through its tall windows onto polished tables and gleaming silverware. It's odd seeing it so empty, so silent, when I've only ever known it alive with chatter, music, and laughter.

"Are you okay?" Penn asks softly.

"Yes... I was just thinking about all the parties I've attended here, the dinners, the celebrations..."

"You sound like you miss it," he says.

"You know," I murmur, turning to face him, "I do. But this..." I wave a hand around the silent grandeur. "With no one here, without the usual chatter and clinking glasses...it's like the whole place has been put on mute. And I...don't hate it."

"I'm here," he says quietly, the warmth in his voice wrapping around me.

"Maybe that's what makes it more appealing," I reply, a playful wink accompanying my words.

"With all the noise and hustle of Christmas, it's like the world hit pause here," he adds.

I step toward the French doors that, in summer, lead to a deck overlooking the golf course. Flicking on the light, I'm met with a blanket of falling snow, each flake illuminated like a tiny diamond. I hug myself, savoring the view. Despite the cold, despite the storm outside, there's a warmth in having this entire place alone with Penn. "Cozy," I murmur, crossing my arms over my chest. "But I'm worried about getting back."

He steps behind me, sliding his arms around mine and warming them with a slow, gentle motion. "How often does the plow get out this way in winter?"

"I don't know. Probably not often since the club's usually closed."

"Shit."

"I need to get back. I have to be there for tonight's festivities. How would it look if the event's director didn't even show up?"

"With this kind of snow, Jay... I'm guessing tonight's events are already canceled."

I pull my phone from my pocket, hoping to call home, only to find no service. "Great. Do you think there's a landline somewhere around here?"

"Probably," he replies, eyes scanning the room.

"Let's keep looking."

We find a narrow set of stairs and begin our descent. The air grows colder with each step, and the dim light does little to push back the unease curling in my stomach.

"You okay?" Penn asks, his voice low and steady behind me.

A nervous chuckle escapes. "Have you... ever seen the movie *The Shining*?"

"Jesus... why did you have to bring that up?" he groans, though I can hear the smirk in his voice.

"I don't know," I practically squeal, my voice bouncing off the concrete walls.

We reach the bottom of the stairs and find a heavy door. Penn steps ahead, testing it. "Not locked." He pushes it open, and I instinctively grab the back of his jacket, clinging like a lifeline.

"Did you hear that?" I tilt my head, straining to locate the faint, squeaking sound again.

"If you heard someone pounding on a typewriter... or see those twins... I'm fucking out of here," he warns.

I chuckle, covering my mouth. "No, it wasn't that. Just... squeaking."

"Probably mice," he mutters, eyes scanning the dim corners.

I shiver and press closer to him. "Great. Now I wish it *was* a typewriter."

Penn flicks the light on. The fluorescent bulbs hum to life overhead, casting a harsh, pale glow over the rows of cardboard boxes stacked along the walls. The air smells of mothballs and peppermint, with a side of industrial cleaner that makes my nose wrinkle.

"This could take all night," Penn says, surveying the space.

"Actually, we might have all night," I admit. "If that snow keeps up..."

He shivers. "I am *not* spending all night in this creepy basement."

I pull out my phone, checking for a signal. "Do you think we should find a phone first?"

"Let's just do a quick sweep of the boxes first. Look for labels," he suggests.

I step forward... and something whacks me square in the face. I scream, flailing like a ninja warrior.

"It's okay," Penn murmurs, gently pulling the offending strand from my hair.

"What was that?"

"Cobwebs," he says, suppressing a grin.

"Eww," I mutter, wiping my face. "Nothing says Christmas magic like a damp basement full of cobwebs."

He smirks, clearly amused, and we dive into a quick search of the boxes. Banquet supplies. Patio furniture. Umbrellas. Old signage and banners. Chafing dishes. Champagne flutes. Artificial flowers. I let out a frustrated sigh.

"Everything but—"

"Found it." Penn's voice cuts through my disappointment. He brushes off dust from a box labeled *XMAS—Fragile* in black marker and sets it down.

"Thank God."

"I don't know... this feels too easy," he says, eyeing me knowingly.

I crouch to open the box, and instead of the star for the nativity set, I find a horde of plastic skeletons staring up at me. "Of course. Wrong holiday. And yeah... no way was it going to be this easy."

"Why the hell would someone mark it *XMAS—Fragile?*"

I shrug, matter-of-factly. "It's the elf. He's getting us back for stuffing him in the closet."

Penn chuckles. "I've no doubt, but don't worry. We'll find your star."

A louder noise suddenly echoes through the basement. I jackknife to my feet, heart thumping. Pulling out my phone, I switch on the flashlight app and sweep it around the corner.

Paint cans, ladders, tool chests, janitorial carts, mops, buckets. HVAC units, boilers, laundry machines, and humming water heaters. The old pipes creak and groan like the building itself is alive.

"It's an old building. Pipes make noises," Penn assures me, pulling me close. His warmth seeps into me, steadying my nerves.

I nod, pointing desperately toward the stairs. "That was the only box marked *XMAS*. Let's try somewhere else."

We hurry back up the stairs, feet pounding as if the twins—or some other horrific characters—are chasing us. Penn slams the door behind us, then points to another set of stairs. "Let's go that way."

We climb quickly, the chill clinging to our coats. At the top, we find a door that opens without a key.

"This is better," he says, a glimmer of relief in his eyes as we calm.

We walk down the hall, the floorboards muted under our steps, and push open the door to a billiards room. Felt pool tables gleam in the dim light, dark wood paneling stretches along the walls, and mounted hunting and fishing trophies stare down at us. The faint scent of cigars lingers.

"Billiards room," I say, stating the obvious.

"That looks fun," he replies, eyes lighting up as he points to the tables.

"I thought you might like that." I slip my hand into his, and for a moment, the world outside feels miles away. "Let me show you my favorite room."

I guide him to a door and open it. Instantly, the rich scent of old books surrounds me, a far more pleasant assault than the basement ever was. The library is massive, the shelves climbing to the ceiling, a rolling ladder resting against them like a bridge to another world. A fireplace stands ready to crackle, and I can almost imagine sinking into a leather armchair with a book in hand.

"It's perfect for you," he murmurs softly, his voice carrying a weight that makes me glance up at him. There's a quiet awe there, like he's absorbing more than just the room—like he's taking in a piece of my world.

His gaze shifts, landing on the old desk in the corner, and before I can react, he's across the room with a landline in his hand. "It works."

For a fleeting moment, a pang of disappointment hits me. I like being locked away from the real world, having this stolen bubble with him. But then I remember my role. I'm the event director, and everyone is probably worried.

I cross the room, leaning over the desk, and punch in my parents' number. My dad answers on the second ring.

"Hey, Dad. I'm at the country club, and the snow is coming down hard. How are things there?"

"I've been calling for the last hour. Are you okay?"

"Bad reception, but I'm okay. I'm inside and safe. But tonight's events—"

"Cancelled," he interrupts, and relief blooms in my chest.

"Ask about a plow," Penn murmurs quietly, his hand brushing mine for a fleeting second, sending a little spark up my arm.

"Is that Penn? He's with you?" my dad asks, his voice tight with worry.

"Yes," I answer, smiling.

"Thank God." Relief floods his tone and hits me square in the chest like a snowball. "Okay, Jaylynn, I'll see what I can do about a plow, but they're busy. It might not be until morning. Really, I don't want you guys on the roads tonight. I want you both to stay safe inside... and keep warm."

"Okay, thanks Dad. We will. Give everyone a hug for me, and we'll see you all tomorrow."

"Will do. Love you."

"Love you too, Dad."

I lower the phone and catch Penn's gaze. His shoulders slump just a fraction, a quiet, almost faint exhale. He must have heard a part of the exchange—the relief that my dad knows he's with me. It's touching him more than he's letting on. I have no doubt that this amazing man wants to belong, to be trusted, to be welcomed.

"Dad was relieved to hear you were with me," I murmur, reiterating what I'm sure he heard, as I lightly brushing my arm against his.

"He said that?" His voice is low, almost hesitant, as he eyes me, needing to hear it again.

"He's been trying to call, worried about us."

"Worried about you."

"Worried about you too, Penn."

"Yeah?" The word is soft, vulnerable.

My chest tightens. "Yeah... he cares about his family. And you're family, Penn." I press my hand against his chest, feeling the solid warmth there. His throat works as he swallows, and I add gently, "He wants us to stay inside... warm."

I watch him shift, taking in the library around us—the floor-to-ceiling bookshelves, the fireplace that could swallow us in its glow, the snow-dusted windows framing the world outside. His expression softens, something tender threading through the mischievous spark in his eyes.

"Well, it's still early. How should we pass the night away?" he asks, that familiar twinkle there again.

14

PENN

"First things first," Jaylynn says, clapping her hands. "We should get a fire going and find some blankets."

I shake my head so fast it probably looks like I'm trying to rattle my brain loose. "I am not going back down in that basement."

Her lips twitch, and then she laughs at the sheer terror written all over my face. "Yeah, me neither. Not unless you want to re-enact every horror movie ever made. But..." she taps her chin thoughtfully. "I bet we can find some stuff by the stage. Costumes, blankets, who knows. And if all else fails, we've got those big ugly Christmas sweaters in the car." She folds her arms and rubs them like she's already half-frozen. "Honestly, I'd like to ditch this coat and get a little more comfortable."

I nod toward the large fireplace. "Maybe we should light the fire downstairs instead. A little less flammable than a room full of books, don't you think? What genius thought a fire-place in a library was a good idea?"

"Right?" Her eyes go wide in mock horror. "Can you imagine if I burned down a library? #GobbleGate would be old news. Everyone would be talking about #FictionFriction."

"Or #HotOffThePress."

She gasps, then collapses into a fit of laughter, bending at the waist. "#Overdue inferno!" she manages between giggles. "Get it? Like overdue books but—" She snorts. "On fire. Oh my god, I kill myself."

"Nothing wrong with being your own biggest fan." I bump her shoulder with mine, grinning. "Although, for the record, I'm a fan too."

That earns me a smile that feels like its own brand of heat.

"Oh! How about #ShelfDestruct?" I add. "You know. Libraries have shelves, and they destruct in fires."

She narrows her eyes, suspicious. "Are you making fun of me?"

"Nope." I widen my eyes, all innocence.

"Uh-huh. Well, for the record, I love #ShelfDestruct. But I'm calling dibs on #LibraryLit."

We laugh until my stomach aches, both of us sounding like kids who forgot the world outside exists. The laughter fades slowly, leaving that hushed, warm afterglow that makes my heart pound a little harder than it should. I slide closer, slip my arms around her, and pull her against my chest. She fits there too well.

"How about," I murmur against her hair, "We avoid making any of those headlines and light the fire in the foyer instead. Pretty sure I spotted a kitchen down there, too." I rub my stomach dramatically. "Hungry?"

"I could eat," she says, leaning into me like she belongs there. "Maybe we'll find some canned goods or something frozen."

"There were big, squishy couches down there. Perfect spot to crash later."

Her face lights up. "And, I have my iPad in the car. I keep my agenda on it, but..." Her lips twitch with mischief. "I may or may not have some Christmas movies downloaded."

"Die Hard."

She jerks back, scandalized. "Oh my god. You're not one of *them*."

"One of what?"

"The guys who think Die Hard is a Christmas movie."

"Isn't it?"

She lets out a scandalized huff so over-the-top it makes me laugh. Could this woman be any more adorable? "I should've asked more questions before I agreed to marry you."

I laugh. "Pretty sure you asked me."

She flings her hand in the air, all dramatic indignation. "Whatever. Doesn't matter. I can't marry a monster, Penn."

"Fine, fine," I surrender with both hands raised. "Die Hard is not a Christmas movie."

She squints at me, then smirks. "Wow, that was easy."

"Does that mean the engagement is back on?"

"It is." She rises on her toes and presses her mouth to mine, soft and sweet and so much more dangerous than a fire in a library.

When she pulls back, her breath fans against my lips.

"Although," I murmur, brushing a stray hair from her cheek, "If I *were* a monster—like in *Beauty and the Beast*—I'd build you a library like this one."

Her eyes soften, her smile curving slow and sure. "Careful, Penn, tempt me with a library and you just might make me fall for you."

The words land square in my chest, and for a second, my heartbeat is way too loud in my ears. I press a kiss to the top of her head, hiding the grin that threatens to give me away. "How about you think on the merits of Die Hard while we head downstairs and see how much wood we've got. Then I'll go get the iPad."

We step back into the hall, our footsteps echoing off the old walls as we take the creaky staircase to the main level. The stone fireplace looms over us like it's been waiting for us all along. I crouch, flip open the wooden box at its side, and grin. "Looks good. Dry. Plenty of kindling and hardwood." I glance at her over my shoulder. "Why don't you find us some paper? Probably behind the desk."

She salutes and heads off, her hips swaying in a way that makes concentrating on firewood way more difficult than it should be. By the time she returns, triumphantly holding up an armful of paper, I've built a little log pyramid on the grate.

"Perfect." I stand and point. "Crumple some up and stuff it in the gaps I left."

She arches a brow at me. "Didn't know you were a boy scout."

"There's a lot you don't know about me," I say, giving her backside a playful swat. "Play your cards right tonight and maybe you'll learn something."

She jerks a thumb over her shoulder. "I saw a deck in the boardroom."

I grin. "Strip poker?"

"Sure. But after a movie, getting me out of my clothes was a given anyway."

A low growl rumbles out of me before I can stop it, and I steal a quick kiss, hot, messy, not nearly enough, before forcing myself to pull away and head for the doors.

"I only said that so you'd stay warm going back out there!" she calls after me.

"Thoughtful," I toss back, grinning. "It's going to be much easier to melt a path to the car."

Her laugh chases me outside, wrapping tighter than my coat as the wind whips and snowflakes sting my face. The car's buried under six inches, but I scrape at it until I can wrench the handle open. In the dim glow, I dig around, finding the bag with the sweaters and her beast of a tote from the front seat. It weighs at least ten pounds. What the hell does she carry in this thing, bricks? But I sling it over my shoulder and trudge back, snow clinging to me like a second skin.

The second I step back inside and lock the door, Jaylynn looks up. Her whole face lights, and that smile... damn. It's not just happy. It's like she's relieved, like she's glad I came back at all. It hits me dead center in the chest, a warmth that burns hotter than the fire will.

"Find everything?" she asks, still smiling.

"Yup." I shake snow off the bags and hurry to her side. I grab the long matches from the mantel, strike one, and touch it to the paper. Flames lick to life, crackling bright and hungry. The dry wood catches quickly, filling the room with the sharp, sweet scent of smoke and the kind of heat you can lean into.

I shrug out of my damp coat and drape it over a chair, then drop down beside her. She's cross-legged on a thick mat, her hands stretched toward the blaze, palms open to soak in the warmth.

For a while we don't say anything, just sit shoulder to shoulder, listening to the wood pop and watching shadows flicker across the old stone. The silence feels easy; we feel like we belong.

"This is nice," she finally says, voice quiet.

"It is nice," I echo, my voice rougher than I mean it to be.

Her gaze drifts over, soft and steady. "I can't imagine anyone else I'd rather be snowed in with."

That's all the invitation I need. I lean closer, slow enough to give her every chance to stop me, and brush my lips over hers. Just a whisper of a kiss, unhurried, unashamed. A promise of all the hours we have stretched before us, uninterrupted.

Except, of course, my stomach decides to ruin the moment.

It growls loud enough to echo. She jerks back and laughs, her eyes sparkling. "Oh my god. Penn, you're ridiculous. Come on, let's go find some food."

Groaning, I push to my feet and offer her a hand. She slips hers into mine, warm and small, and lets me pull her up. The second she's standing, she waves her hand in front of her face. "Wow, it got hot in here fast."

"Come here." I tug her closer, unzip her coat, and slide it from her shoulders. I drape it over the chair beside mine, then dig into the bag for her ugly sweater. She pulls it over her head, her hair puffing up wildly with static.

I laugh, reaching out to smooth it back down. The second my fingers touch, a zap cracks between us. She yelps, I curse, and then we're both laughing so hard the fire crackles in sympathy.

And just like that, the whole world outside disappears.

I yank my hand back and shake it out dramatically. "Jesus, I knew there were sparks between us, but come on."

Jaylynn throws her head back, laughing, before fishing in the bag and pulling out one of the two sweaters she'd picked for me. "I want you to wear this one."

I eye it with suspicion. "Of course, you do."

Still, I tug it on, the wool scratchy and ridiculous, and she immediately bursts into laughter, doubling over as she reads it out loud.

"Deck the halls? Nah, deck my lap with dances."

I look down at the bold red letters stretched across my chest. "What does that even mean? Doesn't deck mean decorate? How exactly do you 'decorate my lap with dances?' Because unless this comes with an instruction manual, I'm lost."

Her grin is wicked as she pokes me in the chest. "Play your cards right tonight and you'll find out what it means."

"Looking forward to it," I say, smoothing the sweater with exaggerated care. "But for the record, I am *not* wearing this in public. I can't decide if it's funny or offensive. What I *am* sure of is that whoever designed it was in cahoots with the creepy elf."

"Most likely," she agrees cheerfully. "But hey, where's your holiday spirit?" She pushes open the double doors to the massive professional kitchen.

I grin. "I decked Santa, remember?"

She snorts, almost tripping as she walks. "What was your hashtag for that again?"

"#SantaSmackdown."

She snaps her fingers. "No, no. Better. #KrisKringleKO."

I pause, nodding like I'm impressed. "Good one."

She bows low, like she's on stage. "Thanks, I'll be here all night."

"Right, you are your own biggest fan."

Her laugh bounces off the stainless steel as she wanders around inside the massive walk-in freezer. A puff of frosty air billows out, and she shivers. "Brr." Wrapping her arms around herself, she disappears deeper inside. A moment later she re-emerges triumphant, carrying two meat-lovers frozen pizzas and a bag of vegetables dangling from her wrist.

"Perfect," I say, holding up my own find. "I scored a box of instant potatoes. Now this is what I call a well-balanced meal. Coach will be thrilled I'm eating right during my suspension."

Jaylynn arches a brow and sets the pizzas down with a thump.

"We're making the best of it." She glances at the box in my hands. "Instant potatoes are my absolute favorite."

I squint at her. "Are you serious?"

She bursts out laughing and shakes her head. "No. Did you just meet me?"

"Kind of," I tease, still smirking.

She rips open the pizza boxes. "You know this place prides itself on fresh, organic, farm-to-table everything. And now? Busted." She waves the frozen pizza in the air. "Turns out they've been taking shortcuts."

"Good thing too," I point out, reaching for a pot. "Otherwise we'd starve."

"Fair." She chuckles and starts searching the cupboards until she finds the right cookware. She sets a baking tray and a couple of pots on the counter, metal clanging against metal.

I tear open the potato pouch, skim the back of the box, and set it aside. "Easy enough. Water, boil, stir, try not to burn the place down."

"Comforting," she deadpans.

I pour water into the pot and flick the stove knob. A low hum fills the space as the burner glows red. The two of us move around the big, empty kitchen in a rhythm that feels... weirdly domestic. Like this isn't going to be the first time we're going to cook together, like maybe it could be the first of a hundred times.

And that thought alone heats me like a runaway puck.

"You actually look comfortable in a kitchen," she says, pulling open the small refrigerator. The cool air spills out, frosting her cheeks pink.

I shrug, tearing open the pouch of potatoes. "I used to do a lot of the cooking growing up. Aunt Elaine said she couldn't stand a useless man." I smirk. "Yet, she married Earl."

Jaylynn laughs, shaking her head as I give the pouch a shake before opening it. "Still," I add, softer, "I'm glad she taught me. Someday maybe I can make you a real meal, with real potatoes."

"Not much in there." She closes the fridge, leans against it like she's weighing her words. "If I get that job in Boston, I'm going to take you up on a real meal."

My chest tightens. "Did you apply?"

Her hands go up in defeat. "Haven't had a chance. I would've tonight, but..." She gestures around at the snowed-in country club, the storm raging outside. "Here we are. No service."

"It's not so bad, is it?" I ask, carefully.

The smile she gives me is small, genuine, and warm enough to thaw ice. "Not so bad, Penn."

Just then, my pocket buzzes. "What the hell?" I dig out my phone, blinking at the screen like it's a ghost. "It's a text. From Jaxon." I look around the kitchen like the walls are playing tricks. "I somehow got a signal in here."

"What's it say?" she asks.

I read aloud. "Hey, heard you were snowed in. Just checking on you."

"Aww," she murmurs, touched. "That's so nice of him."

Something warm stirs low in my chest. "Yeah. Good guy." I thumb back a reply, letting him know we're safe and raiding the kitchen like starving bandits.

I'm about to put the phone down when it pings again. This time it's Rip Hart. "*I hope you're snowed in with a hottie who'll keep you warm.*" I chuckle, flashing the screen at Jaylynn. "Group chat."

She grins wickedly. "So... are you going to tell them you're with a hottie?"

"No," I say immediately. Too fast. She cocks her head. I scramble. "I mean, you are a hottie. Absolutely gorgeous, really. I'd scream it from the rooftops. But if you get that job in Boston, I don't want the guys circling like sharks."

Her brow quirks. "Isn't Rip married?"

"Yeah. But not everyone in that group is."

Her smirk deepens. "Aww, is my little Radman jealous?"

"Fuck yeah," I admit, catching her waist and tugging her against me. "You're my fiancée, remember?" I tease, but the word feels... less like a joke than it should.

My phone pings again, and my blood runs cold. "Oh, fuck."

"What?"

I hold the phone out, groaning. Jaxon's latest gem to the group. *Careful what you say, dude. The girl he's snowed in with is his fiancée.* My screen lights up like a pinball machine as the guys go wild.

"Shit," I mutter. "If you do come back to Boston—"

"You know what?" Jaylynn cuts me off, her hands sliding up my chest as she rises onto her toes. She kisses me, soft and certain, silencing everything—my doubts, the storm, even the buzzing phone. "Tonight, we don't exist in the real world. Tonight, it's just us. No jobs, no group chats, no gossip. Just this. Our own little fairy tale." Her eyes search mine. "When are we ever going to get another chance to be this far away from everything?"

The words hit deep, and I glance around the dimly lit kitchen, the snow and wind outside battering the windows. She's right. This is ours. "Yeah," I whisper. "And no elf in sight."

I flip my phone off and toss it on the counter, then pull her back into me and kiss her like the world won't be there waiting in the morning. The fridge dings behind us, yanking me back to reality, but even that feels like part of the spell we're caught in—like this night is stitched together with magic and mishaps.

When I finally let her go, she lingers, eyes closed, holding on to the kiss like it's a memory she can carry into the future. She exhales slowly as I nudge the fridge door shut, and then she straightens, practical again, flipping the oven on.

I get to work on the potatoes while she fills a pot to steam broccoli. The storm rattles against the windows, the whole world muffled and white, and for the first time in a long time, I feel steady. Like we've carved out something safe here, something that belongs to us.

"How's this for making new Christmas memories?" I ask, half-teasing, half-serious.

Her lips curve into that soft, heart-punching smile. "It's definitely going to be a good memory."

I move closer, brushing her hair back from her face, letting my fingers linger just a beat too long. "And the best part?" I murmur, my forehead dipping toward hers.

"What's that?" she whispers.

I smile. "We've only just gotten started..."

15

JAYLYNN

With the fire roaring, I curl up on the sofa beside Penn, a slice of pizza in hand. We eat like it's our last meal, grease on our fingers, laughter in our voices.

"Who knew frozen pizza could taste this good?" I say between bites, washing it down with a warm soda. The freezer ice cubes looked like they'd been fossilized a century ago, so... warm it is.

"Try this." Penn scoops up a heaping spoonful of buttery mashed potatoes and holds it out. His eyes dare me to refuse. I lean forward, open my mouth, and let him slide the bite past my lips. The salt, the butter—it's stupidly perfect. I close my eyes, savoring.

"Carbs. Heaven," I murmur.

"My turn." I stab a spear of broccoli and lift it to his lips. He takes it without hesitation, chewing with exaggerated seriousness. "No complaints?" I tease, handing him my soda.

"I always eat my veggies." He tips his chin, smug, before drinking straight from the can. "I was a good boy."

"You *were* a good boy, Penn," I say without thinking.

His head cocks, curiosity sharpening his gaze. "What makes you say that?"

"You just... were. You never got in trouble at school. You lived in the library or the rink. You cared about your grades as much as hockey. And you were always nice to everyone." My chest tightens at the unspoken truth, that not everyone had been nice to him.

"Yeah, well..." His mouth twists. "I wasn't nice to Santa."

I snort. "What did he do? If you don't mind me asking."

Penn's eyes darken. "He was drunk. A little girl asked him for a pony, and he told her magic wasn't real. Yanked his beard to prove it. She burst into tears, and he started ranting at the other kids in line. When he staggered off the stage, about to ruin Christmas for a dozen more... I tackled him."

"With your fist."

He shakes his head. "It ended up that way, yes. But dammit, someone needed to stop him."

I blink, then grin. "You did what you had to do. But wait, how do you know she asked for a pony? Don't tell me you were in line too."

He shifts, uncomfortable.

"Penn." I laugh, nudging him with my shoulder. "You were, weren't you?"

"No," he mutters, stuffing potatoes in his mouth. "I went to talk to her mother afterward. To make sure the little girl was okay." He swallows, then drops the bomb. "Now I own a fucking pony."

"You what?" My soda nearly sprays across the room.

"I bought it. Legally, it's mine. But it's hers. I just board it. She takes care of it."

"Oh my God." A laugh bubbles up, uncontainable. "You are the absolute sweetest."

"No, I'm not."

"Yes. You are." I set the soda on the coffee table and lean closer, a grin tugging at my mouth. "If I said I wanted a pony—"

"You're not getting a pony." His smirk is pure trouble. "But if you want something to ride..."

Heat curls low in my belly at his cocky grin. "Oh, but I do," I whisper, laughing before my expression softens. "Seriously, Penn. You're a good man, whether you believe it or not." Warmth moves through my blood as he shrugs, like it's hard for him to take a compliment. "I still remember all the awards you picked up at graduation," I say, nudging him with my knee.

"I needed something to fall back on if the hockey thing didn't work out."

I tilt my head, curious. "What did you study again?"

"Computer science." His lips curve slightly, like he knows it doesn't quite fit the Penn everyone else sees. "It was something I actually enjoyed."

I take another bite of pizza, chewing slowly as I process that.

"That couldn't have been easy, juggling hockey and coding and... everything."

He shrugs, but I hate that he's diminishing the effort he put in. "It's all about time management. You did Public Relations, right? How was that?"

"I enjoyed it. I thought..." The words falter on my tongue, memories pressing down, but Penn finishes them for me, his voice gentle.

"You thought you and Dylan would take on the world together."

A ghost of a laugh escapes me. "Yeah. Something like that."

He notices the shift in me. He always does. To lighten it, I point to the bowl of mashed potatoes. Penn scoops up another bite and feeds me, like we're weaving comfort into every small action. The fire snaps, the storm hammers outside, but here in the empty clubhouse with Penn, the old familiar ache in my chest, born out of humiliation, feels... muted. Almost bearable.

"Do you wish..." His Adam's apple bobs as he swallows, hesitation flickering in his eyes. "Do you wish he'd put the ring on your finger and not Sloane's?"

I snort, the sound surprising even me. His brows rise, like he wasn't expecting that reaction.

"Not even in a million years, Penn." I take another bite of pizza, shaking my head. "Sure, it was strange seeing him with her. And yeah, maybe some small part of me knew it was going to be a disaster, which is why I dragged you into the middle of it." My voice softens with guilt as I glance at him. "That was my mess. I shouldn't have involved you."

"I'm kind of glad you did."

"Because I'm about to rehab your bad-boy reputation?"

His grin is crooked, sincere. "No. Because otherwise I wouldn't be here with you, eating pizza and mashed potatoes in front of a fire." He takes my empty plate, sets it on the coffee table, and before I can blink, he's tugged me effortlessly onto his lap. His hands bracket my waist like I belong there. His voice drops low. "I like being here with you, Jay."

Outside, the wind howls against the windows, but inside, the firelight flickers golden across his face, and warmth spreads through me that has nothing to do with the flames. His palm strokes up my back, and the heat of it sears straight through me.

"I like being here with you, too."

His confession leaves me trembling, and I lean in and press my lips to his. What starts slow ignites in an instant. Our mouths opening, tongues tangling, the kiss going hot and hungry. Hands roam, tugging at clothes, both of us desperate to erase the space between us.

"Stand," he murmurs against my lips, tapping my thigh.

I rise slowly, my knees shaky, my breath unsteady. Standing before him, the fire crackling at my back, I glance down at his shirt and can't help but smirk. He follows my gaze, reading the words across his chest before his eyes flick back up to mine, playful and blazing.

"Have I played my cards right?" he asks, voice thick with desire.

I hook my thumbs into the hem of my sweater and give my

hips a slow, teasing sway. "Well... you did make a mean bowl of mashed potatoes, so I'm going to say yes."

He groans, shifting in his seat, adjusting his pants like they suddenly don't fit. The sight sends a thrill through me.

"Something going on there?" I tease, pulling my sweater over my head and tossing it away.

He doesn't answer with words, only a low, guttural sound, his eyes tracking every flick of my fingers as I unfasten the buttons of my shirt and let it slip off my shoulders.

"Fuck," he growls, the sound rough and needy.

I turn slowly, giving him my back, my fingers working the clasp of my bra. The clasp slips loose, and I toss the bra aside with a flick of my wrist.

"Jay." His voice is raw now, no teasing left, only hunger. "I want to see you."

I glance back over my shoulder, my lips curving, heart thundering, the air between us humming like it might combust. "Then look."

As he watches intently, I slide my hand to the button of my pants and flick it open. The zipper hums as I shimmy the pants down my legs, deliberately slow, pointing my ass right at him as I undress. Behind me, Penn's breathing shifts— deeper, heavier—and the sound sends heat racing through my blood.

I've never given anyone a show before, never teased like this, never bared myself with so much intention. But then again, I've never done a lot of things until Penn. My fiancé.

Hooking my thumbs under the thin band of my panties, I tug them down just an inch, just enough to taunt, before backing up and lowering myself onto his lap. His thighs are hot and unyielding beneath me, his body buzzing like a live wire under my skin.

"Babe," he rasps, brushing my hair from my neck so his mouth can find my bare skin. His lips burn a trail up my neck, his breath ragged. "You are so fucking sexy."

I wiggle, grinding deliberately against the thick hardness straining inside his pants. His groan vibrates through me, low and guttural, and I know it's killing him, being trapped like that. With a wicked grin, I rise, pivot, and straddle him, facing forward this time. I hover just above his lap, arching my back, my breast brushing his mouth like an invitation.

He takes it without hesitation. His lips close over me, hot and wet, sucking until my head tips back and a moan slips free. His tongue teases, laves, and the scrape of his teeth has me clutching at his shoulders, desperate for more.

When he finally pulls back, his hands roam lower, sliding down the curve of my spine until they're gripping my ass, squeezing hard enough to make me gasp. Then, in one swift move, the band of my panties snaps tight around my hips before he yanks, tearing them clean off.

"Penn," I gasp, half shocked, half exhilarated by the raw urgency in him.

"Need you naked," he growls, scattering hot kisses across my throat, my collarbone, anywhere he can reach.

I'm still balanced on my knees when his hand slides between my thighs. The first brush of his fingers makes me shiver, and then he's there—pressing, parting, finding me wet and aching for him.

"Baby," he groans, voice breaking as his finger slips inside me. "You're so wet for me."

My head falls back, a desperate sound ripping from my throat as my body clenches around him. He works me with deliberate precision, curling his finger, stroking my most sensitive spot until I'm trembling. His thumb finds my clit, rubbing hard and fast, sending shockwaves of pleasure radiating through me.

"Penn..." My voice is breathless, unraveling as heat builds, sharp and consuming.

"Come for me," he whispers against my skin, his free arm wrapping tight around the back of my thighs, holding me up as my legs threaten to give out.

I can't fight it. I don't want to. The pressure spirals higher, faster, until it bursts. My whole body seizes, every muscle tightening as wave after wave of release crashes through me. I cry out, clutching his shoulders, the world blurring, shaking apart in his arms.

And when I open my eyes, he's staring at me like I've just given him something priceless, something sacred. His expression is almost awed, as if he can't quite believe I came undone for him like that.

My chest heaves, my skin still trembling, and my heart slams harder than it should. Because I've had sex before. I've gone through the motions, even fooled myself into thinking there was intimacy. But this? With Penn? It's different. It's raw and consuming, threaded through with something deeper, something real.

For the first time, I understand what it's supposed to feel like when it's not just your body giving in... but your heart.

"Penn," I whisper, still trembling as aftershocks ripple through me. I feel boneless, but the need pulsing between my legs is far from satisfied.

He cups my face, his forehead pressing to mine, his breath hot and uneven. "I need you, Jay. Right now. I can't wait anymore."

My answer is a nod, a shaky, desperate sound escaping my throat as I reach for the button of his jeans. He groans when my fingers brush against the hard length straining inside, and together we fumble, urgent and messy, until his pants and boxers are shoved low enough for him to spring free.

The sight of him steals my breath. Thick, hard, the head already slick. He looks carved for me, like every part of him was made to fit every part of me.

I straddle him again, and his hands grip my hips like he's afraid I'll disappear. "Are you ready for me?" he rasps, his eyes searching mine.

Even though I'm sure I was never ready for him, I kiss him hard, sealing the answer with my mouth. "Yes, Penn. I want you inside me, now."

His control fractures in an instant. One hand guides himself to my entrance, the other steadying me as I sink slowly onto him. The stretch makes me gasp, my body clenching tight around the thick intrusion.

"Jesus Christ," he groans, head tipping back, jaw tight. "You feel... so fucking good."

The burn melts into bliss as I take him inch by inch, until I'm seated fully, filled in a way I've never been before. My hands clutch his shoulders, nails digging in, as my body adjusts.

When I shift, the friction sparks white-hot pleasure. He swears again, gripping my hips and holding me still. "Don't move. Not yet. I'm already so close."

But I can't stop. I rock against him, slowly at first, then faster, riding the wave building between us. He meets me thrust for thrust, his hips slamming up, driving him deeper until I'm crying out, until every stroke has me clenching tighter, wetter, needier.

"Penn," I gasp, my voice breaking, "Don't stop. Please…"

"I couldn't if I tried," he grits out, kissing me hard, devouring me like he needs me to breathe. His hand slips between us, finding my swollen clit, rubbing furiously as he pounds into me.

The world shatters again. My body locks down on him, my release tearing through me in violent waves. I scream his name, every nerve alight, and he curses, thrusts once, twice, before groaning my name into my mouth as he explodes, spilling deep inside me.

For long moments, the only sound is our ragged breathing, the crackle of the fire, and the storm raging outside. My body collapses against his, and his arms caging me in as though he'll never let go.

When my heartbeat finally slows, I lift my head. His gaze is locked on mine, intense and raw, no trace of cockiness left, only truth.

"Jay," he whispers, brushing his thumb across my cheek. "You're going to wreck me."

Emotion squeezes my chest so tight it almost hurts. Because for the first time in forever, I'm not broken, not abandoned, not someone's second choice. In his arms, I'm exactly where I'm supposed to be.

But isn't this just all pretend? If it is, it sure as heck doesn't feel it and I'm not sure what to do about that.

We hold each other for a long while, bodies tangled, skin slick and cooling in the firelight. His heart still beats fast against mine, and I let myself listen, memorizing the rhythm. Eventually, Penn taps the back of my thigh, his voice rough but gentle.

"We should get some blankets. And maybe add more wood to the fire before we both freeze."

Reluctantly, I slide off his lap. He brushes a kiss across my temple before we pull our clothes back on, piece by piece, sharing small touches between buttons and zippers like neither of us can quite stop. He adds wood to the fire and when I tug my sweater over my head, he's already lacing his fingers through mine, tugging me along as if letting go isn't an option.

"Where are we going?" I ask quietly.

"I thought I saw blankets in the ballroom."

We walk down the long, shadowed hallway, the old boards creaking beneath our steps. His thumb strokes lazy circles across my palm, and that simple gesture is enough to make warmth pool in my chest all over again.

The ballroom yawns open in front of us, wide and echoing, the storm rattling against tall windows. My breath once again catches as I take it in. "This is such a beautiful room," I whisper, my gaze snagging on the stage. "Years ago when I went to summer camp here, I actually did a play on that stage."

Penn glances over, one brow raised as he heads toward the storage closet. "Yeah? Which play?"

"Mamma Mia. It was a musical." I smile faintly, memory tugging me back to those sticky summer nights, nerves before curtain call, and the giddy joy of pretending to be someone else.

He digs through a stack of boxes, pulling out feather boas and glittery hats, until he finally finds a pile of wool blankets and tosses a couple my way. "Really? So, you can sing?"

"Not well." My laugh echoes in the cavernous space.

"Did you play the lead?"

"Sophie." I tug the blanket closer to my chest, a little embarrassed but also warmed by the memory.

Penn straightens with another armful of blankets, a teasing glint in his eye. "Do I even want to ask who played the male lead?"

I shake my head quickly. "Nope." It was Dylan and he knows it. "But..." I gesture to the closet with a grin. "I bet the costumes are still in here somewhere. I think they still put the play on every summer."

He shuts the closet door firmly and catches my hand again, like it's the most natural thing in the world. Together we wander back toward the hall, our footsteps echoing, the scent of old wood and dust mixing with the faint tang of smoke from the fire.

I glance back at the stage, remembering my lines, the songs, the applause. But this time, another thought threads in, an image of Penn up there with me. Not as some awkward teenage boy fumbling through choreography, but Penn now.

Strong, confident, magnetic. My perfect counterpart. And I can't help but wonder what it would have been like if he'd been the male lead. Not just in that long-ago play, but here. Now. In real life.

Oh boy...

16

PENN

The coolness in the room pulls me awake, and when I peel my eyes open to find Jaylynn wrapped snugly around me, my lips curve into a smile I couldn't stop if I tried. Her breath is warm against my chest, her leg tangled with mine, her arm slung over me in a way that feels... possessive. Like she belongs here. Like I belong to her.

I lift my head, eyes drifting to the fireplace. The flames have died, leaving only a bed of glowing embers. Careful not to wake her, I slip out from under her body and draw the blanket higher over her shoulders. She stirs faintly, sighs, then settles deeper into sleep.

I pause, caught in the pull of her beauty. My heart gives a hard thump as I stand there, just staring, drinking her in. The curve of her lips, still a little swollen from my kisses. The faint pink flush across her cheeks from the heat of the fire... and from the way she opened to me only hours earlier. Something deep in my chest twists, equal parts awe and fear.

A shiver runs through me and I crouch at the hearth, quietly feeding logs onto the embers until they crackle and flare back to life. The warmth seeps into my skin, but it's not enough. Not compared to the warmth I just left behind. I stay there, crouched low, mesmerized by the flames and by the thought of what I risk every second I let myself fall harder for this woman.

Just as I'm about to stand and slip back under the covers, I feel a soft, familiar touch. Warm hands slide over my shoulders, down my chest, and every muscle in my body goes taut. Need and tenderness collide inside me, swelling until it's hard to breathe.

"Hey," I murmur, covering her hands with mine and rubbing them gently. She presses her front against my back, her cheek brushing my shoulder. I turn slightly, catching her sleepy smile, and it hits me—hard—that I have no idea how I'm supposed to walk away from her and still keep my heart intact. "I didn't mean to wake you."

"You didn't wake me," she says, her voice low and raspy from sleep.

God, she's stunning like this. Sleep-tousled hair falling across her face, eyes heavy-lidded but soft, lips curved in that lazy smile of contentment that can only come after a night of passion. Firelight glows across her skin, making her look almost otherworldly. And I can't stop thinking about how much I want her again—not just her body, but *her*.

I tug her gently into my lap, guiding her to sit between my legs. She settles with a soft sigh, her back pressed to my chest, her warmth sinking into me. My arms wrap around her automatically, hands linking together just above her heart as if to keep her there forever.

"This is so nice," she whispers, her voice stirring heat low in my body.

I bury my nose in her hair, breathing her in. "Yeah. It is."

For a long moment, we just sit there, the fire crackling, the storm outside eerily silent. I glance toward the window, snow still plastered thick against the panes. "Looks like the storm's finally died down."

We listen together. No howling wind. No rattling shutters. Just quiet.

"It's still pitch-black," I say, my voice low. "Morning's not close...or maybe it is, and the snow's just blocking the light. Do you know what time it is?"

"Don't know," she murmurs, sinking deeper against me. "Don't care." Her contented sigh vibrates against my chest, and I tighten my hold on her like I could anchor this moment in time.

A yawn pulls at me, but instead of exhaustion, there's a restless hum inside my veins. "Maybe we should try to get some more sleep," I suggest, though even as I say it, I don't want to move.

"I actually don't want to sleep."

I get it. Sleep feels like wasting something we'll never get back. Despite what that drunk Santa said about there being no such thing as magic, tonight feels charged with it. Like the world outside has stopped, the storm locking us into a bubble of warmth and firelight where nothing else exists. I want to stay awake with her. To talk about everything and nothing, or sit in silence and just let her weight against me remind me I'm not alone.

"Want me to make coffee?" I ask, even though it's the middle of the night.

She eyes me playfully. "You're not going to do weird stuff to it are you."

I laugh. "Never, and it's you who does weird stuff—that I don't want to know about—to your enemies' coffee."

"Yes, that's true." She stretches her arms wide, her sweater slipping from one shoulder, baring smooth skin to the flickering glow of the fire. I lean down and press a kiss to the side of her head, unable to resist. She makes this soft little sound —half sigh, half moan—and leans into me like she needs the contact just as much as I do.

"Go get under the blankets. I'll be right back." I help her to her feet, reluctant to let go even for a moment. She pads toward the sofa, wrapping herself in the throw while I head to the kitchen.

The space is dark and quiet, the only sound the drip and hiss of the coffeemaker as I pop in the pods I'd found last night. The smell blooms instantly, an aromatic richness filling the air. I fill two steaming mugs. Black, because there's no milk or sugar to be found.

I head back to the door when something from the corner of my eye catches my attention. Was that...a racoon? Either I'm seeing things, or those strange noises came from that very swift mammal. I blink, but the vision is gone. Best not to mention it to Jay, partly because it might freak her out, and partly because it's possible I'm seeing things.

When I return, she's curled on the sofa, legs tucked beneath her, staring into the fire. But the second she hears me, she turns with a smile so bright and genuine it slams into my chest like a fist. God. I don't want this to end. But it will. It has to.

"Black okay?" I ask, offering her the mug. "It's how I drink it, but I saw you put cream and sugar in yours at the inn."

"It's perfect." She wraps her hands around it, cradling it between her palms. She inhales deeply, eyes fluttering shut. "Smells so good."

I sink beside her, and she immediately tugs the blankets over both our legs, drawing me into her cocoon of warmth. Our shoulders brush. Our knees bump. So easy. So right.

"You know, we never did find the star," I remind her, taking a sip.

She groans, tipping her head back. "God, I know."

"If you were a gigantic star for a nativity set, where would you be?"

She blows on her coffee, steam spiraling into the air between us. "Hidden away in some storage room, probably. We need to find out who packed it up."

"Whoever was in charge of the country club float, I'd guess."

"That could be half the town," she says, lips pursed in thought. "Hopefully by morning we'll have better reception, and I can start making calls."

She rests her head on my shoulder, like it's the most natural thing in the world. I feel her weight sink into me, her hair brushing my jaw, her breathing syncing with mine. Together, we sip our coffee in silence, the crackle of the fire and the occasional pop of sparks the only sounds in the room.

And damn it, I don't think I've ever been more content in my life. Not in the locker room after a win, not even in the quiet moments alone when everything should've felt good but never really did.

This—her, here with me—feels right.

But it's not real.

At least, it's not supposed to be. Sure, the sex was great, and being with her feels effortless, but at the end of the day we're trading favors, aren't we? She needed a fake fiancé. I needed an image adjustment.

Except it isn't simple anymore. Because the fiancé part might be pretend, but the rest—the warmth, the intimacy, the way my chest tightens just looking at her—that's all terrifyingly real. And that...that's not good. Especially since I'm still not convinced a part of this is because she wants Dylan back.

"Jay." My voice is rougher than I mean it to be.

"Hmm?" she murmurs against my shoulder.

"Do you miss Boston?"

She exhales slowly. "I really do."

"What do you miss the most?"

She tilts her head, considering. "Work. Shopping. The big city vibe. There's just...energy there, you know? It's so different from Snowberry Falls."

I glance down at her, at the way her lashes brush her cheek, at the way she looks perfectly at home here with me despite her words. "You like it here too, though, don't you?"

"Yes, but the city has more to offer." She glances at me, eyes bright with ambition. "More opportunities for me."

I nod, my chest tightening as I think about what she's been through to claw her way back. "I really hope you get the job. It'd be nice. We could hang out." I nudge her playfully, like we're just friends, even though it doesn't feel that way. Not anymore.

"I could come to your games. It's been a while since I've seen you play in person."

"Yeah," I manage, but the word scrapes raw in my throat. My stomach knots. Jesus Christ, I want to stay on the Bucks so bad it hurts.

"You know I loved watching you play, right?"

"You did?" My brows lift. "I thought you just went to hang out with your dad."

She smirks. "Sure, but you don't spend that much time around a coach without picking up a few things."

I tilt my head, curious despite myself. "So, what did you learn, Jay?"

Her gaze holds mine, steady and unflinching. "That you're really talented."

A laugh escapes me, but it sounds hollow. "Yeah, I can take a guy down when I need to."

She doesn't answer right away. Her silence stretches, weighted, until finally she says softly, "I really loved watching you."

My head jerks toward her. "Wow, I didn't know you were such a creeper."

Her lips curve, teasing. "Well, now you do." She inches closer, until her thigh brushes mine, the heat of her body seeping through the blanket. Her voice drops, quiet but sure. "You've got a lot of skill."

"As an enforcer, you mean."

She shakes her head. "You handle a stick as well as you handle an opponent. You've got more going on than you let on." There's a caution in her tone, like she knows she's stepping into dangerous territory with me.

"That's not what anyone wants," I mutter, shifting in my seat, restless.

"I'm not so sure that's true. What's the worst that could happen if you showed them your stick and puck work?"

"That's not what they pay me for," I snap more sharply than intended. My jaw flexes as I drain the last sip of my coffee. "And if I step out of line, if I stop being what they expect, I get sent back."

Her eyes soften, but she doesn't back down. "What if you don't?"

When I don't answer, she traces her finger around the rim of her mug, choosing her words carefully. "You know, after #GobbleGate, my confidence was wrecked. I was terrified to put myself out there again. So, I hid. Came back here. But when you've lost it all. When you've already hit rock bottom..." she shrugs, lips twisting. "There's nowhere to go but up. So, I took on the parade. Small steps, right?"

"Nothing small about that," I say quickly.

"Well, that's turning out to be true. But now I'm applying to the Bucks. Maybe I'll get it, maybe I won't. But what do I have to lose in trying?"

I run her words through my head, unsettled. "Nothing, I guess."

She nods, quiet but certain.

We fall into silence, but my mind won't stop spinning. What she's saying echoes too close to what Jaxon told me yesterday. It rattles around in my chest, scraping against the fear I don't talk about, the fear that if I stop being the guy who does what's expected—the fighter, the protector, the one who never steps out of line—I'll lose the only thing keeping my spot on the team.

But hell, doing the right thing, the thing people wanted, never brought my parents back, did it?

The thought rips through me like barbed wire, leaving me raw and aching. I drag my gaze back to Jaylynn. Her face is open, warm, lit by firelight and filled with a concern so genuine it almost undoes me. She wants me to believe I could be more. That I *am* more. But no one else has ever believed that—not the team, not the coaches, not even me.

I was never even enough for my parents.

But right now, I don't want to unpack it. Not tonight. Not when the walls between us feel this thin, and I'm one breath away from giving her more of myself than I should.

"Come on." My voice comes out rougher than I'd like. I stand and hold out a hand, needing to move, to break the heaviness before it swallows me whole. "Let's go check out the billiards room."

She hesitates, eyes narrowing like she sees right through me. Like she knows I'm running from something. But then she slips her hand into mine anyway.

Her fingers curl against my palm. Warm. Trusting. And as I lead her into the darkened hall, one thought pulses like a warning I can't shake—

Why does she want this for me? Sure, I'm an NHL player, and enforcer, fourth line. Does she need me to be more, to be something else, something better? Something equivalent to mayor?

What if I can't be what she wants?

17

JAYLYNN

I tilt my chin in mock indignation as I tug Penn toward the grand ballroom. "I won, which means we're doing what *I* want."

"You won?" His voice drips with disbelief. "Oh, puleeeze." He drags the word out with such dramatic flair I almost snort. "What you did doesn't even qualify as a win."

I bite back a laugh. "Excuse me? I sunk every single ball, including the black one. That's *literally* the definition of winning a game of pool."

His eyes gleam wickedly. "Every time I lined up a shot, you lifted your shirt and flashed me. That's called cheating."

I blink my lashes innocently. "Is it my fault you're so easily distracted?"

The next thing I know, his hands are on my waist. He hoists me effortlessly into the air, spinning me until I squeal. "Yes," he growls, grinning up at me. "It's *absolutely* your fault."

My laughter spills out, loud and free, as his lips brush the sensitive curve of my neck. Heat licks through me. God, I love this playful side of Penn—the side that laughs and teases, the side that lets me in. Sure, things got heavier earlier, my words poking at the fears he tries to bury. Fear of not measuring up, fear of being benched, fear of being abandoned all over again. But right now? He's light. He's alive. And I ache to keep him here.

When he finally sets me down, I blow a strand of hair from my face. I probably look like a complete mess, but the way his eyes darken as they track me... Yeah, he's definitely not bothered.

I slip from his arms and dart toward the storage closet, tugging free a dusty box of costumes. "Okay, show time."

His groan echoes through the room. "You're not seriously making me do this."

"Yes," I say sweetly, dragging out the word. "I won. My rules."

His shoulders slump like I've just sentenced him to death by karaoke. "Jay, I can't sing."

"Who cares?" I shake my phone. "I'll play the music. You just have to...pretend." With a triumphant flourish, I toss him a white suit jacket from the box. "Here."

He stares at it like it's a crime against the fashion world. "Really? You think I can squeeze into this? It's three sizes too small."

I cock my head. "Hmm. True." I dig out another one, slightly bigger but still far from his size. I grin wickedly. "Stuff your-self into this. It'll be hot."

"Jesus."

I pull out the white dress I wore years ago, the one that won't fit me now either. But I don't care. "Come on. I want to sing and dance."

His lips curve into a grin, as he shakes his head. "Fine. But only because I can't say no to you."

My heart does a little flip. God help me, I like that too much.

"What if we filmed it?" I tease, eyes sparkling. "You, doing a play just for me? Adorable. And for once you'd be in the spotlight in a *good* way."

He narrows his eyes. "You are not filming this. No one is ever seeing me in that getup. Besides, Rowyn already has enough footage from yesterday. Plus, she'll get more when I play 'nice' Santa and don't punch myself in the face."

I laugh as he wrestles with the jacket, watching his broad shoulders strain against the seams. Meanwhile, I shake out the dress and drape it over a chair. Then I hook my fingers under the hem of my sweater and tug it over my head.

That's when I feel it. Penn's gaze on me, hot and heavy.

"Turn around," I murmur, my cheeks heating.

He cocks his head, eyes glittering with disbelief. "Really?"

"Yes," I insist, trying for firm but hearing the crack in my own voice.

And he just stands there, daring me with that look that says I'd have to be insane to think he's going to miss a second of this.

"Babe," he says, moving toward me like an animal stalking its prey and a hot streak of want races through me. My God, the man is hot when he acts all possessive. "I've been inside of you."

He runs his fingers down my arm. His touch, along with his words, bring on a shiver.

"Yeah, that's true," I manage to get out.

His hands trail up, brush my hair from the curve of my neck. He focuses in on that spot of my throat that sends shivers through me, and wets his lips. "So why do you feel weird about getting naked in front of me?"

"I don't know." I glance at the window. We spent a long time in the games room playing and now dawn is upon us. Early morning rays of light are filtering through the glass, casting long shadows across the floor. "I guess because...it's the light of day, and this situation feels different and you're really going to look at me." Am I worried that he won't like what he sees? No one has to tell me I'm not his usual type. But I do see the way his eyes glaze with lust when we're naked together. Heck, maybe this really is all for show and underneath this nice guy image, he's just a brute who punches Santa.

Do you really believe that, girlfriend?

No, not really. But maybe I'm just worried about getting my heart broken.

Ah, there it is.

"Don't you remember?" he asks, his tone deep, husky. "Last night you told me to look."

"I guess I did." I flick my lashes slowly. "I think, I'm just not used to anyone looking at me the way you do, and right now, under these bright lights." I point to the window. "And dawn...." I let my words fall off, because I don't want to say...it makes this all feel too real.

"You feel seen," he says quietly, finishing my sentence. I nod, but I wonder if he really knows what he's saying. That for the first time in my life, I do feel seen...seen as more than the girl who was humiliated at the Christmas festival, more than the girl who wore light up pants and people laughed at. The girl who lost her job and was publicly ridiculed for being incompetent, and had to come crawling home.

Right now, however, I feel seen as more. I feel admired, cherished. Honestly, no man has ever made me feel the way this one does. And that scares me. What if it really is all just for fun, for the act. One I set into motion, because clearly I was never as bright as those light-up pants.

After I've been quiet for too long, Penn backs up a bit and says, "Jay, if it makes you uncomfortable—"

My heart jumps at the warm sincerity in his tone, the way he wants to respect my space and boundaries. "Do you want to look?"

"Always."

That one answer. So honest and simple. I take a step back, and work the buttons on my blouse. I let it fall, and then kick off my pants, standing in front of him in only my bra.

He gives a small shake of his head, his eyes briefly closing like he's in agony. "You are so goddamn perfect."

My throat tightens, and when his eyes lock on me again, and my heart starts hammering, I know I'm in real trouble here. But I can't go there with him. This is a fake relationship, and in two weeks he's back in Boston and I might never get out of Snowberry. I'm going to damn well try, but I've failed before.

Needing to lighten things, I grin. "Wait, is this a distraction? A way for you to get out of singing and dancing in a musical?"

His lips curl up, the hungry look in his eyes still there, but dimming. "Is it working?"

"No," I blurt out, and grab the dress. I pull it over my head, and contort, nearly putting a rib out as I try to get into it. Once it's on, I try to breathe.

"That might have been more entertaining than the strip tease you did last night."

I smack him. "Stop. I feel like a stuffed sausage."

"This was your idea," he laughs.

I put one hand on my hip and glare at him. "So, you're saying I do look like a stuffed sausage?" I challenge.

"Yes, and I look like..." He tugs on the arms of the suit, but they won't reach his wrists.

"A popped sausage?" I suggest.

"Well, I was going to say, dangerously irresistible, but I think your description is more accurate."

I go up on my toes and kiss him. "Two things can be true at once," I joke. I crinkle my nose and look around. "I wish there was a karaoke machine."

"I don't."

"It was for your benefit. To help you learn the words."

"You know they don't really get married in Mamma Mia."

"So, you have seen it."

"It's kind of a classic, Jay," he huffs out, looking a bit sheepish. "I guess Donna and Sam got married."

The fact that he knows that makes me laugh. "Ohmigod, you're killing me." I twirl in the bohemian dress. "I kind of like that Sophie and Sky head off to see the world." I grin. "Let's sing the song from the beach scene. Lay all your love on me."

"Shouldn't we be in bathing suits for that? On a beach, not locked in a country club during a snowstorm?"

I roll my eyes at him as he tugs on the sleeves again. "We're working with what we have, Penn."

I find the song, and put up the lyrics on my phone. "Okay, you sing Sky's part, and I'll sing Sophie's part."

"Yay."

I whack him and laugh. "Where's your enthusiasm?"

"Must be back at the peppermint room. Maybe the scary elf stole it."

Ignoring his grumpiness, I put on the song, and give him the phone. I don't need to read the words. I know them by heart.

"Let's go."

He starts, a little stiff, and I twirl around him, grinning like a fool when he stumbles over the words. But he keeps going. He's trying. For me. And that makes my chest ache in the best way. Honestly, I couldn't love him more for it.

Love.

No, not love. Appreciation is more like it. I belt out the next few lines and he stands there and watches me perform. His smile is soft, proud, like I'm the only thing worth seeing in the whole world. The best part? He doesn't dim me. He doesn't tease me for being too much. He lets me shine, and then shines with me.

I hold my hand out to him and he comes to me, and then I point to the phone because he's missing his lines.

"Oh, right." He glances at the phone as I take his hand and spin around him. He belts out the lyrics and a joy I haven't felt in a very long time...a joy I might not have ever felt in my life...wraps around my soul and hugs tight. We sing and dance and laugh and by the time the song is over we're both breathless and laughing like fools.

"You're incredible," he says and pulls me to him. "You were meant for the stage, Jay."

I shut my phone down and that's when I hear it. My eyes go wide. "Penn."

He glances over his shoulder, looking terrified. "What? It's not the twins, is it?"

That makes me laugh all over again. "No, I think I hear a truck. Maybe the plow is here." In that moment, I have mixed feelings. Sure, we need to get out of here because I have a job to do, but I could stay locked away with Penn like this, for at least another week, and never get tired of him.

Just then my phone rings and I nearly jump out of my bohemian dress. "It's my mom." I slide my finger across the screen and realize she's video messaging.

"Mom."

"I didn't wake you, did I?"

"No, uh. We were up." I jerk my head toward the window. "I think the plow is here."

"That's why I was calling. We got a hold of Frank early and sent him straight to the club." She narrows her eyes. "Did you guys get any sleep?"

"A bit," I say, and she narrows her eyes even more.

"Are you wearing a…wedding dress?"

"Oh, yeah, uh. We were…"

"Oh, Jaylynn. You were seeing if the country club was a good fit for your wedding. I'm so happy you're considering it."

"Hi, Judy," Penn interrupts like he's trying to come to my rescue. He stands behind me and gives a strange wave.

"Penn, look at you in a white dress coat. So handsome."

"Jesus," he murmurs under his breath.

"Um, we should go. Check on the plow," I say, desperate to cut this off before she starts Googling catering packages.

"Right. Okay, drive home safely." She gives me a big smile that makes my heart sink into my stomach. "I'm so glad you're considering the country club, Jaylynn." With that I end the call and turn to see Penn running his fingers through his hair and blowing out a rough breath.

"So…" I begin. But I can't find my words because I secretly love the idea of a wedding here, and even though it's ridiculous and foolish and Penn and I aren't a real couple, I can't help but imagine what it would be like standing here, in real wedding attire, exchanging vows.

He exhales sharply. "That couldn't have gone any worse…"

My heart plummets, but that's crazy. I mean, come on. Did I really expect him to want to set a date, to follow through with the wild, glittery, slightly unhinged, hot toddy-fueled idea?

Sheesh.

18

PENN

"Are we almost done?" I grumble, my voice low enough that only Jaylynn can hear.

She jabs her elbow into my ribs, sharp enough to make me grunt. "Come on, Grinch. Everyone is loving this but you."

"I told you I can't sing," I mutter, though even I know this whole caroling thing isn't about hitting the right notes. It's about neighbors leaning on each other, about belonging, about letting the season work its magic. But did we really have to do it on the coldest night of the year? Christ, I'm pretty sure my balls just retreated north for hibernation.

"There's cold beer after caroling," she promises, her words puffing out in little clouds of white.

I shove the flimsy songbook into my pocket and rub my hands up and down her arms, pretending it's to keep her warm, when really it's because I can't stop touching her. My fingers itch for excuses. My body leans without asking permission. Out of the corner of my eye, I catch Dylan the

Douche watching us, his gaze narrowed, and the caveman part of me wants to sling an arm around her and stake my claim.

"I want hot beer," I grouch.

Her nose crinkles, adorable in a way that should be illegal. "You do?"

"No." I dip closer, my lips brushing her ear so no one—especially not her parents—overhears. "What I want is you in my bed, with us warming each other up."

She laughs softly, the sound sending heat straight through my frozen veins. "That can be arranged, but right now..." She pokes me in the side again. "Sing."

So, I grumble, drag the book back out, and half-heartedly join in. But the truth is, somewhere between "Deck the Halls" and "Silent Night," I'm not thinking about my lack of pitch. I'm thinking about how, in just one week, Jaylynn has somehow dragged me into a whole new life.

Ugly sweater contests, storefront decorating, wrestling a stubborn oversized star out from under a stage, then assembling the life-size nativity set in town square with her dad. Arts and crafts with kids sticky from hot cocoa and marshmallows. Teaching ankle-biters how to skate. Family dinners where laughter was louder than the clatter of forks. Hockey games on the frozen pond that ended with everyone breathless and rosy-cheeked.

And then there's my team. The guys blowing up our group chat, wanting to know all about my fiancée. Rip demanding proof of life. Roman insisting 'pics or it didn't happen'. For the first time in forever, their chirps didn't feel like noise.

They felt like...invitations. Like maybe I wasn't just skating on the outside, waiting for the call to pack my bags.

A smile tugs at my mouth before I can stop it. I've never really felt like I belonged anywhere, and hell, maybe a part of me didn't want to. But something's shifting.

And let's be real. Jaylynn is the reason.

But...reality check. Getting close to her, to this family, to these teammates, only to lose it all if I get sent back down? That'll gut me.

Still, standing here, singing off-key with her shoulder pressed into mine, my breath mixing with hers in the cold air, I know one thing with bone-deep certainty. Every ridiculous, festive, uncomfortable thing she's made me do this week...I loved it.

And the scariest part?

I loved it because of her.

Fuck. What is happening to me?

I don't know. I only know what the next two days will bring. Me in a Santa suit and the lighting of the town's Christmas tree, and making better memories for Jaylynn. I want to over-write the humiliation Dylan dumped on her that night years ago, when he left her crying on the stage, laughter in the air instead of applause for all her hard work with the festival. If it kills me, she'll have new memories, ones that wash those old painful ones away, forever.

"Oh, we have to go to Penn's house," Judy says, her cheeks flushed pink from the cold.

My head lifts. "It's too far to walk," I remind her. We've been making our way through the downtown blocks, but Aunt

Elaine's place is miles away. No way we're dragging everyone through the snow and ice.

"Come on, son." Will throws his arm around me like it's the most natural thing in the world.

Son.

My heart stutters and suddenly it's a little harder to swallow.

"You're family now," he says again, with that simple conviction that always rocks me back on my heels. "And we have to sing to family."

Do we, though?

I don't say it. Instead, I stand there, feeling foolish—and maybe a little raw—for loving the way this man treats me. Not just like his daughter's fiancé. Not just like a guy passing through. Like a son. Like the father I never had, and never let myself admit I wanted.

And the craziest part is I already know I'm going to miss all of them—Jay's big, loud, messy, rambunctious family. I used to swear I liked solitude. Convinced myself it was freedom. Maybe that was just the story I told to cover up the fact that I'd never been invited into something worth missing before.

"Oh right, I forgot you lived out there in the middle of nowhere," Dylan cuts in, his voice sharp enough to scratch. He snorts, then pretends to think, tapping his temple. "You lived with... what was it? Oh, that's right. Your aunt, Elaine."

"Yes," I answer through clenched teeth. He's got that familiar smirk on his face. The same one I remember from high school. He's winding up for a punchline, ready to drag me down in front of her family. But here's the thing. I'm not a teenager anymore. And I'm not about to let Jay watch me snap and give Dylan what he wants.

As if she senses the storm brewing inside me, Jaylynn slips her hand around my arm. Her touch steadies me, tells me. Not who Dylan tries to paint me as, but who I really am.

"Come on," she says lightly. "We'll drive out with Mom and Dad."

"Dylan, I'm cold," Sloane whines at his side, tugging at his sleeve. "Can we just go home? You can warm me up." Her smile is filled with promises, but he doesn't take the bait.

Dylan shakes his head, puffing up like he's so fucking important. "It's Christmas, Sloane. As mayor, it's my obligation to be here for the people." Then, to her, "Why don't I drop you at my parents' place and I'll meet you there later?"

"Fine," she huffs, then Dylan tilts his head toward Jaylynn.

"Jay, you can ride with me if your father's car isn't big enough for everyone."

Like hell she will.

I wrap an arm around Jaylynn's waist and pull her flush against me. "There's plenty of room," I say, voice low, even, deliberate. I meet Dylan's eyes and don't blink. "She's with her family. Where she belongs. And there's no need for you to drive out to Elaine's."

"Wouldn't miss it for the world," Dylan fires back, his smirk stretching wider, like he knows exactly which buttons to push.

My jaw locks so tight it aches. Because what I want more than anything in this moment is to rearrange his smug face with one clean right hook. But I fight it, for Jaylynn. She doesn't want that from me.

Instead, I climb into the back of Will's vehicle with Jay pressed to my side. Will blasts Christmas songs, everyone singing at the top of their lungs. Everyone but me. Because while they sing, I'm stewing. Not just at Dylan's digs or his smirk.

No.

I'm stewing over the question that won't leave me alone. What the hell is Dylan up to? He can mess with me all he likes, but if he fucks this up for Jaylynn or hurts her heart, or her chances at pulling this off and getting the job of her dreams, I'll destroy him.

Every now and then I catch the way Jay's eyes flick toward me —soft, worried, protective. She senses it too. Dylan's circling, looking for cracks to pry apart. I give her hand a squeeze, trying to reassure her, even though the truth is I'm wound tight as barbed wire inside. The last thing I want is for him to ruin this festival for her.

"Penn," Will calls from the front seat, catching my eye in the rear-view mirror. His chin jerks toward the town square. "Check it out."

I follow his line of sight to the massive nativity set standing proud in the middle of town. My grin spreads when I see the big star—the same one that started it all. The storm. The country club. The night that changed everything.

Jaylynn glances at me, a smile on her face and I know she's thinking the same things as I am. She leans into me and whispers, "If only we could have bottled that night so it would last forever."

I nod, my heart pounding a bit harder as my gaze strays to the wooden panel on the nativity set. It looks broken, the box underneath leaning wrong.

"Looks like the winds knocked it around. Maybe you and I can grab a hammer tomorrow and patch it up."

My stomach knots. A hammer? I couldn't hammer a nail straight if my life depended on it. "Uh, yeah, sure," I manage, my throat tight. The old familiar shame prickles under my skin—never handy enough, never skilled enough.

Jaylynn feels it instantly. She threads her fingers tighter through mine, her thumb brushing the back of my hand. That one small touch tells me she doesn't give a damn about my useless hammer skills. Does that mean to her, I am enough?

"I really hope Elaine will join us for Christmas dinner," Judy chimes in, her voice bright with genuine warmth.

I shrug, trying to keep it light. "She's set in her ways. Crowds aren't her thing. But...I'll ask her."

We head toward the edge of town, and my chest grows tighter with every mile. Other cars are already parked outside Elaine's place, headlights cutting through the dark. A lump rises in my throat. It's not shame—not exactly. It's just... this house, this woman, this life—it's mine. And the idea of Dylan standing on this porch, peering into the corners of my world, makes me want to barricade the door.

The front door creaks open as we pile out. Elaine, wrapped in her robe, beams when she sees us. "Oh, this is lovely," she says, her voice touched with the same eccentric warmth she's always carried. She ducks inside for her coat, and when she joins us again, her smile is so wide it damn near splits her face.

We gather around, singing into the night. She claps, hums, even throws in a few notes off-key, and my heart clenches. God, I love this woman. She raised me when no one else would, and I'd burn down the whole damn town if anyone mocked her for it.

Especially Dylan.

When the carols fade, I step up and wrap her in a hug, breathing in the familiar scent of her lavender lotion. "Elaine, Judy was hoping you'd join us for Christmas dinner."

Her brows lift. "We're not having our own dinner here?" There's a flicker of disappointment, like I've let her down without meaning to.

"It's the cats, Elaine. I can't." Right on cue, Muffin barrels against the screen door with a yowl, and my nose instantly starts itching. I sneeze three times in a row.

"Oh, Penn," she murmurs, guilt lacing her tone. "If I'd only known..."

I cup her hands. "I like that you took them in. But I also want to spend Christmas day with you. So, come with me. Please."

Her face softens into a smile. "I'll come."

Relief floods me as I hug her again, but the moment's shattered by Dylan's voice, slick and sharp.

"So, you didn't know Penn wasn't going to spend Christmas with you?"

The words land like a stone in my gut. He says it with just enough edge to stir doubt, to make it sound like I'd left her behind.

Elaine stiffens, turning toward him. Her expression flickers, recognition, followed by a carefully polite smile. "Dylan. Is that you?"

Her tone is brittle, like glass about to crack, and my body coils tight. Because I know Dylan. He's not here to sing carols. He's here to poke holes, to take shots, to remind me—and Jay—of every place I fall short.

And why is he doing that, Penn?

Because he wants to prove that he's better than me, and maybe that's because he wants her back…

But why now? It has to be more than the fact that she's engaged. More than the fact that he wants what he can't have. I mean, I know that trick has worked before, but my gut is suddenly telling me something else is going on with him. I tuck that thought away to examine in depth later.

"Nice to see you again, Elaine." Dylan cocks his head, his smirk tight, still waiting for her answer to his little trap.

"No, I guess I didn't know," she says, voice polite but thin.

His smile sharpens. "But you did know about the engagement, right? That Penn and Jaylynn were supposedly dating in Boston?"

Supposedly.

Okay, here we go.

Elaine straightens, then turns her eyes to me with a soft smile. She cups my face in her palm like she used to when I was a kid. "Of course, I knew. Penn calls me every week. He was smitten with Jaylynn from the beginning." She makes a tsking sound. "Heartbroken when she moved home. They didn't think long-distance would work, but the moment he came back, one look at her and he knew. I always knew they belonged together." She shoots Dylan a deliberate wink.

His face falters, the smugness cracking, and I bite back a grin. Who knew Elaine had such a wicked slap shot?

I lean down to hug her, whispering, "You did good."

"That guy's a douche," she mutters back.

"Elaine," I scold lightly, though a laugh breaks through.

Her eyes twinkle. "Jaylynn was too good for him. I'm glad she found the man she needed."

I pause, heart squeezing. For a second, I almost worry she believes all this is for real.

"Elaine—"

She waves me off. "Go on, get back to the inn and get warm. It's freezing out here. You don't want to catch your death of cold before the parade."

"Speaking of the parade, I'll swing by and pick you up. We'll get there early and you can help us set up. Wait, you do want to come, right?" I ask.

"Wouldn't miss seeing you play Santa," she says proudly.

"It's good for my image," I joke.

"As long as you don't deck anyone." Her eyes cut toward Dylan. "Though I wouldn't blame you if you did. And I can get myself there. I'm not feeble, you know."

"I know, but I don't mind."

"You have a lot to do, so I'll just meet you there."

Jay moves in beside me, slipping perfectly into my arms like she was made for the space. Elaine beams at the sight, and I swear my chest feels too full. No wonder she thinks this is real.

We're all about to leave, but Elaine holds a hand up. "Wait, it's National Oatmeal Muffin Day." She comes back with a huge tray. "Help yourselves."

"They look amazing," Jay says, grabbing one. She takes a bite and moans softly. "Even better than they look."

"Come on, everyone," Elaine calls, and the carolers swarm, while Earl—her evil cat, Muffin—glowers at me from behind the screen door."

"Elaine, I do hope you'll come for dinner," Judy says.

"Wouldn't miss it for the world," she responds, and I glance at Dylan. Is he going to try to get himself an invite to Christmas dinner too?

"Oh, that's wonderful!" Judy beams, then gives Elaine a co-conspirator wink. "I can't wait to start the planning."

My stomach lurches. Planning. Wedding planning.

Elaine claps. "Oh, it's going to be so exciting."

Jay opens her mouth, probably ready to pump the brakes, but I press a hand to her side to quiet her. Not here. Not now. Soon enough, when I'm back in Boston, and hopefully she is too, we can say it didn't work out.

Is that the real reason you don't want to say anything, dude?

Yes.

Oh, it doesn't have anything to do with the fact that you're enjoying all this, that maybe you like being a fiancé and would one day love to marry Jaylynn at the country club?

No.

Okay maybe.

Dammit.

That's when Dylan strikes.

"Wow, looks like Penn's aunt is more excited than the bride to be. What about your parents, Penn, are they just as excited?"

Jay curls her arm around me, holding me tight as my pulse thunders, my control hanging by a thread. But one thing is clear, Dylan is looking for trouble, looking to take me down. He's still the bully he was in high school. But yeah, he can say what he wants to me. But so help me if he hurts Jaylynn.

"Maybe they're busy," Dylan adds with mock sympathy. "Or wait, do you have any other family? Family is such an important thing in this small town."

I feel Jay stiffen beside me. Her grip on me tightens, like she's trying to keep me from lunging at him. I'm not going to do that. I'm not going to do anything to mess this festival up for her.

"Of course, he has family," Jaylynn snaps, her voice sharp as broken glass. She exchanges a quick, loaded glance with her father.

Dylan just shrugs, feigning innocence, like he hasn't just ripped open a scar that never fully healed. "Oh yeah? Then where are they?" He lets his gaze sweep the crowd in exaggerated mockery, as though proving a point.

And then something miraculous happens.

Before I can answer, Jaylynn's family moves. One by one, her brothers and their wives, the kids still sticky with candy canes, her parents, and even the neighbors—all the carolers standing around in the frosty night—step in closer. Forming a wall. Closing ranks.

Around me.

For me.

My chest tightens, my throat going raw as my heart grows two sizes bigger, threatening to burst clean out of me. For the first time in too damn long, I'm not standing alone.

Dylan's smile falters, his fake bravado cracking. Good. Let him choke on it.

Elaine clears her throat, stepping in to smooth the edges. "You all need to get home before you catch your death of cold," she says again and reaches out to give my hand a squeeze. Her touch says more than words ever could. "Thank you for coming."

"Elaine's right," Judy agrees warmly. "We can't have Santa sick before his big day." She glances at my aunt, her tone genuine and sweet. "It's always so good to see you, Elaine."

Dylan slinks back, his moment ruined, while Jay presses tighter against my side, as though to shield me with her body.

Back in the car, silence hangs heavy until the heater hisses on. Jay's thigh presses against mine, a quiet reassurance, her careful glances softening the raw edges Dylan left behind.

He'd meant to humiliate me, to remind me of everything I don't have—but instead he showed me exactly what I do.

Family.

Maybe it's borrowed. Maybe it's fake. But tonight, wrapped in their circle, it feels real. And for once, I let myself bask in it.

"Are you guys warming up?" Will calls from the front seat, breaking the quiet as he steers us back onto the road.

Jay wiggles closer, burrowing into my side like she belongs there. "Nice and toasty," she says, tilting her face up at me, mischief sparking in her eyes. "So… you still up for the beer fest? There will be karaoke."

I groan. "Kill me now."

But inside, with her tucked so perfectly against me, there's no denying the truth. If she wants me to sing, I'll sing. Hell, I'll do anything for her.

19

JAYLYNN

After going with Penn to BJ's place for his suit fitting, I step through the double doors of the community center and pause, letting the warmth and buzz wash over me. The air hums with chatter and laughter, the kind that floats above the clinking of coffee cups and the rustle of paper bags.

To my left, rows of vendors line the walls, their tables overflowing with knitted mittens, jars of homemade jam, and delicate ornaments that shimmer beneath the twinkling strands of white lights draped overhead. The faint sound of a carol drifts from the old speakers, scratchy but charming, adding to the nostalgia of it all.

From the adjoining room comes the happy chaos of children's voices. I peek inside long enough to see kids bent over paper and glue, little fingers sticky with glitter and ribbons. The sweet, spicy scent of cinnamon bursts into the air from their craft table, hitting me square in the chest and reminding me of every Christmas cookie my mom ever baked. I breathe it in, savoring it before drifting toward the cozy café corner tucked against the wall.

"That looks good," I murmur to Mom and Aunt Maureen, nodding toward the rows of pastries glistening under glass domes. Flaky croissants, sticky buns drizzled in icing, and steaming cups of cocoa topped with whipped cream.

They've come simply to shop, their arms already carrying tote bags, while I'm here to keep an eye on things, to make sure the festival I poured my heart into runs smoothly. Still, my gaze strays to the vendors, to the sparkle of holiday magic on every table, and I think maybe—just maybe—I'll pick something up. My shopping is done, gifts wrapped and hidden, but I'd like something special for Penn. Something that says thank you for everything he's doing, for all the ways he's standing beside me when I need him most.

Just the thought of him sends a soft, syrupy warmth through me. I decide then and there to bring Penn and Dad something sweet, maybe coffee and cinnamon rolls, as they work on fixing the nativity set. A small gesture, but one that might make them smile.

"I'm going to check out the knitted sweaters," Aunt Maureen says, already wandering off, her eye for handmade goods as sharp as always.

Mom lingers, though. She squeezes my hand, her mitten rough against mine. "The festival is going so well, Jaylynn. You've done a remarkable job."

Of course, she'd say that—she's my mom, my forever cheerleader. But the pride in her voice warms me anyway.

"Let's just hope the parade goes off without a hitch," I reply, though a knot tightens in my stomach. Memories of #GobbleGate flicker like a bad movie reel. I know how quickly things can spin out of control.

Mom's smile widens, unshakable. "It's going to be perfect."

And I believe her, because she's always believed in me. That's the thing about parents—they're your safety net when the rest of the world feels like it's waiting for you to trip. Not everyone is lucky enough to have that.

Which makes me think of Penn. My chest tightens. Dylan was cruel to bring up Penn's parents, cruel to dig at a wound that never healed. I can't fathom what it must have been like for him, abandoned, left on his aunt's doorstep with no good-bye, no promise to come back. Just silence.

But Penn isn't alone. Not anymore. He has me. He has Dad. He has this community that cheers for him louder than he'll ever know. He just needs to believe it, to believe *in himself*. Until then, I'll believe enough for the both of us.

"Thanks, Mom."

She gives my hand another squeeze before hurrying after Aunt Maureen, their laughter trailing behind them as they disappear down a row of knit hats.

I take my time wandering through the aisles, pausing to admire the way the fairy lights glow against jars of cranberry chutney, the sparkle of snowflake earrings, the rows of hand-painted ornaments. The energy in the room is alive, festive, the air thick with pine and cinnamon and community spirit.

At one booth, I stop to admire the stockings, each one stitched with care. "Hey, Janice," I say warmly to one of the town's long-time crafters. "These are beautiful."

I lift a stocking patterned with peppermint sticks, the red and white stripes bold against quilted fabric. My fingers trace the stitches, neat and perfect, and a grin tugs at my lips.

Janice nods, her silver hair catching the light. "That one's been popular this year."

I can't help but laugh softly. If anyone should have a peppermint stick phobia by now, it's Penn. And yet, my grin deepens. "I'll take two." Later when I have the time, I'll personalize them.

Her eyes brighten with curiosity. "For you and your fiancé?"

The word sends a little flutter through me. I nod, returning her smile, though my heart beats faster, skipping like it knows the truth before I've dared to say it out loud. "Yes," I say, voice soft.

"Will you be going back to Boston with him?"

The question lingers heavy, and I nod automatically, though the truth is murkier. Boston isn't a certainty. Not with him, at least. Maybe I'll be in the stands, cheering for Penn when the Bucks hit the ice, especially if the PR position comes through. Maybe we'll still be friends. The future feels like a snow globe that hasn't settled yet—everything swirling, glittering, but impossible to see clearly.

What do you want, Jaylynn?

That part I know, at least in the secret corners of my heart. But what Penn wants? That's the real question, and the one that keeps me up at night.

After I pay for the stockings, I slip back into festival mode. Row by row, I check in with vendors, making sure their tables are stocked, their cocoa warm, their smiles genuine. Everything about this reminds me why I love this community. But despite that, the big city is still calling.

When I push through the door into the back room, the hum shifts. The air is sticky with glue and glitter, the tables a kaleidoscope of craft paper and pipe cleaners. Laughter bounces off the walls, full of joy.

"Where's Penn?" Little Liam pipes up, his eyes shining with the kind of hero-worship only a child can give.

I grin, my chest softening. Somehow, between hockey and hot glue guns, Penn has become a local celebrity. "He's working on the nativity set." I lean down to peek at Liam's project. "What are you making?"

"It's for the tree." He holds up a crooked but dazzling ornament—a hockey stick drowning in glitter.

"It's perfect," I say with conviction, because it is. His toothy grin makes me laugh, and I ruffle his hair before drifting on to chat with a few more kids, their sticky hands leaving smudges of sparkles everywhere.

By the time I return to the main hall, the crowd has doubled. The air is alive with energy—boots stamping snow from the entryway, voices overlapping, the faint jingle of a bell from one of the volunteers by the door. I glance around, pride swelling in me at the turnout.

And then I see her.

Sloane.

My stomach knots. Because where Sloane is, Dylan usually lurks nearby, and the last thing I want right now is a forced conversation with my ex. Especially knowing in two nights' time, after the parade and tree lighting, Dylan will be front and center in the community center's kissing booth. Good for fundraising, sure. Great for the children's hospital. But the only thing I'm certain of is I won't be lining up to pucker up.

Sloane lifts her head, as if she can feel my gaze tugging at her. She smiles, but it's brittle, sliding across her face without reaching her eyes. Something about it makes me hesitate. I could turn away, bolt for the café and bring Penn and Dad their well-earned coffee and snacks. But my gut tugs me in the opposite direction.

I weave through the crowd, the scent of cinnamon and pine clinging to my coat. Up close, Sloane looks... different. Her makeup isn't flawless, and for the first time, her phone isn't glued to her hand, documenting her every move. Instead, she stares down at the merchandise on the table.

"Hey, Sloane," I say, careful to sound casual. "Are you enjoying Snowberry?"

Her voice is flat. "It's okay."

"Dylan not with you today?"

She shakes her head, a small movement that seems to take effort. "No, he said he had some business to deal with. I thought I'd come over here and check things out."

There's a shadow about her, a loneliness that feels heavier than all the glitter in the room combined. Before I can think better of it, words tumble out. "I'm just about to bring Penn and my father some coffee and snacks. They're out in the cold fixing the nativity set. Want to help?"

Her head jerks up, eyes sparking. "Really?"

"Sure."

For the first time since I spotted her, Sloane smiles, an actual smile that reaches her eyes, softening her entire face. "I actually didn't think you liked me," she admits shyly.

To be fair, maybe I just hadn't given her a chance. "Of course, I like you, come on." I gesture toward the café, and she falls into step beside me, close enough that her shoulder brushes mine.

"What did you buy?" she asks, her tone lighter now, almost curious.

I can't help but grin as I pull the bag open. "Oh, this is the first Christmas Penn and I are spending together here in Snowberry, so I grabbed us matching stockings."

She peers inside, her hand brushing mine as she tugs the fabric gently. "They're so cute." Then her voice dips, almost wistful. "I don't even have a stocking at Dylan's parents' place."

The ache in her words surprises me. Sloane, with her million followers, her curated perfection, suddenly seems... alone.

"They have more," I say quickly, my heart tugging. "We can go back."

She gives a quick, almost violent shake of her head. "No. I don't think so."

The firmness in her voice makes me pause, but her eyes—flat, tired—say more than she wants to admit. Something's wrong, but I don't press. We reach the café, and the warm, sugary air rushes over us like a blanket, thick with the scent of cinnamon, nutmeg, and fresh-baked bread. Behind the glass case, pastries glisten under the lights.

"My treat," I say lightly, and Sloane's gaze locks on a cinnamon roll like she's been starving for more than just food.

"I shouldn't," she whispers, almost guiltily.

"Yeah, you should. I should too," I tease, trying to coax her into softening. When I reach the counter, I order four cinnamon rolls and four steaming coffees, ignoring the amused look the barista gives me.

When the order's ready, I busy myself at the little self-serve counter, adding cream and sugar to mine and Dad's cups, leaving Penn's black, just the way he likes it. I glance at Sloane out of the corner of my eye. Her cup sits untouched, and she makes no move to change that.

"You know," she says suddenly, letting out a laugh that tries for casual but breaks in the middle, "I don't even think Dylan would know how I take my coffee."

The words are so raw they snag at me. I force a smile anyway. "Oh, I'm sure he would," I offer, even though I'm not sure at all.

As I balance the cups in a cardboard tray, she takes the bag of cinnamon buns and we head outside. The cold slaps us the second we're on the sidewalk, our breath puffing into clouds. "They're just down the road," I say. "Are you okay to walk?"

She nods, tugging her coat tighter, and we fall into step together, weaving through the crowd on the sidewalk.

"You and Dylan," she begins after a few steps, her voice tentative. "You dated for a long time?"

The question lands like a stone in my stomach. The last thing I want is to dig up old history with his fiancée. "Yeah, a while ago," I answer shortly, my tone clipped. Then I pivot.

"What's keeping him so busy that he has to work at Christmas?"

She shrugs, her lashes lifting just enough to meet my gaze. "He doesn't tell me much about his work. Just the positive things he wants me to post about."

"You help him with his social media?"

"I don't have a degree or anything. Not like you." Her voice cracks on the admission, a flash of vulnerability slipping through. "Maybe if I did, I'd be able to…"

Her words trail off, collapsing into silence. She glances down quickly, lips pressing shut as if she regrets saying even that much.

"Hey," I say gently, "It's not too late to get a degree, if PR's your thing."

She gives a hollow little laugh. "Yeah, maybe. I guess that would help him."

Help him what?

The thought circles in my mind, heavy and unsettling. But I don't ask. I don't want to peer too closely into Dylan's life anymore. Not my circus. Not my monkeys.

What I do know is that the polished image Sloane and Dylan broadcast online—the smiling selfies, the champagne toasts— suddenly looks thinner than tissue paper. And I can't ignore the sting of irony. Here I am in a fake relationship with Penn, yet somehow Sloane's real one feels just as fragile.

"What about you?" I ask instead. "Is PR something you'd want to do for *you*?"

Her silence stretches, filled only by the sharp click of her impossibly high heels on the snowy pavement. They're all wrong for the slick sidewalks, and every step sounds precarious. Finally, she exhales, voice small. "You and Penn are really good together. I see the way he looks at you."

Her words catch me off guard. "Thanks," I murmur, because what else can I say? Things suddenly feel awkward and I fill the silence. "You and Dylan are good together too." She simply nods, and I continue with, "You must be excited about the wedding."

"I was," she says, then stops herself. Her voice cracks on the word, and she looks away, eyes shining with something she doesn't want me to see. "Until…"

The silence she leaves behind is louder than any confession. Something's unraveling in Sloane's world, and for the first time, I wonder if she's standing on the same kind of shaky ground I once was.

"Hey," a familiar voice calls and I lift my head to see Penn waving at me from beside the nativity set.

"Hey," I echo, quickening my steps. Sloane keeps pace beside me, her heels clicking against the frozen pavement. My arms are heavy with the cardboard tray, but my chest feels light at the sight of him. "I thought you guys might be hungry after all this work."

I let my gaze sweep over the nativity scene. The carved wooden figures stand tall against the frosted backdrop, halos of light catching on their sanded edges. "It looks great."

Penn practically beams under my praise, that boyish grin of his tugging at something deep in me. When Dad rests a firm hand on Penn's shoulder, giving it a fatherly squeeze, I swear I can hear the pounding of Penn's heart in the space between us. His chest lifts, just a little, like the weight of that touch means more than he can say.

"Penn was a great help," Dad says proudly.

I catch the subtle flicker of Penn's eyes toward Sloane, just a brief acknowledgment before he refocuses. "I ran into Sloane at the craft fair," I explain. "She helped me carry these treats for you guys."

"Thanks," Penn says, his voice low, and I hand out the steaming coffees while Sloane passes me the bag. One by one, I dole out cinnamon buns still warm in their wax paper sleeves.

"Damn, that's good," Penn says around a mouthful, his lips curling into a laugh. "You know, Roman Marinelli loves these things. He's constantly sneaking them during the season." He shoots Dad a playful look, eyes glinting. "Wait, you're not going to tell on me, are you? I know you and Coach are tight."

Dad waves him off, already chewing, crumbs catching in his mustache. "Nope, too busy stuffing my face."

The laughter that follows rises into the crisp air, and something swells in my chest—big and warm and aching. I love the way Dad has taken Penn under his wing, as if it's the most natural thing in the world. I love the way Penn is opening up, piece by piece, like a door that's been locked for too long finally easing on its hinges. If there's ever been a man in desperate need of a family, it's Penn. And somehow, without fanfare, mine is becoming his.

I sip my coffee and step aside, nudging a life-size wooden sheep closer to the manger. The wood is cold beneath my palms, but when I stand back, the scene feels fuller, more complete. Penn and Dad's conversation drifts back to me—hockey talk, tomorrow night's game, who's watching where. Apparently, Penn, along with Jaxon—who is arriving back home today—will be catching it with my brothers.

That's good. It gives me the perfect window to slip out later, to make the drive to The Memory Chest, an eclectic shop over in Rutledge. It's a big store where you can find old treasures stacked floor to ceiling, things you didn't even know you needed until they called to you. I'm not sure I'll find what I'm looking for, but I'll try. For Penn, I'll try.

"I'd better get going," Sloane says suddenly, her voice cutting into my thoughts.

Since the guys are knee-deep in sports stats and don't need me hovering, I nod. "I'll go with you. I have a couple of things to check on anyway."

I turn back to Penn, my heart tugging. "I'll catch up with you later," I promise, sliding into his arms for a quick hug. His warmth lingers, but with Dad standing right there, a kiss feels too exposed, too intimate. So, I let go, and Sloane and I head back down the sidewalk, the cold nipping at our cheeks. Snow crunches beneath our boots and for a stretch we walk in silence. But I notice the way she keeps glancing sideways at me, her teeth catching her lip, like she's working up the courage to speak.

"Everything okay?" I finally ask.

"It's just... strange."

"What's strange?"

She exhales, a foggy plume dissolving into the air. "Dylan thinks you're up to something with Penn."

My blood runs cold, sinking straight to my toes. *Up to something.* The words coil tight in my gut. Why did I ever concoct a fake dating plan? It had seemed so harmless, so controlled. Now it feels like a snowball rolling downhill, gathering speed, impossible to stop. If Dylan knows—if Dylan suspects—we could both end up crushed beneath it.

"He just thought it was rather strange that you two were suddenly engaged," Sloane continues, her voice softer now. Then her eyes flick to mine, steady. "But I can see it. I can see how good you are together."

My laugh comes out sharper than I intend, more defense than amusement. "Why does Dylan care anything about me anyway?" I huff, trying to brush it off, even as unease claws at me.

Her steps slow, and she lifts her left hand, the diamond catching in the glow of winter sun. Her voice hitches. "Because I think..." She swallows hard, gaze fixed on the ring that suddenly seems too heavy for her finger. "...he might still have feelings for you."

20

PENN

"If I'd known that this is what you meant by catch up with you later, I might have made myself scarce."

She nudges me from beside the roaring fire. "Oh, come on. You're having fun. Admit it."

I glance at the stack of letters before us. "This is going to take all night."

"Come on, Santa. This is your job."

"I think Santa's job is delivering the gifts, not responding to Santa letters." I wink at her. "And I believe Mrs. Claus' job is lap dances."

"Well, that's not on the table right now, because Mrs. Claus' job is to put the final touches on this application." She bites her lip nervously as she glances at the laptop she has balanced on her thighs. She finished the application the other day. I read through it for her, but she keeps going over it. I think she's too nervous to send it. Too nervous of failure. But hey, she already said she hit rock bottom and there's nowhere to go but up.

Jesus, who am I to talk? I'm terrified of failure myself because if I try and fail, I won't be going up, I'll be going down...right back to the Grizzlies.

"You'll get it," I whisper, and give her arm a little squeeze.

She smiles, and then it turns playful, like she's trying to hide her insecurities. "Once I'm done, I'll help you with the letters, and then we'll see about putting that lap dance back on the table."

The bell over the inn's door chimes as the door opens and as people file in, I lean in close to Jay. "As long as it's not on this table." I am so not sharing her with anyone. "Unless, of course, you're into that kind of thing," I add, knowing she's not.

She chuckles playfully. "No, I'm not. Now get to work. This is going to take forever."

"Fine," I grumble, and tear open the next letter. I read the scribbling and write back with warmest greetings from the North Pole. I mention the elves are working hard for all the boys and girls then remind them to be kind and to leave cookies and carrots. Jay told me not to mention anything about the wish list because there's no guarantee they can get it.

"Anyone ask for a pony yet?" she teases with a grin.

"I never should have told you that."

She leans in and kisses my nose. "But you did and now I know that you're a cinnamon roll."

"I'm a what?"

She laughs. "A cinnamon roll. You know."

"Because I ate one today."

"No, that's what we call tough heroes who are soft inside, in romance books."

"You're strange, Jay."

"What did you say the pony's name was?"

I shift, the room growing warmer. "I didn't."

She stares at me, and I go to work on the letters under her scrutinizing gaze. "Oh my God," she finally bursts out.

"What?"

I seal the letter, and plunge the personalized Santa stamp in the ink before I press it to the envelope.

"It's something cute isn't it, like Muffin?"

I shiver at that name. "No."

"What is it?"

"Nothing."

"Did you name it, or was it already named?"

"I named it," I grouch ready to give up because this is Jay and she's not going to stop until I spill.

"Tell me."

"Fine. Her name is Strawberry."

"Strawberry. Why?"

"Because...the little girl. She had strawberry blonde hair and I thought she'd like it. I told her she could change it, but she loved it, so see. I was right."

Jay puts her hand on her stomach and leans forward.

"What are you doing?"

"Holding on to my ovaries, because I think they're going to explode."

I shake my head. "This is why I never wanted to tell you."

As she laughs, I take in the firelight dancing in her eyes. Jesus, she's beautiful. Catching me off guard, she sits up, throws her arms around me, and despite the bustle of people around us, presses her lips to mine.

It's a slow, easy kiss, the kind that makes the noise of the inn fade to a soft hum. When she pulls back, she licks her bottom lip like she's savoring the taste of me, and I fight the urge to lean in again. Instead, I grab my hot cocoa, taking a long sip, trying to distract myself from the very real possibility of a lap dance later.

She goes quiet, staring at her screen, but I can tell she's somewhere else. I tilt my head. "Something on your mind? You know I'm a pretty good listener."

Her smile is soft. "You and Dad. You seemed to have fun fixing the nativity set."

My chest tightens, a little squeeze I can't quite shake. She's right. I did have fun. Felt like I belonged to something bigger. "I earned how to use a hammer today," I say, trying to lighten things, though there's a trace of truth under the joke. "You have a nice family, Jay."

She nods, letting out a small huff that carries every ounce of worry she's been holding. "I do. They're...very supportive. Even after #GobbleGate, they didn't... they didn't lose faith in me. I just…" She swallows hard. "I don't want to let them down again."

"Babe, you could never let them down," I say, reaching for her hand. "What happened was a mistake. It could have happened to anyone."

She shakes her head, the faintest frown tugging at her lips. "Why do all my big mistakes have to happen center stage?"

"Not this time," I assure her, squeezing her hand. "When you step up there for the tree lighting, I've got you. Nothing —*nothing*—is going to happen. You have my word."

The tension in her shoulders eases, the lines around her eyes softening. "My big Madman," she murmurs.

"That's me. Radman the Madman."

"You're so much more than that." She gives me a kiss, and stares at me for a moment, like she's waiting for me to see that too.

I glance down at the envelopes, but my hands stop moving. "Do we even have stamps for these?"

"Nope," she says, a mischievous glint returning to her eyes. "When the kids come to see you after the parade, you'll hand them out personally."

I frown at Chloe's letter. "I realize Santa's supposed to know every child in the world, but…no idea who Chloe is. And she lives in Snowberry?"

Jay laughs, brushing back a strand of hair. "I'll help."

I groan, dramatically, as if the weight of the world just landed on my shoulders. "My God, the pressure. Why did I agree to this again? Do you have me under some kind of peppermint spell?"

"Possibly," she teases. "And for the record, you did this to yourself."

"Yeah," I mutter, grimacing at the memory. "Because there's no way I'd want you on the float with...him." I make a face like I just bit into something sour, then take another long sip of my cocoa to wash it away.

She nudges me gently. "You did it for me, Penn. I really appreciate it. I was dreading playing Mrs. Claus with him."

I stare at her a moment too long, trying to decide if I should say something. "What?" she asks, catching me.

"Nothing," I mutter, glancing at the fire, fighting the swirl of emotions I can't quite untangle. Did she start this whole charade to get him back, and maybe that's none of my business...except Dylan is a colossal jerk, and engaged—not to mention my growing feelings for her—makes it feel impossible to ignore.

I feel her eyes on me, and I look up. The firelight dances in them, and my chest tightens. Jesus. She's beautiful.

"My family...they really like you, Penn." I nod, but my stomach tightens. At the core of all this...we're deceiving them. My chest feels heavier than it should. "Dad always liked you. He saw so much potential in your game." A pause. Then, "Do you think you'll maybe...ever try for a different position on the team?"

There it is again. A quiet reminder that maybe I'm not enough, that maybe I don't measure up.

"I don't know," I mutter, trying to mask the sting, and switch topics quickly. "I was surprised to see you with Sloane today." Her face drops. My back stiffens, something niggling in the back of my brain. "What?"

She shakes her head, brow furrowed. "She...uh...she was alone, and I felt bad for her, so I invited her along."

My heart beats a little faster. "Of course, you did," I say quietly.

Her voice softens almost to a whisper. "I don't know what she was thinking, to say..."

"Jay?" My voice is cautious, because I can feel the tension crawling under her skin.

Her eyes find mine, turbulent and raw. "She said something... about Dylan still having feelings for me. That's absolutely crazy." I stay quiet. The words hang between us, heavy and uncomfortable. Her brow furrows as she turns toward the fire, a storm brewing in her expression. "Why would she ever say that? He humiliated me years ago, and he's engaged, for God's sake."

I swallow hard. I'm not surprised, but that doesn't make it any easier to watch. If he and Sloane ever do break up, if some hidden part of Jay—one she might not even know exists—still entertains a thought of him, it could open a door I don't want her to see. My jaw tightens. I have to figure out what Dylan's up to before he can even think about touching her life.

And damn it, I know I'm falling for her. For Jaylynn...for her family too. I have no clue how I'm supposed to handle that.

The inn door creaks open, and a gust of icy wind sweeps through, ruffling the letters on the table. I reach for another card, trying to bury myself in work—but my eyes catch a figure in the corner. Dylan. Of course. And Sloane is with him, looking…unhappy.

"Don't look now," I murmur, but Jay's gaze shifts automatically toward the door.

Sloane gives us a hesitant, awkward little wave, and Jaylynn's frown deepens. "What are they doing here?"

"No idea," I mutter under my breath, my teeth grinding.

Dylan strolls toward the counter, that infuriatingly smug grin plastered across his face. Sloane follows like a shadow, and the next thing I know, Belinda is handing him a key.

I shake my head. "You've got to be kidding me."

"Ignore them," Jay whispers, but Dylan clearly has a different idea.

He strides over, grin still in place. "I didn't realize you two were staying here too."

I narrow my eyes. "Yeah…we are," I growl, the words sharp. He knew. I told him we were at the town hall meeting.

"What are you working on?" Sloane asks, settling herself in the big wingback chair beside Jay.

As Jay turns toward Sloane I can't help but turn to Dylan and comment, "I thought they were fully booked here."

Dylan smooths a hand through his hair and unzips his coat, that wry, infuriating grin firmly in place. "When you have clout like I do."

Clout.

Ah, that explains the stench.

He drops into the seat next to me, all casual arrogance. "You know, I've been thinking. I should probably be the one playing Santa. I am the mayor, after all."

"Not the mayor of Snowberry," I point out, trying to keep my voice steady.

"Sure, sure," he says, shrugging like it's obvious, "But still… and Sloane mentioned something about being in line for the booth if you were going to be in it. You know, for charity."

What the actual fuck? Is he trying to hook us up or something?

"We really should stick to the original plan," he mutters, trying to sound reasonable, though my knuckles tighten around the edge of the table.

"Nope," I blurt out firmly. No way this guy is going on the float with Jay. "BJ already did all the work letting the suit out." I rub my hands over my thighs, working to keep them busy. "I tried it on earlier, and it wouldn't be fair to ask her to take it in again this close to the parade."

Judging by the scowl carving deep lines into his face, I've clearly struck a nerve. I pick up my drink and take a long, slow sip, trying to look innocent, but inside, I'm practically dancing. Jesus. I really do belong on Santa's naughty list.

"I'm sure it'll be fine," Dylan says, turning to Jay with all the practiced charm of a man who thinks the world bends to him. "Hey, Jay, how about I play Santa? The town's expecting it, and…" His eyes flick toward me, that casual, mocking superiority I want to wipe off his face, "…I'll make sure everything goes smoothly. We wouldn't want an incident, especially if you ever want to leave this town and work in the city again."

Goddammit. Not only is he insulting me, he's insulting her, too. My jaw tightens. My gaze sweeps the room and lands on the enormous light-up candy cane by the door.

No Santa in the world would put me on the naughty list for that, right?

I take another steadying breath and force myself to sink back into the chair. No way am I going to deck Dylan. That would be exactly what he wants. A fight. Drama. Proof that I'm... reactive, impulsive, predictable. Besides, I already promised Jay I wouldn't let anything ruin her festival. So, I clamp down on the fire inside me, letting it burn quietly. But that doesn't mean I'm not plotting other ways to make my point. Like putting a creepy elf in his room.

21

JAYLYNN

After a day of making sure the festival continues to stay on track—fingers crossed—I grab my purse from the dresser and tug on my hat.

"You guys have fun tonight," I call to Penn as he steps from the bathroom, hair damp, skin still flushed from the shower. He looks so good, I nearly scrap my plans and climb back into bed just to get tangled up in him.

"You're still not going to tell me where you're sneaking off to?" he asks, pulling me into his arms before I can answer. Not that I'm going to actually tell him. His mouth claims mine in a kiss so deep, so consuming, I forget the day, the season, my own name.

When he finally eases back, I'm breathless. "What?" I manage, dazed by his clean, soapy scent and the heat rolling off his body.

He grins. "So much for kissing the answer out of you."

"There was a question?"

"The question," he says, tucking a stray lock under my hat, "Was whether you're going to tell me where you're going."

"Christmas shopping is all you need to know," I tease, poking his stomach.

His smile fades, replaced with a seriousness that tugs at something deep inside me. "I don't want you out on those roads after dark. Not because of me."

I roll my eyes, but inside, my chest tightens. The truth is, I'm chasing down a gift, one, I hope that will mean a lot to him. After a loud, chaotic Christmas dinner, I want nothing more than a quiet Christmas night with Penn right here—in this room—before he has to return to Boston. My stomach knots at the thought, because I don't just want stolen nights with him. I want to go back with him. Not as a friend. Not as the team's PR manager.

As his.

"Why do you always think everything's about you, Penn?" I shoot back as I roll my eyes. "Such a narcissist." I pause and crinkle my nose. "Wait, do narcissists think everything is about them?"

"Probably."

"Okay then. That explains Dylan." I get a foul taste in my mouth just saying his name.

"Why are you thinking about Dylan?"

"I'm not."

His head tilts, his eyes scanning my face like he wants to ask something but then a slow smile breaks out. "You're coming back tonight though, right?" His gaze drops to the bed, his voice roughening. "Because I'm going to need you here.

Naked. Between the sheets." His hand skims down my body, slides between my thighs. "And my mouth right here."

A sharp shiver wracks me. God, it's insane. The more I have this man, the more I crave him.

A door slams down the hall, yanking me back to reality. Dylan. Sloane. Their room is across the hall are a constant reminder that this cozy inn isn't our private haven anymore. And Dylan—of course—swears he booked his stay here ages ago. A few nights with his family and then a romantic Christmas getaway with his fiancée. I don't know if it's true, but I do know that last night at dinner—which he managed to weasel himself into having with us—he was far too flirty with me.

Surely to God, Sloane wasn't right about him wanting me back.

Penn stiffens and as if he's reading my mind he says, "Surprised he didn't weasel an invite to your parents' place to watch the game tonight."

"Yeah, me too." My mind flickers to Sloane. She seems so out of place, maybe even lonely. Behind all her glossy posts and polished smiles, there's a real person with real cracks in her armor. I know the feeling. Things aren't always what they look like. And I'm the biggest proof of that.

Should I invite her to go to Rutledge with me? I consider it a moment longer, then change my mind. Last night after dinner wrapped up, she said she wasn't feeling well. While I actually like her now that I've glimpsed behind the curtain so to speak, she's quite sweet and...vulnerable. I really shouldn't have judged so harshly based on her social media. I honestly know better than that, and feel pretty awful about it. But it's probably best that I don't get involved deeper at this point. Especially after what she said, and I wouldn't put it past Dylan to use her against me somehow so he could weasel his way back into playing Santa. I can't believe how manipulative the man is.

What am I even saying?

Of course, I believe it.

Dylan thrives on the limelight. I'm just grateful Penn shut him down, and now I get to look forward to sharing the float with Penn. A laugh bubbles in my chest. Crazy to think when I first saw him trying to check in at Snowberry Inn, I lumped him in with Dylan. Wrong. So wrong. Penn is every kind of different—every kind of better.

He moves to the window, pulling back the curtains. "Checked the weather. No snow in the forecast."

My heart wobbles at the simple thoughtfulness, and I can't stop staring at the way his shoulders shift as he scoops up my mittens and carries them to me. That's when it hits me.

"Wait. Where did the creepy elf go?"

Penn bites his lip, like he's holding back a grin. Mischief dances in his eyes.

"What did you do?" I march to the closet, yank the door open. No elf. Spinning on him, I narrow my eyes. "Penn?"

He whistles. Innocent. Too innocent.

"Oh my God, you did. How?"

He brushes a hand over his shoulder. "Douchebag isn't the only one with clout."

My brain races. "Belinda. You charmed Belinda, didn't you?"

"What happens at the check-in desk at Snowberry Inn," he says solemnly, "Stays at the check-in desk at Snowberry Inn."

"Penn!" I half laugh, half yell.

"I may have told her I wanted to give him a welcome gift."

My eyes narrow. "And?"

"And... she'll be getting signed jerseys for her nephews." He presses a finger to his lips. "But it's a secret, so shhh..."

I laugh so hard I fling my arms around him. "Oh my God, Penn, I love you."

His hands pause mid-stride around my back. My breath stalls. Did I really just—

"I mean—I love that you did that." My voice wobbles. "Who knew you were so naughty."

He leans close, his breath hot against my ear. "You knew," he murmurs, and those two words promise all kinds of wicked.

Heat floods me, stealing my composure. "Yeah. Guess I did." I glance at the clock, fighting the urge to drag him back to bed. "You'd better get going before the guys start wondering what's making you late. I don't even want them imagining..." I cringe.

"Right." He straightens, grabs his phone. "Let me check if Jaxon is ready. I'm catching a ride with him."

I grin, warmed by how much more comfortable he seems with his teammate. They're even planning ice time together after Christmas, before heading back to Boston. As he fires off a text, I blow him a kiss and slip into the hall.

I'm seconds from the lobby when Dylan turns the corner and I slam right into him. I'm about to apologize when the mistletoe alarm shrieks. Oh, hell no. Belinda's head pops up. Of course. I swear I'm dismantling that damn thing tonight.

"If you'll excuse me," I mutter, trying to sidestep.

But before I realize what's happening, Dylan's hand clamps around my back and his mouth crashes onto mine. His tongue slides into my mouth, and I shove him hard, swipe my sleeve across my mouth, sputtering. "What the hell, Dylan?"

He only grins, brushing off my disgust like it's nothing. "We had no choice." He points at the mistletoe just as the alarm dies down.

"We absolutely had a choice. Don't you ever do that again." Fury propels me past him.

I stop at the desk where Belinda is watching with wide eyes. "I'm heading to Rutledge," I say briskly. "Going to hit The Memory Chest. Want me to stop at that candle shop you love?"

Her face brightens. "Oh, you're a lifesaver. I've been too swamped to get there." She scribbles a list, hands it over. "Thank you, sweetie."

"My pleasure."

I tuck the note in my bag and escape outside. The winter sun beams down, glittering off the snow. No need to borrow Penn's SUV. My old car will do just fine today.

Sliding behind the wheel, I yank off my mittens and crank the radio. Christmas music floods the car, sweeping away the sour taste Dylan left behind. The day is gorgeous, the festival is on track, and I have a hot fiancé who plays tricks with elves, teaches hockey to kids, is bonding with my family, and warms my bed every night.

And that thought makes me smile all the way to Rutledge.

The sun is already slipping low on the horizon by the time I reach town square. The streets glow with holiday lights, strings of gold and red zigzagging overhead, storefront windows dressed in evergreen garlands and frosted displays. The air smells faintly of cinnamon and wood smoke, carried on the crisp bite of evening. Main Street is bustling, couples with linked arms, kids darting between parents, last-minute shoppers hurrying from one store to the next. I blend right in, another face in the holiday rush.

First stop is the candle shop. Belinda's list is short, but the line isn't. The place is warm, heady with vanilla, balsam, and cranberry spice. I shoulder my way through the crowd, juggling armfuls of jars, and grin when I finally manage to snag everything she wanted. Errand complete.

But it's the next stop that sends my pulse skittering. Just weeks ago, I never would have imagined picking out a gift for Penn Radford. Radman. Madman. Now the thought alone makes me a little dizzy, a little giddy.

The Memory Chest is quieter, a different kind of busy. The moment I step through the door, the scent of old paper and cedar hits me, and the hum of nostalgia wraps around me. Rows of shelves stretch deep, crammed with everything from antique toys to vinyl records to delicate glass figurines. I wander slowly, letting myself get lost in the aisles. Bits and pieces tug me back to my own childhood—a worn teddy bear, a stack of Nancy Drew mysteries, a puzzle missing one piece. But I'm not here for me.

I'm here for him.

I search for what feels like forever, weaving in and out of aisles until my throat catches on a squeal. There it is. The gift

I wasn't sure still existed, something so perfectly, uniquely Penn, I want to clutch it to my chest and never let go. I snatch it up, heart thudding.

And then I turn.

Straight into Dylan.

Again.

What the ever-loving hell?

"What are you doing here?" The words snap out before I can swallow them. My stomach plunges, instinct telling me this is no coincidence. Did he overhear me mention Rutledge to Belinda? Did he follow me?

He laughs, easy, casual. "I'm the mayor of this town. Had to check on something at the office."

My gaze skims the store. "Where's Sloane?"

"She's back at the inn. Still not feeling well." His eyes flicker to the box in my hands. "I popped in for some shopping, thought I spotted you. What've you got there?"

I tighten my grip. "Just last-minute things. I'm done now." I step to move past him.

He shifts easily in beside me. "I'm headed out too."

I keep my tone light, though unease prickles the back of my neck. "Did you find what you were looking for?"

His smile is thin, sharp. "Not yet. But there's still time."

I pay quickly, shoving my purchase into the bag. He lingers close enough that I feel the heat of his presence, and my skin crawls. When I push through the door into the sharp night air, he follows.

"Let me walk you to your car. It's dark out."

"I'm fine, Dylan."

"I'm sure Penn would appreciate me making sure you got there safely."

I pick up my pace. By the time I reach my car, I'm borderline jogging. I toss the bags into the trunk, slam it shut, and circle toward the driver's seat. Dylan's voice cuts me off.

"You're not going anywhere."

My heart stutters. I whirl. "What?"

He points at the ground. "Your tire. It's flat."

"You're kidding."

"Nope. Do you have a spare?"

"In the trunk." I shove past him, pop the latch, but when I circle around, my stomach sinks.

"Oh no."

"What now?"

I squat, pressing my palm to my other back tire. The rubber sags beneath my touch, limp and useless.

"This one's flat too."

Dylan squats beside me, phone already out, his flashlight beam cutting across the sagging rubber. "Damn," he mutters, running the light along the gash. "Looks like they've been cut."

A cold knot coils in my stomach. My first instinct is Penn. Call Penn. "How could this even happen?"

Dylan makes a low tsk and shakes his head, scanning up and down the street as if the culprit might still be lurking. The crowd here is thinner than it was earlier, people rushing to finish their shopping before night closes in. "Kids these days," he says finally. "Lot of mischief going around lately."

"Should I call the police?"

"They won't do much." His shrug is dismissive, practiced.

"Then I'll call Penn—"

"Nah." His interruption is smooth, casual, but firm. "No need to drag him out here tonight. He's watching the game, isn't he?"

I glance at the ground, unease prickling the back of my neck. "Yeah, but—"

"I'll call a tow truck."

I shake my head, already fishing for my phone. "I have Triple A." My thumb fumbles across the screen until I find the number. I rattle off the location to the operator, then tuck the phone away. "Half an hour," I say, exhaling. "Thanks for walking me out. You might as well head back to Snowberry. I'll grab a coffee while I wait."

"I'll give you a ride home." He jerks his chin toward his car parked a few spaces down.

"No thanks. I can catch a ride with the driver."

His smile doesn't budge. "Then I'll wait with you. Keep you company."

"Suit yourself."

I stride down the sidewalk and duck into the nearest café, grateful for the blast of heat and the hum of conversation.

Through the wide front windows, I can still see my car under the streetlight. At least it's in plain sight.

"I'll grab us coffee," Dylan says, heading for the counter.

I sink into a chair, fingers worrying my phone. Penn. I don't want to pull him away from the game, don't want to make him walk back to the inn to fetch his car, but I do want him to know. It's instinct already, checking in with him. Like we're a real couple.

I type a quick message. Flat tire. Called Triple A. Waiting at café in Rutledge.

Fifteen seconds later, my phone rings. Relief sweeps through me at the sight of his name.

"Hey," I say, smiling despite myself. "You didn't have to call. Everything's under control."

"Are you okay? I can come get you." His voice is steady but tight, protective.

"No." The one word comes out soft. Honestly, just hearing his voice has calmed me. "You're with the guys, and you caught a ride with Jaxon. Don't worry about me. Besides, you'd have to walk back to the inn for your car."

"Jay." His voice is low, almost offended. "You think a walk is trouble? I'm coming."

"No," I say again, firmer this time, though my chest swells at his insistence. "I'm okay. Really. I just wanted you to know."

Rustling filters through the line. "I'm already putting on my coat. I'll fix your tire."

My throat tightens, emotion pressing hot behind my eyes. God, the way he doesn't hesitate. "No, you can't. It's actually two tires. Someone punctured them. So please. Stay. I promise I'm fine. The tow truck will be here any minute."

That's when Dylan's voice cuts through the cozy café hum, loud enough to carry across the table, and the phone line. "Wasn't sure how you liked it," he says, setting down a steaming paper cup. He drops a couple of creamers and artificial sweeteners beside it. The ones I never use.

Penn's voice drops an octave. "Is that Dylan?"

Guilt—stupid, unnecessary guilt—flashes through me. I force a light laugh. "Yes. I ran into him at the store. I'm in Rutledge," I explain, too quickly. Why does this feel like I'm defending myself?

"Rutledge?"

"There was a shop I wanted to hit."

"What's Dylan doing there?"

"He said mayor business."

A beat. Then, rougher, "I bet he did."

I don't miss the edge in his voice—jealousy, distrust—and though part of me appreciates it, I hate that Dylan has us both on edge. I dislike him. I distrust him. I just hope Penn knows he can trust me. Even if, God help me, I sound a little guilty for no reason at all.

"He's going to stay with me until the truck comes."

"Okay."

"Are you having a good time with the guys?" I ask, injecting enthusiasm into my voice.

"Yeah, it's all good."

I lift the lid from my coffee, an uncomfortable knot in my stomach at how strained the conversation is becoming. "Okay, I'll see you later then."

"Keep me posted."

I wait a beat, hoping he'll say more, but the line clicks dead. For some reason, that silence weighs heavier than words ever could. Without saying anything, I stand, snag two sugar packets from the counter, and return to my table. Dylan's eyes track me the whole way, sharp, calculating.

"That was Penn," he says.

Not that it's any of his damn business. "Yes."

"Did you tell him you were in good hands?"

I arch a brow and shake my head, refusing to dignify his smug question with an answer. I stir my coffee, keep my eyes fixed on the window, my car still in view. Silence stretches between us, taut as a wire as we sip.

"How does Sloane take her coffee?" I ask, and his brows pull together.

"That's a strange question."

"Just curious." He doesn't answer, which is, in itself, an answer, as his gaze strays to the window. I turn, and relief floods me when the tow truck pulls up sooner than expected.

"They're here." I leap to my feet, dump my empty coffee cup in the recycling bin, and hurry outside. After talking with the driver, I ask if I can catch a lift. But when I open the cab door and see the mess of tools—and another guy already in the passenger seat—I freeze.

"You can't ride in there," Dylan says smoothly, almost too quickly. "Come on. I'll take you. I'll get you home safely."

I hesitate, but practicality wins. "Fine."

The second I slide into his car, I angle my body toward the door, as far from him as possible. He merges into traffic, the hum of the tires filling the silence until he decides to break it.

"You know," he says with a casual laugh, "I thought you and Penn might have been faking an engagement."

My heart trips. I school my face into neutrality. "That's ridiculous."

"Yeah," he says, though his tone suggests he doesn't buy it. "I thought maybe you were trying to make me jealous."

"You thought wrong."

Partly. None of this was to make him jealous. Rather it was so I didn't look like such a failure, a girl who couldn't make it outside of Snowberry. But at the end of the day, why did I even care what he thought? I shake my head, angry with myself. Although, I'm not angry that I've gotten to know Penn, not at all angry about the time we've been spending together.

"It worked," he says with a smile.

I roll my eyes. "I'm with Penn."

"You and me," Dylan starts ignoring me, and I almost shut him down, because there is no 'you and me'. But he rushes on. "We could have been something."

Don't engage.

Don't engage.

"Maybe you should have thought about that before sticking your tongue down Tamara's throat."

Why am I engaging?

"Come on, that didn't mean anything."

"It meant something to me." My glare cuts across the car, but the pain of that night is now a distant memory, thanks to Penn. Did I pine after Dylan for a while? Sure. Did he know it? Yes. But now, he can't feel anything from me, except dislike. "What are you even doing, Dylan?" Could Penn have been right? Does he only chase what he can't have? Or is this just about power, control, image?

"I've grown up, Jay Jay."

"Don't call me that." The old nickname stings like lemon on a cut. When he opens his mouth, I cut him off with a sharp shake of my head. "You lost the right to call me that a long time ago."

"Fair." He exhales, but his voice carries a smug undertone. "But I want you to know, I'm not the same person I was. I've changed. One day I'm going to be President, and I'm going to need the right woman by my side."

I nearly choke on my own tongue.

"Sloane is the right woman," I point out, even though I don't think that's the case, because the woman can do so much better.

He ignores me and says, "Do you have any idea what my political position could do for your career?"

That's what this is about? He wants to use me to help him get ahead? Guess he should have thought about that before the Tamara tongue incident. But wow, am I ever glad it happened.

No way would I want to be married to a guy who could cheat so easily, and now, what he's doing to Sloane, saying about her, is horrible.

"The places we could go."

"Right now I just want to go back to the inn." I consider calling Penn, or shooting him a text, but I think he's already upset that I'm with Dylan. He doesn't trust him any more than I do. Besides, I really don't want to reiterate any part of this conversation with him. It would only upset him, and it's Christmas. Soon enough he'll be back in Boston, Dylan a distant memory, which means he doesn't need to know about that horrible kiss either.

Honestly, it's embarrassing to think Dylan only wants me because he wants to use me. Embarrassing to think, even back in high school he was using me, until the mayor's daughter came along and he thought she would be a better fit for his career. I'd invested so much time into us, but he never loved or cared about *me*.

"I honestly don't know what you're doing with a guy like Penn. He's nothing." He snorts out a humorless laugh. "An enforcer who's likely going to get sent back to the Grizzlies. A guy who only knows how to use brute force. I mean, he did punch Santa. Who does that?"

"He had good reason."

"There's no good reason to act like that in public. None. He'll do it again. You'll see." A pause and then he continues, "At the end of the day, Jay, he's a thug, and I'm the guy who can take you where you need to go. The guy who will always show up for you. The guy who'll do right by you. Not Penn."

"You're engaged," I snap. Engaged or not, he'll never be the man Penn is. And while I could spend hours defending Penn to him, is it worth it? Dad always says, never wrestle with a pig in mud, you both get dirty, but the pig enjoys it.

"Can I make a confession?" he asks.

"No."

"It's about Sloane. She—"

"I like Sloane," I cut him off. "She's actually really sweet, Dylan." I shift, tugging my purse closer to my chest, a barrier between us.

"Yeah, sure, but she's not you." His voice is deceptively casual. A beat, and then, "She's not educated...or even all that smart."

Heat rises in my chest. "Don't say things like that. She's smart and doesn't deserve that comment. Have you seen her social media? She's fantastic." It's not a lie. She tricked me into believing she had the perfect life. But no matter how good she is, she could never convince me she's with the perfect guy because she's not.

"She might be good at social media." He waves his hand like it negates her existence. "But she doesn't have the finesse with the media—not the way that really counts. This—us—it would do wonders for your image."

I stare straight ahead, forcing my hands to unclench. Is he really suggesting we get back together for my benefit, when really, this is about his image and what I can do for him.

"Forget about this little festival. That's nothing. It's meaning-less compared to what I can give you."

"The festival means a lot to everyone in town," I argue, stubbornly.

"You know, Penn is never going to give you what I can."

What—heartache, sleepless nights, uncertainty? No, he's never going to give me that. "You have no idea what you're talking about." Penn is real, safe, and kind, everything Dylan will never understand.

"He's only going to let you down. I mean, come on, he might be in the NHL but he can't even get off the fourth line. He's never going anywhere."

"He has a lot of skill," I blurt out in his defense. "One of these days he's going to be more. You'll see."

"He told you that."

"No, but..."

"But you've talked about it?" When I don't answer, he continues, "I'm the guy you can count on, Jaylynn."

Stop engaging.

"All I'm going to say, again, is that you have no idea what you're talking about."

"Yes, I do." Dylan's eyes lock on mine, unflinching. "He'll prove to you who he really is soon enough. Guaranteed."

Why the hell is he saying that like he knows something I don't?

22

PENN

With unease weaving its way through my blood, I step back into the living room, the glow from the big screen pulling everyone in. The guys are glued to the hockey game, their shouts rising and falling with every play. Jaxon leaps to his feet, hands tugging at his hair as he screams at one of the players like the guy can hear him through the TV.

My gaze drifts from their rowdy energy to the mantel above the fireplace. Two peppermint stockings hang there, side by side. Penn. Jaylynn. The careful stitching catches in the firelight, and something inside me squeezes tight. Jaylynn did this. For me. She didn't make a big deal out of it. She just quietly hung it there. I've never had a stocking. Not one with my name. This...this gesture is her quiet way of making me a part of something bigger, something important, something I never knew I always needed. It's so goddamn touching that my chest aches in ways I can't even name.

I clear my throat during a lull in the game, trying to steady myself. "I'm going to take off."

Will glances over, and I try, unsuccessfully, to mask my upset. He sets his beer down and stands. "Everything okay?"

"Yeah," I say quickly, too quickly, scrambling for casual. "Jaylynn is in Rutledge. Flat tire. She called Triple A. I'm sure she's already on her way back."

Will's brow slams together. "Damn."

"I offered to go, but..." My words tangle. "She's with Dylan."

That pulls Jaxon's attention. His head turns, curiosity flickering in his eyes.

I rush to fill the silence. "He just happened to be in town. They ran into each other. Had coffee. He's staying with her until the tow comes. I'm sure she's fine." I force a laugh that feels like gravel in my throat. "I'll just head back to the inn, wait for her there."

"Want me to drive you?" Jaxon offers.

I shake my head. "I'm good. I'll catch you guys later."

Outside, the night slams into me. Wind cuts at my face as I zip my coat higher, breath steaming in the dark. A part of me hates that she's with Dylan, but another part clings to relief that she isn't stranded alone on the side of the road. Still, the thought of him beside her makes the cold seep deeper, like it's in my bones now.

I walk fast, boots crunching over frozen patches, the streets empty. No cars. No voices. Just the hush of a town curled in on itself, families tucked close together, hockey on their screens, Christmas lights glowing in their windows. Together. Warm.

By the time I push through the doors of the inn, the blast of heat and the scent of hot cocoa hit me like an embrace.

The fire roars in the hearth, throwing sparks of light into the lobby's shadows. God, I could use something stronger than cocoa, something to burn away the chill clinging to me.

I nod to Belinda at the desk and head for the hall, but stop short. Sloane is sitting alone near the fire, her legs tucked up beneath her, glass in hand. When she turns and spots me, her face brightens, though there's something tired in the edges of her smile.

"Hey, Sloane," I say, shrugging off the night air as I walk closer. "How are you feeling?"

"This helps," she says, lifting her glass. The steam curls above the rim, but it's not cocoa—there's too much amber glinting through it. "Hot toddy." Her gaze flicks over me, noting the cold still radiating off my skin. "You look like you could use one."

"Or two," I admit, hanging my coat on the rack.

"Sit. I'll grab you one."

Before I can protest, she disappears, and I lean toward the fire, letting the flames thaw the ache in my fingers. When she comes back, she hands me the warm glass, the fragrant heat rising to my face.

"Thanks." I take a sip, the burn sliding down my throat. "Perfect."

Sloane sinks back onto the sofa, phone in her hand but untouched. No scrolling. No posed selfies. Just her, staring into the flames, shoulders weighted.

"You enjoying Snowberry?" I ask, easing into the chair across from her.

Her laugh is soft, almost wistful. "Jaylynn asked me the same thing. It's quaint, and...small. Everyone seems to know everyone, and outside of Dylan and his family, I only know you and Jaylynn."

"Where's home?"

"California."

I whistle low. "You're a long way from sunshine and palm trees."

She nods, her eyes flickering toward the fire. "Yeah. I am."

"Missing your family?" I ask gently.

Her lips tilt, but it's not quite a smile. "Every day. But Dylan wanted to spend Christmas here, with his family. He said he can't stand being somewhere without snow at Christmas."

"How did you two meet?" I ask.

"I came to Vermont to ski. We met on the hill." A laugh escapes her, brittle and humorless. "Next thing I knew, I was packing up my life in California and moving to Rutledge."

I lift my glass in a silent toast. She clinks hers against mine with a hollow *ting*. "Well, at least Rutledge is bigger than Snowberry."

We fall quiet, both of us watching the fire crackle and spit, the flames chewing at the logs. Then she breaks the silence. "I really like Jaylynn. You two are great together."

She's not wrong. "Thanks."

"You should lock that in," she adds, half teasing, though her eyes don't hold humor.

I tilt my head, studying her. "I already did."

A slow nod and then quietly, "Right."

Just one word. But it lands heavy. Not agreement. Not approval. Just...doubt. She doesn't buy it. Which means Dylan probably doesn't either. My jaw clenches. If he says or does anything to ruin this festival for Jaylynn, I swear...

"Sloane," I start, but the shrill BZZZZZ of the mistletoe alarm cuts me off.

We both turn toward the lobby, watching a couple lean in, laughing as they kiss beneath the sprig dangling overhead. When I glance back, I catch it, the flash of pain in Sloane's eyes, there and gone.

"You okay?" I ask quietly.

Her throat works as she swallows. "Dylan and Jaylynn got caught under that earlier."

My chest tightens. "Under the mistletoe?"

"Yes."

"Surely to God they didn't—"

"They did."

Heat surges through me. My hands curl into fists before I force them to loosen. I am *not* going to hit Dylan. I won't do anything to upset Jaylynn.

"I was coming from the dining room and saw it," Sloane says, her nose wrinkling like she wants to block out the memory. "And I've had this awful feeling ever since...well, since I arrived." Her voice wavers, but instead of pressing into that feeling, she pivots. "Do you think he—"

"No," I cut in firmly. "I don't think it meant anything."

The lie tastes bitter, but what good would the truth do? She loves him. I can see it in her eyes, the way they go glassy, the way she's clinging to hope like it's all she's got. So, I swallow my own anger, my own distrust, and let her keep the scraps she needs.

"They simply got caught under the mistletoe," I add. "And you know the saying—when in Rome."

"Yeah, I guess." Her gaze drops to her drink. "He went into Rutledge earlier. We had plans, but out of nowhere he said he had to check on something at the office." She checks her phone, thumb flicking across the screen. "He's been gone a long time."

My gut coils tight. A bad feeling gnaws at me. "He ran into Jaylynn. She had a flat tire. He stayed with her until the tow truck came." Why the hell didn't he call or text to let her know. I drain half my toddy in one go, the burn scalding down my throat. "He'll be back soon."

"He's with Jaylynn?" she asks, her voice catching on the name.

"Yeah." I force calm I don't feel. "They just happened to run into each other."

The words scrape out of me, and don't at all sound convincing. Because even as I sit here, trying to assure Sloane nothing is happening, alarms blare in the back of my brain—insistent, ugly whispers that maybe, just maybe, I'm wrong.

I glance toward the inn's door, willing it to open. Willing Jaylynn, not Dylan, to step through. But when it finally swings wide, it's only another couple. The mistletoe alarm chirps again as they kiss, and something in me snaps. First chance I get, that damn thing's coming down.

Sloane and I linger, trading small talk. I ask about California, about her family. And for a moment, the heaviness lifts. A smile finally curves her mouth, genuine, brightening her face. We laugh softly, sip the last of our drinks, and the exhaustion creeps in, tugging at the edges of us both.

She picks up her phone again, checks it, and her face falls when the screen stays blank. No messages. No Dylan.

"I think I should call it a night," she murmurs, the fight draining out of her.

I check my phone again. Nothing. I'd asked Jaylynn to keep me posted, but she hasn't sent a single message. A knot tightens in my stomach. Maybe I should call, make sure the tow truck actually showed. My thumb hovers over her name when the front door creaks open, and there she is.

Jaylynn.

Relief barrels through me. But it lasts only a second, because right behind her, too close, is Dylan. I'm on my feet before I know it, crossing the room in three strides. I slide an arm around Jaylynn's waist, pulling her close, and press my mouth to hers. The kiss is deliberate, claiming. Possessive. When I pull back, her eyes are wide, her smile unsure.

"You okay?" My voice is softer than I feel.

"Yes." She glances over her shoulder at Dylan, who is peeling off his jacket like he owns the place. "I ended up getting a ride home with Dylan. The tow truck was full. Tools everywhere, another guy in the cab, so it made sense to come with him. Guess it was lucky I ran into him." She gives a quick laugh, but it's shaky, nervous. My gut twists. Something's off.

"Debatable," I mutter, eyes narrowing on Dylan. "So. Two tires slashed, huh?" My tone is sharp, laced with suspicion I don't bother hiding. "What's going on in Rutledge these days?"

He shrugs, all casual indifference. "Kids."

"Kids, huh?" I step closer, my stare locked on him.

"Yeah." His voice drops lower, his shoulders squaring. It's the stance of a man ready to go toe-to-toe.

Fine by me.

Before the room can combust, Jaylynn slips her hand into mine, her tone bright, almost too bright. "We should get to bed. Big day tomorrow." She gives Sloane a warm smile. "Goodnight, Sloane. I hope you're feeling better."

We turn down the hall. The mistletoe alarm goes off—again. My teeth grind. I bend and give Jaylynn a quick kiss, all while one thought hammers in my skull—is she going to tell me she kissed Dylan earlier?

In our room, she doesn't. She just grabs her pajamas and disappears into the bathroom. Water runs as I strip the pillows from the bed, tension buzzing in my muscles. When she finally emerges, she's soft and warm in her flannel PJs, her hair damp, her face scrubbed clean of makeup. She slips under the covers without a word.

I take my turn in the bathroom, then slide in beside her. I curl my arms around her, pulling her close. I'm about to pull her underneath me, make love to her but stop when she speaks.

"Night," she whispers, already drifting. Her breathing evens out, but mine won't. My mind is still lit up like a storm, replaying every glance, every pause, every lie of omission. Dylan's shadow lurks even here, in the dark.

I sleep restlessly, and while I trust her, she was acting strange last night. I know there's something she's not telling me. I hate that she feels she can't be completely honest. When dawn finally bleeds through the curtains, I'm wide awake, watching her.

And in that quiet, Sloane's words come racing back.

You should lock that in.

She's right. I have to tell Jaylynn how I feel. I have to tell her that I'm in love with her. That I want her in Boston with me. Even if she doesn't get the job, she'll find something else. We'll find a way. Because I'm not letting her slip through my fingers.

She stirs, lashes fluttering, and I lean down to kiss her awake.

Her lips curve into a sleepy smile. "That's a lovely way to wake up." She slides her arms around me, pulling me closer. I'm just about to roll her beneath me when her eyes snap open.

"What time is it?"

I glance at the clock. "Nine."

"I didn't mean to sleep this late." She bolts upright, scrambling. "I have to go."

"Go where? The parade doesn't start until five."

"I know." She's already climbing out of bed. "But I've got a million things to check on like the floats, parade route, security, crowd control, lights for the tree, the horses, costumes, photographer and booth for Santa, elfie selfie station..." She vanishes into the bathroom before I can stop her.

"Is there anything I can do?" I call.

Her voice floats back, muffled. "Actually, yes. Collect the ballots for the best-decorated shop and tally them for me to announce after the parade."

"That's easy. But what else can I help with?"

"Nothing." She reappears long enough to bend down and kiss me. "I've got plenty of volunteers, but I want to keep an eye on things myself. No way I'm letting another #GobbleGate happen."

I grin despite myself. "Fair enough. Just promise you'll call if you need anything."

"I will. Just be at the community hall by four-thirty. Your suit will be waiting."

"Okay, Mrs. Claus."

And just like that, she's gone—rushing out the door with her list, her smile, and her secrets.

I roll over and drift back to sleep for another hour. When I finally wake, I shower, check my phone—still nothing from Jaylynn—and grab a quick breakfast at the inn. The dining room is quiet, the kind of quiet that hums with anticipation, like the whole town is holding its breath for the night to come.

On Main Street, I collect ballots shop to shop, greeting merchants, admiring windows strung with garland and glittering lights. In one store, something in the display catches my eye—a small item, simple, but with the right touch it could become the perfect Christmas gift for Jaylynn. A grin spreads across my face as I tuck it under my arm. I'll swing by her parents' later for help with the finishing touches.

Excitement warms me, pushing back the chill of doubt I've been carrying. I finish my rounds, return to the inn, tally the ballots, and check the time. Fifty minutes until the community center. Plenty of time. I decide to walk, but first, I want to do a little digging into Dylan Hayes. I spend the next half hour doing a deep dive on social media, and news outlets.

Misappropriation of funds.

I shake my head as understanding dawns. The guy could be in big trouble. He needs someone to spin this, change the narrative, and that someone is obviously Jaylynn. I shut my laptop, a hollow ache inside my stomach.

He doesn't love her or want her. But if she knew why it could only open up old wounds, create new ones, and really hurt her. Fuck. I check the time again, pull on my coat and head outside. I walk to the center and when I enter, the place is buzzing. Costumes, props, decorations, a kissing booth for later when the adults convene after the tree lighting. It's chaos wrapped in Christmas. But no Jaylynn. My gaze sweeps the crowd, heart skipping when instead of her, I spot Dylan.

I angle to leave, but he intercepts me, genuine concern on his face. "Hey, everything okay with Elaine?"

I stop cold. "What are you talking about? Is she here?" My eyes scan the room.

He shakes his head. "No. Drove past her place earlier. The screen door hanging off the hinges, cats everywhere on the lawn."

My stomach drops. Cold panic slices through me. I dig for my phone, calling Elaine over and over. Voicemail. Again and again. Finally, I leave a message, my words clipped, urgent.

"You better get out there," Dylan says. "Things don't look good."

I'm not sure I buy his concern, but if something is going on, and I don't go, I could never live with myself. "Where's Jaylynn? I'm supposed to be dressed and ready in fifteen minutes."

"Didn't she tell you? Things are delayed. Parade's pushed back a half hour."

"Shit."

"Don't worry. Not her fault. Mayor Banks misplaced his bell."

Now that's something I can believe. "I'm going to text Jaylynn. If you see her before she gets my message, tell her I'll be back on time."

"Will do."

Something in his voice needles me, but I push it aside. I fire off a message to Jaylynn as I stride out the door. A second later, a phone pings behind me. I whip around, expecting to see her. But she isn't there.

The unease spreads.

I jog to the inn, jump into my SUV, and hit the road, my grip is white-knuckled on the wheel. Don't panic. Don't imagine the worst. Still, my mind won't stop spinning. If anything happened to Aunt Elaine. No. I'm not going there. She's fine. Forgetful, maybe. The cats probably slipped out. Muffin/ Earl —hell, I can practically picture him staging a feline coup to sabotage Santa's parade.

But when I reach her house, the world feels too quiet. The lawn is empty, the screen door shut tight. My pulse hammers as I bound up the steps and pound on the door. No answer. I dig out my key, push inside. The sound of hissing greets me, cats streaking past my legs.

"Elaine?" My voice echoes through the house.

Her car is in the garage. She has to be here. I tear through the rooms, calling her name, checking corners, checking each floor. My heart races harder with each empty hallway, each unanswered call.

Still nothing.

I grab my phone again, call Jaylynn this time, but she doesn't pick up either.

Dread coils tight in my chest. Maybe Elaine walked into town. Maybe she's at the hospital. Maybe—

My phone rings. Relief surges when I see her number. I snatch it up. "Elaine? Are you okay? Where are you?"

A beat of silence. Then, "I think I'm the one who should be asking you those questions."

23

JAYLYNN

Dressed in my Mrs. Claus costume, I hurry through the chaos of the community center, my red skirt swishing around my legs. Kids are darting between tables, volunteers are shouting orders, and somewhere in the back, a brass band is warming up. It feels like I'm at the center of a snow globe someone won't stop shaking.

Where the heck did I put my phone?

I nearly collide with Sheriff Reynolds. "Can you call my phone for me? I can't find it, and I don't have time to look."

"Sure thing." He pulls his cell from his belt and punches in my number. We both pause, scanning the echoing room. Nothing. The noise is so loud we wouldn't hear a rocket launch.

"Thanks. I'll keep looking," I say breathlessly. The parade is going to start in five minutes, and still no sign of Penn. A knot of worry tightens in my chest. I almost ask the sheriff to call him, but then, right there. From the corner of my eye, I catch a glimpse of red velvet and snowy white trim disappearing into the back room. Santa. My Santa. Penn.

Relief surges through me so fast my knees go weak. He's here. Of course, he's here. If there's one thing I know about Penn, it's he's dependable.

De—Penn—dable.

Oh my god, I crack myself up. If I had time to laugh I would. I'm already half-turned to go to him when Cassie barrels into me, her cheeks flushed. "There's no candy on the daycare float. The kids can't throw candy if they have no candy. Weren't you supposed to handle that?"

My heart lurches. "Right. Yes. On it."

I sprint to the locker room, find the massive bag of candy, and haul it out myself. Cassie's already vanished, juggling a dozen other fires, so I drag the sack to the float and start handing it out to eager little hands. Just as I finish, Mayor Banks, dressed in his town crier costume, and moving at the pace of a snail, starts ringing his brass bell. The sharp clang ricochets off the brick walls, signaling that the parade is about to begin.

The building erupts into motion. Families, volunteers, costumed performers—everyone floods out toward the street in a merry rush. Convinced Penn is among them, I climb aboard the last float and settle onto my bench, finally allowing myself to breathe.

The crowd outside is a blur of mittens and twinkle lights. I search through the faces until I spot Santa striding toward me. My chest unclenches. It's been nonstop chaos all day, but now—now that Penn is here beside me—I can relax. Everything will be okay.

I wave at my mom and dad, who beam and wave back as they jockey for a spot along the curb. When I turn back around, I see Santa climbing up onto his seat beside me. My smile freezes. My pulse slams against my throat.

Dylan.

My stomach drops, the world tilting under me. "What are you doing here?" I manage to croak, the words scraping past the lump in my throat.

He adjusts the hat, smugness in every move. "Penn didn't show, Jaylynn. Someone had to take his place."

"What do you mean he didn't show?" I lurch forward, panic clawing at me. "I need to go find him."

His gloved hand clamps on my arm, pressing me back into the seat. "He's not here."

"Let me use your phone."

"It's in the locker," he says flatly.

"I need—" I push to my feet, but the driver flicks the reins. The horse lurches forward, the float rolling, and I nearly topple. "Where is he?" My voice cracks, desperate.

Dylan only shrugs, his lips curving in a self-satisfied smile. "Beats me. But if I had to guess? After seeing us together last night, Penn finally realized what I've been saying all along. You and I are the ones who belong together. He probably stepped aside, gave us the space we need."

My blood runs cold. "You have no idea what you're talking about."

"You said that last night too. But here we are. Penn's gone, just like I told you he would be. He will always let you down, Jay. Always. You just didn't want to see it."

"No." My denial is fierce, but it doesn't stop the ache in my chest, the whisper of fear curling inside me. Where is Penn? "I need to get off this float."

Dylan leans back with a smug little smirk. "Too late. The parade's moving. So why don't you do what you're supposed to do?" He gestures to the crowd, his voice low and cutting. "Smile and wave, sweetheart."

I turn my head and plaster on a smile, lifting my hand to wave as the float creaks along the snowy street. On the outside, I'm Mrs. Claus—warm, merry, picture-perfect. On the inside, I'm unraveling, scanning every face in the crowd, searching.

Where is Penn?

My heart insists he didn't bail. Not on me. Not on *this*. Dylan has his fingerprints all over this mess. I can feel it in my bones.

"I'm the guy you can count on, Jaylynn," Dylan murmurs at my side, his voice smug beneath the roar of holiday cheers. "The guy who's here for you now, and will be here for you in the future."

My stomach twists. I keep my smile fixed for the children lining the sidewalks, but my voice is tight. "Did you say something to him?"

"I didn't need to." He waves at a family in the front row like he's the real Santa, like he owns this. "He sees how good we are together. That's all it took."

Anger pricks at the corners of my eyes. I refuse to let him see me break. "Do I need to remind you that you're engaged?"

"Sloane and I broke up." He shrugs as if it's nothing, but my heart hurts for her. "There's nothing standing in our way now. Not even Penn." His grin slices through me, and I swallow hard against the bile rising in my throat. I really, really need a phone.

"Everything I said about him was right," he adds smoothly. "He's a thug. You'll see soon enough."

I turn away, my smile faltering but still there, because if I let the mask slip, the kids will see. And this moment—the lights, the joy, the magic of Christmas—isn't mine to ruin.

The street is strung with twinkle lights, red and green bulbs glowing against the dusk. Wreaths sway from lampposts, the air filled with the scent of pine and hot cocoa. The crowd is beaming, faces lit with pure holiday wonder. Everything looks perfect. Everything should *feel* perfect.

But it doesn't. Not even close.

When we pass my parents, I spot Jaxon with Rowyn at his side. Their smiles falter, confusion etching across their faces as they realize it isn't Penn riding beside me. Whispers ripple through the nearby crowd, curious eyes darting toward me, toward *us*.

I close my eyes for a heartbeat, wishing the earth would open and swallow me whole. Just get me through this. Just get me off this float.

Dylan doesn't notice—or doesn't care. He keeps talking, spinning out his future as though it's already written in stone. Him as president, me running his campaigns, the two of us unstoppable. His voice is a steady drone, a nightmare lullaby I can't tune out no matter how hard I try.

Minutes stretch like hours until at last, the float lumbers into the town square. The massive spruce tree towers above us, its branches heavy with ornaments, waiting for the moment the lights will blaze to life. Children are bouncing on their toes, clapping their mittened hands, shrieking with excitement as they line up for their turn on Santa's lap.

The driver pulls the reins, and the horse slows to a stop. The float shudders, and Dylan rises to his feet with a booming laugh, as though this is *his* moment. He leaps down, playing the role to perfection, reveling in the applause.

Then he turns, all gallantry, and extends his hand to me. His smile is for the crowd, but the glint in his eyes is for me alone, warning me that if I do something, I could destroy any chance at a real career. Every instinct in me screams to recoil. To refuse. To let the world see just how false this is.

But the children are watching. Wide-eyed. Believing.

So, I swallow the revulsion clogging my throat, press down the panic clawing at my chest, and slip my hand into his.

For them, I play the part of the adoring Mrs. Claus.

Even though it feels like betrayal.

The crowd in the square is electric, humming with anticipation. Children cluster at the base of the towering spruce, their mittened hands clasped as they chant, "Santa, Santa!" A hundred little faces watching, waiting for magic.

Beside me, Dylan basks in it. He puffs his chest, waves like a celebrity, and soaks in the attention as though he earned it. He leans closer, his voice a low murmur. "This is our moment, Jaylynn. Don't ruin it."

I don't answer. My heart is hammering too loudly, every nerve in my body stretched tight.

And then—I see him.

Penn.

He's cutting through the crowd at the edge of the square, no costume, just jeans and his dark leather coat. His jaw is locked, his shoulders rigid. Anger radiates off him, a storm barely contained. For a heartbeat, relief crashes over me so fierce my knees weaken. He's here. He didn't leave me.

But when his eyes find Dylan at my side, his expression darkens.

"Jay." His voice cuts through the chatter like a blade.

Dylan turns, his mouth curling into a smug smile. "Well, well. Speak of the devil."

Penn strides forward, stopping just short of the float. Children squeal at the sight of him—some recognizing him as one of the town's hockey heroes—but Penn doesn't break his glare. His hands clench at his sides, the only sign of the restraint it's costing him not to grab Dylan.

"What the fuck, Dylan?" Penn's voice is low, dangerous. He's trying, for the kids' sake, but I hear the fury under every word.

Dylan spreads his arms, Santa suit gleaming under the lights, playing to the crowd. "Someone had to step in when you didn't show. Can't disappoint the children, right?" He smirks.

"That's not how this happened, and you know it." Penn's chest rises and falls with a sharp breath, like he's wrestling the urge to lose control. His gaze flicks to me, and that's when I see it. Penn Bradford. Radman. Madman. The enforcer.

Mayor Banks takes to the platform and picks up the over-sized switch for the tree, beaming at the crowd. "Ladies and gentlemen, in just a moment, Santa Claus himself will light our Christmas tree!"

Cheers erupt, and the children scream with glee. Dylan soaks it in, and makes a move toward the stage. Penn steps closer, his voice dropping so only we can hear. "You and me, we need to talk."

Dylan chuckles. "Careful, tough guy. Wouldn't want to throw a punch in front of all these witnesses. Bad for your image. And hers." He nods toward me, his voice pitched just loud enough to needle.

Penn's eyes blaze, his fists flexing. For a split second, I see the storm break through the cracks in his control. Then he takes a step back, jaw tight, forcing the fury down. For the children. For me.

Penn's voice is low, ragged, barely contained. "You can say whatever you want to me. Do whatever you want to me. But don't think for one second I'm going to let you mess anything up for Jaylynn."

Dylan scoffs, spreading his arms as though the entire town square is his stage. "Mess it up? You didn't show. I did her a favor, Penn. I saved the day."

Penn's eyes flash. "You tried to sabotage this parade. You sent me on a wild goose chase, had me tearing across town thinking my aunt was in trouble. Do you have any idea the hell you put me through? What this could have done to Jaylynn's career?" His voice shakes with fury. "Tell me, did you flatten her tires on purpose, too?"

I jerk my head toward him, shock stealing my breath. Tires? His aunt? What goose chase? My brain scrambles, trying to catch up.

Dylan smirks, like he's relishing every second. "Jaylynn doesn't even have a career to sabotage. But I'm going to rectify that. Me. I'm the guy who's going to do that. She's not going to make it out there in the real world without me. She tried once, and look how that turned out."

Penn's jaw clenches. His voice drops, but it vibrates with unshakable conviction. "You're the one who needs her to..." He falters, turns toward me. For a split second, I see the storm in his eyes—the war he's waging inside. What is it he's trying to say to me?

He faces Dylan again, voice steady and fierce. "For the record, she *does* have a career. And don't you ever diminish her like that again. She doesn't need you—or anyone—to make it. She's strong, and smart, and she can do anything she sets her mind to."

Dylan barks a laugh. "Smart? I wouldn't go that far. Not if she's wasting her time with you." His voice sharpens like a blade. "You're an enforcer, Penn. A thug. A nothing who's never getting off the fourth line. Even she knows that."

Penn stiffens, his mouth opening—ready to fight—but Dylan keeps pressing, the knife twisting deeper. "Let me guess, Jaylynn's been pushing you, hasn't she? Telling you to be more, do more? She deserves better than a thug for a husband. Even *you* know that."

Penn falters, his throat bobbing as he swallows hard. His gaze flicks to mine, and I know—God, I know—Dylan has used my words against him. Words I never meant to hurt Penn with.

"Penn." My voice cracks. My heart is pounding so loud I can hardly hear. We can't do this here, in front of everyone. Our private lives spilled out under the glow of Christmas lights. "Penn, don't—"

I reach for him, my hand trembling, but he doesn't move.

Dylan tilts his head, the predator who smells blood. "You think she can live up to her potential with *you?*" He sweeps his hand toward the float, the stage, the staring crowd. "Look around, Penn. This is the best you can give her? This is her life with you?"

Penn's voice is tight, each word ground out between clenched teeth. "You're the one who's messing this up for her."

"No." Dylan leans closer, his voice dropping to a vicious hiss. "You're the one who's going to mess it all up, and prove to her exactly who you are."

Penn's brows knit. "What are you talking about?"

Dylan pivots to me. "Let's not kid ourselves, Jay. Without me, you're nothing. *I* saved this parade. I'm the one who can give you the career you dream of. With Penn?" He sweeps his hand toward the children at the edges of the crowd. "This is all you'll ever have." He looks back at Penn, his eyes glittering with malice. "That kiss we shared under the mistletoe was just the beginning."

Fire burns in Penn's eyes. "Penn, it's not what you think. I didn't—"

"I know," he responds through clenched teeth, his gaze never leaving Dylan's. "Don't you go near her again."

Ignoring him, Dylan adds, "Oh, and you were right about her tires. I did that. I needed alone time with her after our kiss.

She just doesn't see it yet, but she will. She'll see we're meant to be together."

The words land like a bomb.

Penn's entire body goes rigid. His fists curl tight, his breath tearing through his chest. When he finally speaks, his voice is a growl that makes the hair rise on the back of my neck. "You put her in danger."

He stalks forward, each step deliberate, deadly. My heart leaps into my throat. This is going bad, fast.

"Penn, wait." I lunge for him, reaching for his arm.

But I'm too late.

His fist arcs through the air, a loud crack. Dylan stumbles back, crashing into a display of light-up peppermint sticks, strings of red-and-white bulbs tangling around him as he crumples. Gasps ripple through the crowd, children cry, and a stunned silence swallows the square.

"Penn!" My scream rips from my throat.

He spins toward me, his chest heaving, his eyes wild. And then—just for a heartbeat—I see every emotion flicker across his face. Fury, shock, regret, sorrow... and then the one that guts me most.

Shame.

His shoulders sag, his fists unclench, and he looks at me like he's already lost. "I'm so sorry, Jaylynn," he whispers, voice raw. "I ruined this for you. The one thing I swore I'd never do." He swallows and looks at the tree. "Christmas, the tree lighting...I wanted to give you new memories. To wipe away the painful ones."

His gaze sweeps the square—the crying children, the horrified faces, the chaos he's unleashed. His chest rises and falls in quick, ragged bursts.

And then he turns.

Before I can reach him, before I can call him back, he's gone.

Gone from the stage. Gone from the crowd.

Gone from me.

Dylan pushes to his feet, rubbing his jaw with a grimace, the tangled lights glowing around his legs. He smirks. "What did I tell you, Jay? He just proved exactly who he is."

24

PENN

It's Christmas Eve, and the guys keep calling, their voices upbeat, inviting me over tomorrow for dinner, promising food, beer, and distraction. I know what they're doing and appreciate it, but no. I can't go. Not after what I did. I'd rather stay curled up in my bed, staring at the ceiling, hating myself for the spectacle I made at the festival. For hurting the one person I swore I'd protect.

There's no universe where Jaylynn deserved that. Yeah, sure, Dylan deserved to get decked for slashing her tires—among other things—but not at Jaylynn's expense. Not at the cost of her reputation, her dream, her faith in me.

My phone pings again, lighting up with familiar names. There's only one person I want to talk to, only one person I want to beg forgiveness from. Jaylynn. I want to tell her I'm sorry a thousand times, in every language I can think of, until she believes me. But I'm too afraid to call, too afraid of what she'll say to me.

And maybe... maybe Dylan was right.

The thought slices through me like a blade. Maybe she really does deserve better. Someone who isn't a coward on the ice. Someone who isn't defined by his fists and his failures. They call me the enforcer, but I have more than brute force in me—I know I do. Still, the Bucks never wanted that from me. They wanted the hits, the penalties, the chaos. And if I try to be more, if I push for a role beyond that and fail? What then? Sent down to the Grizzlies? Cut? Forgotten?

But the truth is… that wouldn't even feel like rock bottom anymore.

Because losing Jaylynn? That was it. That was the lowest I could fall.

But what do I have to lose now? Maybe I should go to Coach. Maybe I should demand the chance to be more, to prove I can be more. It won't bring Jaylynn back, but at least it would honor the way she saw me—like I was worth something. Like I wasn't just fists and fury.

She wanted me to believe in myself. She told me I was more. But no one else ever has—not my team, not my coaches. Not even my own damn parents. I've spent my whole life following the rules, thinking that would make me enough. Look where that got me.

The buzzer jolts me out of my dark thoughts. Someone's at my building. I roll over, pull my pillow over my face, and groan. Whoever it is, I don't want to see them. I don't want to see anyone.

Buzz.

Buzz.

Buzz.

"Go away," I mutter into the pillow, even though they can't hear me from the street.

It can't be Elaine—she called earlier, and I talked to her before I left Snowberry. She wouldn't come all this way, not on Christmas Eve.

Buzz.

Buzz.

Buzz.

Jesus Christ. Whoever it is, they're relentless. I throw my pillow across the room, shove myself upright, and stomp over to the intercom, ready to tear into them. My finger slams the button. "What?"

There's a beat of silence. Then a familiar voice. "Hey, Penn. It's Will."

My heart stops. Will. As in Coach Quinn. As in Jaylynn's father.

What the hell is he doing in Boston? On Christmas Eve? He should be at home with his family, not standing outside my building. Unless... oh God. Unless I ruined Christmas for him, too.

Perfect. My gift of screwing up keeps on giving.

I hesitate, a hundred scenarios running through my head. Maybe he's here to tear into me, to finish what Dylan started. Maybe he's here to punch me in the face and call it justice. And the worst part? I'd let him. I'd take every hit. I deserve it.

I press the buzzer to let him in and back away from the door, my stomach in knots.

The elevator dings down the hall a few minutes later, echoing like a death knell in the silence of my apartment. My chest tightens as the doors slide open. I take a step back, bracing myself. For anger. For judgment. For the blow I probably have coming.

Because if anyone has the right to make me pay for what I did to Jaylynn, it's her father.

"Coach," I say automatically, my voice rough, and I edge back a step as he closes the door behind him.

"It's Will, remember."

My throat tightens. Will. Not Coach. Not Mr. Quinn. Just Will. The way he insisted I call him when things between Jaylynn and me felt real, felt permanent. But things aren't real anymore, are they? She's gone. I lost her. So, I shake my head, bitter.

"Since Jaylynn and I aren't together anymore, I figured I should probably go back to calling you Coach. Especially since I'm pretty sure you're here to kick my ass."

To my surprise, he chuckles—low, genuine—and shakes his head.

"No?" I ask, confused.

"Have a seat, son."

Son.

The word detonates in my chest.

It should be comforting, but it feels like someone tearing the bandage off a wound I've been trying to ignore. All I can think about is never earning that word again. Never being his son-in-law. Never sitting at their table with Jaylynn at my side, pretending I belong in their world. The ache scrapes me raw, leaves me hollow.

My legs give out and I stumble back, dropping into the couch. My apartment looks like a disaster zone—takeout boxes, empty bottles, the kind of mess that screams *loser*. I can practically feel his disappointment crawling over the walls. Some role model for his daughter. Some catch.

The first words tumble out before I can stop them. "I'm sorry."

His eyes soften. "I know you are."

"I never meant to hurt her," I rush on, the words thick with guilt. "God, that's the last thing I ever wanted. She's the best thing that's ever happened to me, and I blew it. I humiliated her. I'm sure she hates me."

Will leans forward slightly, his voice steady but sure. "No, son. She doesn't hate you."

The word *son* again. My throat closes around it.

"In fact..." He lets a slow smile creep over his face, then deliberately lets the sentence dangle, unfinished.

"In fact, what?" My heart's hammering so hard I can hear it in my ears.

"I'll let her tell you that herself."

"Tell me what?" My voice cracks.

"Why don't you come back to Snowberry with me and find out." He glances at his watch. "If we leave now, and I speed just a little, we can be there in time to watch the Grinch before bed. It's Christmas Eve tradition."

I shoot to my feet so fast I nearly trip over a pizza box. "You've got to be kidding me?" My laugh is almost hysterical. "After what I did? I ruined everything. I traumatized a crowd of kids. Ruined Jay's career." I can barely force the next words out; they taste so bitter. "She deserves better than me."

Will doesn't flinch. He just arches a brow. "You think she's better off with Dylan?"

"Fuck no." The answer tears out of me before I can stop it. The thought alone makes bile rise in my throat. Will tilts his head, the tiniest flicker of a smile tugging at his mouth, and I cringe, running a hand through my hair. "Sorry," I mutter, heat crawling up my neck. "Didn't mean to swear." But the truth is, every ounce of me meant it. Jaylynn with Dylan? Over my dead body.

"I need to tell you something, Penn. Can you please sit?"

The seriousness in his tone knocks the wind out of me, and I sink back onto the couch, my chest tight. "What?"

"Jaylynn always came to the rink with me. She loved watching practices."

I swallow hard, already feeling where this is going. "Yeah. I saw her there sometimes."

"She liked watching you."

The words sting with disbelief. "Me? Really? Why?"

"Because she saw something in you. Skills you didn't think anyone noticed. When you were out there alone, running drills, pushing yourself after everyone else left, she quietly watched. She told me to give you a chance, told me that once you got your shot at the big league, you'd show the world what you were really made of." He folds his hands together, his voice steady, certain. "Penn, she's the reason you were called up. She's the one who always believed in you."

Tears burn hot behind my eyes, and I squeeze them shut, pressing my palms into my face. She believed in me. Not because she wanted bragging rights or because she needed me to be some star for her benefit. She believed in me *for me*. She saw value in me when I couldn't find any myself.

Jesus.

As if reading the avalanche of thoughts in my head, Will leans forward. "She doesn't want you to change positions because of her. She wants it because she wants you to live up to your full potential. Just like you want her to live up to hers. People who love each other... that's what they do. They see more in you than you see in yourself, and they push you toward it."

I drag in a ragged breath and work to calm my chaotic thoughts.

I was always enough for her—but she wanted more for me. For me.

My throat is raw when I whisper, "And look what I did with that. Look how I repaid her."

"What you did..." Will says firmly, but kindly, "...was protect her. Defend her. Yeah, decking Santa in front of the kids wasn't exactly your proudest moment. But between you and me?" His mouth quirks. "If you hadn't done it, I would have."

My head jerks up, eyes wide. "Are you serious?"

"Dead serious." His smile fades as his expression turns somber. He shifts in his seat, his gaze never leaving mine. "I hope I'm not overstepping here, but... I noticed Jaylynn didn't have a ring."

The words slice me open with guilt. Fuck, if he didn't hate me before, he's going to now. "Will—"

He raises a hand. "It's okay. I know everything."

Fuck.

"I'm so sorry. Jay came up with this plan. We never meant to deceive anyone." My voice drops. "Did she tell you? Did she tell everyone?" I'm not sure why I'm worried about everyone hating me for this, they already hate me for ruining Christmas.

He shakes his head slowly. "No. She's not really talking much at all right now. I only had my suspicions. You just confirmed them."

"Jesus," I groan, scrubbing a hand down my face. "I just confessed without even meaning to. You're a sneaky son of a bitch."

Will laughs, and then reaches into his pocket. When he pulls out a small velvet box, my chest seizes.

"What's that?" I rasp.

He opens it, revealing a delicate diamond that catches the light, glowing like it's carrying the weight of generations.

"Uh, Coach. I mean Will. I appreciate the gesture, but you're not my type."

That gets a belly laugh out of him, his eyes crinkling in the corners. "This was her grandmother's ring. Jaylynn always loved it. We've kept it put away, waiting for the right time. And I thought..." He pushes the box toward me, his voice steady. "...this is my way of giving you my approval, Penn. You're the son-in-law I've always wanted."

My head jerks back as my heart thumps wildly. "Are you kidding me? After everything I've done?"

"Yes," he says simply. "After everything. After watching you stand up for my daughter, after seeing how deeply you care for her, after the way you've fought—sometimes poorly, sometimes too hard—but always for her." He pauses, his eyes piercing mine. "Especially after seeing how much you love her."

The truth rips out of me, raw and unstoppable. "I do love her," I choke, tears spilling hot down my face. I bend forward, elbows braced on my knees, face buried in my hands.

Will's voice softens, full of quiet conviction. "Then you need to tell her."

"She's not going to talk to me," I say, muffled by my palms, every ounce of me terrified of the rejection I deserve.

"Penn."

I lift my head slowly. He's watching me with a kind of patience and hope that feels like a lifeline.

"There's only one way to find out."

For most of my life, I've been too much of a coward to try—to step out of line, to risk failure, to push past what others expected of me. But right now, failure isn't an option. Not when it comes to Jaylynn. If there was ever a time to fight, it's now.

I wipe my face, stand on shaky legs, and nod. "Let's go."

25

JAYLYNN

My hotel room is dim, only the faint glow of the string lights above my window casting soft shadows across the walls. I've been curled up in the bed I'd shared with Penn for a couple days now, the weight of the blankets no match for the heaviness pressing against my chest.

Dad called earlier to check in on me, wanting me to come home to watch the Grinch. It's our favorite family tradition, but I just want to lay in this bed, tucked away from the real world. Everyone thinks I'm hiding because I'm angry. Because Penn ruined everything. But the truth is... I'm not mad at him. Not at all.

I keep replaying the moment in my head. The way he stepped between Dylan and me, the way his jaw set, the fury in his eyes. He didn't hit Santa for himself. He hit him for me. Because in that moment, I mattered more than anything else.

And God help me, I love him for it.

What breaks me most is that he's probably sitting somewhere right now, tearing himself apart, convinced he ruined me, convinced he isn't good enough. Penn has always been his own worst enemy, and I know he's drowning in it. I want to call him. I want to talk, but he hates himself, and no doubt thinks I'm better off without him. I need to give him space, time with himself to figure things out.

I push from my bed and walk to the window, the gift I bought Penn wrapped and sitting on the desk. Will I ever be able to give it to him? I turn, and a small laugh escapes me despite the heaviness in my chest. The creepy elf—the one we'd both claimed wasn't judging anyone—has been put back in the room, perched on the shelf like it's silently keeping tabs on me. Its plastic eyes glare in my direction, and for a second, it feels like the elf *really* knows everything that has gone down.

"Yeah, yeah," I mutter, shaking my head. "I know. You've seen it all and I know what list I'm on."

A knock sounds at the door, startling me. It could be Belinda or Jaxon's parents, who've been bringing me food and have also been keeping tabs on me, but I have zero appetite tonight. I jump back into my bed, bury my face in the pillow, and pretend not to hear.

Another knock. Louder.

My heart stutters, because when I don't answer them, they don't persist.

Who is at my door?

And then...his voice. Rough. Unsteady. Aching in a way that makes my own chest splinter.

"Jay. It's me."

I press my hand to my mouth, biting back a sob.

Penn.

He's here.

Back in Snowberry.

But...is he here for me?

Us?

"Please," he says, desperation threading through every sylla-ble. "Don't shut me out. Not yet."

Tears blur my vision. He really thinks I don't want him here. That I hate him. That I could ever hate him. I sit there, trying to breathe, to think...to make my legs move.

He keeps talking, words tumbling like they're being ripped from someplace deep. "I screwed up. Worse than I ever have. I embarrassed you, I hurt you. I should have had more control, done better. And I will regret that until the day I die."

I shake my head into the pillow. No, no, no. That's not what happened. That's not what I feel.

"But I need you to know..." His voice cracks, broken and shaky. "...I love you, Jaylynn. I love you so damn much it terrifies me. And if you never forgive me, if you tell me to walk away right now, I'll do it. But I couldn't let another night go by without saying it."

He loves me...

My whole body trembles. Not from anger. From the sheer force of his love, his guilt, his inability to see that what he did wasn't failure, it was proof. Proof of how much I mean to him. Proof that to Penn Radford, I am worth fighting for.

The tears spill over, hot against my cheeks. I can't let him stand out there thinking the worst for another second. My legs move before my brain can catch up, and I stumble across the room. My hand trembles as I twist the lock.

The door opens slowly, and there he is. Shoulders tense, eyes haunted, clutching something in his hand. He looks at me like I'm the air he hasn't breathed in days. And all I can think is, he has no idea that the only thing broken here is him, and all I want is to put him back together. I reach for the man I've loved this entire time, my hand trembling.

My voice is barely more than a whisper. "Penn…" He flinches, like he's not sure if he deserves to hear my voice. I capture his rough, calloused hand and pull him a little closer. "You… you didn't ruin anything. You stood up for me. For me. That's… that's everything."

His eyes widen, disbelief flashing across his face. "Everything?"

"Everything," I repeat, firmer this time. My heart is pounding. "You didn't hurt me. You… you showed me how much I mean to you. And that… that's all I've ever wanted."

He swallows hard. The tension in his shoulders eases, just a fraction, and I feel a tiny spark of hope flicker between us. "But your job…your future."

"Everything will work out." In my heart, I believe that.

"I… I just…" His voice falters. "I thought I'd ruined everything. I thought I wasn't enough."

"You're more than enough," I say, gripping his hands. "You've always been enough. You just didn't see it yet. And now… now I want you to see it too."

"Your dad came to see me. He told me you were responsible for getting me called up. You...you saw my worth...you saw me."

"I see you, Penn."

"I see you too, Jaylynn." His lips quiver. His eyes shine with tears, and I feel my own spilling over. We stand there for a moment, letting the weight of everything pass between us—regret, fear, love, hope—all tangled together.

And then, slowly, he leans forward. I don't pull back. Our foreheads touch, and it feels like the world has narrowed down to just this. Just us. Then he inches back and holds his hand out, and my gaze goes to the snow globe in his palm.

"What is this?"

"I got this for you... for Christmas." He holds it out, shaking it gently so I can hear the soft swish of something inside. My eyes catch the snow falling over the country club inside the globe.

"You once said you wanted to bottle that night," he murmurs, his voice low.

A laugh escapes me, bubbling up before I can stop it. Not because it's funny, far from it. It's the most thoughtful, ridiculous, perfect gift I've ever received. But when I tilt it, peek through the glass, my chest tightens. There, glued carefully to the back, is a picture of us. Just us. From the night he had dinner at my parents'.

"You did this?" I whisper, incredulous. "You glued us on there."

He grins, that easy, crooked smile that has me melting from the inside out. "You don't like it?"

I shake my head, tears threatening to spill over. "I love it... Penn. I love it so much."

He steps closer, the warmth of him brushing against me, and I can't stop the small smile tugging at my lips. "Good," he says softly. "Because I love you."

"I love you too," I reply, my voice breaking as emotions well up inside of me.

And in that moment, standing in the quiet of our peppermint-themed room, I don't know what our future careers hold, but as long as we have each other, that's all that matters.

I feel him shift slightly in my hands, and then he hesitates, pulling the small velvet box from his pocket. My breath catches.

"Penn..." I murmur, heart hammering so fast I can barely speak.

He swallows hard, eyes flicking to mine, searching, needing permission, and I nod. He opens the box. Inside rests my grandmother's delicate diamond, small but brilliant, catching the light in the dim glow of my room.

My hands fly to my mouth. "Oh... oh, Penn..."

"Your dad also gave me this." He swallows again, voice low. "I want to spend the rest of my life proving that I'll protect you, care for you... love you. Always."

Tears spill down my cheeks as I stare at him, at the man who would fight the world for me, at the man who finally sees himself the way I've always seen him. "Penn... I, this..." My words falter, but the meaning is clear. I love him. I want him. I always have.

He swallows and lets the box hover between us. "You... you don't have to answer now. I just needed you to know how much you mean to me."

I step closer, closing the space between us. My fingers brush his, gripping the edge of the box. "Penn... The answer is yes. It's always been yes. Yes, I want this. I want you."

His eyes go wide, and then, finally, a smile breaks across his face. Genuine, shaky, but radiant. Relief floods him, and it hits me how much he needed that affirmation as much as I needed him.

He leans in slowly, pressing his forehead to mine as he slides the ring on my finger. "I love you," he whispers again.

"I love you too," I whisper, then admire the ring on my finger. "I also have a present for you."

"You do?"

I tug him inside, letting the door click shut behind us, and point toward the bed.

"Oh," he says, waggling his brow. "I like the way you think."

I burst out laughing, shaking my head. "That's not what I was thinking." Well, that might not be entirely true. I hand him the neatly wrapped box on the desk.

His fingers tremble a little as he rips the paper, and his eyes go wide when he sees what's inside. An old board game —*Trouble*. A laugh bubbles up from deep in his throat. "My favorite."

"I wanted to recreate your quiet Christmas morning," I say softly, smiling. "You said you loved them."

"I do," he murmurs, his voice low and full of something that makes my chest flutter. "Maybe with this one, I'll get lucky and pop a damn six."

I nudge him playfully. "Oh, I think you might get lucky."

He chuckles, but then his gaze drifts across the room, and a look of horror flashes in his eyes. "What the hell is he doing back here?"

I tilt my head toward the elf perched on the shelf, its tiny eyes staring at us. "Judging," I say simply, smirking.

Penn's laugh rumbles against my ear as he pulls me toward him, and before I know it, we're collapsing onto the bed together, tangled limbs and laughter spilling through the room.

"How about we give him something to judge," he murmurs against my hair, his voice low and playful, "And really secure our spot on the naughty list?"

"Now I'm the one who likes the way you think." I snuggle closer, letting the warmth of him and the absurdity of the elf fill the room.

"Wait, I think your dad wants us to come over to watch the Grinch."

"We don't need to go anywhere. Not when I've got my own Grinch in my bed." I wink at him. "I mean, you did deck Santa."

He smiles back. "Twice."

I laugh. "Maybe there's something else you can do twice?" I tease.

"No maybe about it."

Penn

The puck smacks my stick and I take off down the wing, Jaxon right there with me. He gives me a quick pass, I send it back, and for the first time, it's not about brute force or clearing a path. It's about rhythm. Timing. Trust.

It's about connection.

Being part of this team. Part of the play.

The scrape of my skates cuts sharp against the ice. The cold air bites at my cheeks. The crowd's roar vibrates through my chest like a drumbeat. Jaxon barrels toward the net, pulling the goalie with him, then threads it back to me in the slot. Instinct takes over. I wind up and snap the puck forward.

It rockets past the goalie's outstretched glove. The goal light flashes and the alarm blares.

Goal.

The horn blasts so loud it rattles my ribs. The crowd leaps to its feet in a sea of jerseys and foam fingers, the noise crashing down like a wave. Jaxon pumps his fist, looping back and slamming his glove against mine.

"Not bad for an old enforcer," he grins. The chirp feels more like brotherhood than anything else.

I laugh, breathless, heart pounding for reasons that have nothing to do with the win. Because when I look up into the stands, I find her.

Jaylynn.

Headset snug around her ears, tablet balanced in one hand, phone pressed to the other. Her pen tucked behind her ear like she's been born for this job. The Bucks' PR director, commanding the chaos of the arena with sharp precision and calm fire.

And still, she feels me looking. Her gaze flicks up, just for a second, and locks with mine.

Everything else falls away.

Her lips curve in that smile. The one that says she sees me. Not just the fists. Not just the mistakes. Me.

The pile of bodies swallows me as the guys mob Jaxon and me, but that look—her look—stays burned in my chest all the way back to the locker room. I step inside and wince. The place reeks of sweat, tape, and victory. Laughter and chirps bounce off the concrete walls. Water bottles spray like champagne. Someone blasts music from a speaker. And for once, I'm not standing on the outside, half-dreading the night's headlines. I'm in it. I belong here.

"Hey, Penn," Brady calls, ripping tape from his pads. "You hitting Kilting Around later?"

"Can't," I say, tugging off my jersey. "Jaylynn's folks and my aunt are in town. Wedding planning." I groan dramatically, but inside, I can't wait. I can't wait to stand in front of everyone—her family, my team, the whole town of Snowberry if they want to show up—minus Dylan of course, and finally make her my wife. Dylan, ugh. I don't like to take pleasure in other people's misfortunes, but hearing he was back home, licking his wounds after getting kicked out of the mayor's office for misappropriation of funds, made me a little happy.

Groans, whistles, chirps. Jaxon chucks a roll of tape at my head.

I duck. "Hey."

"Look at you. Already whipped," Nicklas says laughing.

Yeah, I am and I love it.

"Careful, Nicklas," I warn. "You'll get yours one of these days."

"The only thing I'm getting is a double dose of bunnies tonight, Radman." He flips me off and saunters to the showers. I follow and shower quickly, anxious to get outside to my big family. I pull on my jeans and a Bucks hoodie before slipping out the side door. The March night air is cool, crisp, buzzing with leftover energy from the win. Reporters hover nearby, fans press up against the barriers waving jerseys and signs, but none of it matters. Because there's only one person I'm looking for.

Jaylynn comes running over, hair tumbling loose from her bun, headset hanging around her neck. I don't wait. I scoop her up and spin her once, catching the laugh that bursts from her throat.

"Good game, winger," she teases, her voice low just for me.

"Good game, PR queen." I kiss the top of her head, breathing her in, my heart soaring with all the things I feel for her. How did I ever get so lucky?

When I set her down, I glance up, and my chest goes tight. Her family is everywhere. Her dad is ribbing Jaxon about an open net he missed in the first period, hands waving as he exaggerates the play. Her mom is deep in conversation with Aunt Elaine, both of them laughing like old friends already. Her nieces and nephews are in full chaos mode, darting around in oversized Bucks jerseys, hockey sticks made of foam whacking at each other as if the sidewalk is their own private rink.

It's loud. It's messy. It's perfect.

And for the first time in my life, I know exactly where I fit.

Right here. With Jaylynn. With her family. With my aunt. With the team that finally feels like more than just sweaters and ice time.

This... this is home.

Jaylynn slips her hand into mine, her thumb brushing over my knuckles like she knows exactly what I'm thinking.

"Mom wants to check the country club again tomorrow," she says, wrinkling her nose. "Something about the floral arrangements clashing with the drapes."

I groan, and she laughs.

"Stop being a Grinch. You love it," she says and gives me a playful whack.

I do. Because it means we're building something together.

"I thought you liked me being a Grinch," I tease.

She rolls her eyes. "By the way," she adds slyly. "Sloane texted me. She's coming to the wedding." I honestly love that the two have grown close. Behind the glitz and glamor, and the curated social media posts, Sloane turned out to be really sweet and caring, a woman who simply needed a friend. Leave it to my girl to make sure she had one. "I might introduce her to Nicklas. They'd be cute."

I snort. "I don't know much about matchmaking. I only know Nicklas likes the bunnies. You'll have your work cut out for you."

She wags playful brows. "Yeah, well, we'll see about that."

I smile, because this—planning the future, teasing about teammates, the way the WAGs have taken her in—it all feels like proof. Proof of what we've built. A life bigger than bruises. Bigger than my past. Bigger than I ever thought I deserved.

I tug her closer until she's right up against me, the arena lights glowing behind her like a halo. "You know something, Jay?"

She tilts her head, eyes curious. "What?"

"I spent years thinking I didn't belong anywhere. Not in the league. Not in the locker room. Not even in my own skin. But then you..." My throat tightens, but I push through. "You made me see it. I do belong. With you. With this family. With all of it."

Her eyes soften, and that warmth that always undoes me pools there. "Penn..."

I kiss her before she can say more, right there in the middle of the chaos. Kids laughing. Teammates yelling. Families colliding like one big quilt stitched together by love and loyalty and hockey.

When I finally pull back, she's grinning, breathless. "You sound like a man who's found his forever."

"I am."

And for the first time in my life, I believe it down to my bones.

Forever is right here.

***

Thank you so much for reading, **PEPPERMINT STICK in my Boston Bucks series.** I hope you loved this story as much as I loved writing it. Stayed tuned for Jaxon and Rowan's story in Broken Stick.

Interested in leaving a review? Please do! Reviews help readers connect with books that work for them. I appreciate all reviews, whether positive or negative.

Happy Reading,

Cathryn

Hard Burn (Rivals)

End Zone

Fair Play

Enemy Down

Keeping Score

Trading Up

All In

Blue Bay Crew

Demolished

Leveled

Hammered

Single Dad

Single Dad Next Door

Single Dad on Tap

Single Dad Burning Up

Players on Ice

The Playmaker

The Stick Handler

The Body Checker

The Hard Hitter

The Risk Taker

The Wing Man

The Puck Charmer

The Troublemaker

The Rule Breaker

The Rookie

The Sweet Talker

The Heart Breaker

In the Line of Duty

His Obsession Next Door

His Strings to Pull

His Trouble in Talulah

His Taste of Temptation

His Moment to Steal

His Best Friend's Girl

His Reason to Stay

Confessions

Confessions of a Bad Boy Professor

Confessions of a Bad Boy Officer

Confessions of a Bad Boy Fighter

Confessions of a Bad Boy Doctor

Confessions of a Bad Boy Gamer

Confessions of a Bad Boy Millionaire

Confessions of a Bad Boy Santa

Confessions of a Bad Boy CEO

Hands On

Hands On

Body Contact

Full Exposure

Dossier

Private Reserve

House Rules

Under Pressure

Big Catch

Brazilian Fantasy

Improper Proposal

Boys of Beachville

Good at Being Bad

Igniting the Bad Boy

Bad Girl Therapy

Stone Cliff Series:

Crashing Down

Wasted Summer

Love Lessons

Wrapped Up

Eternal Pleasure Series

Instinctive

Impulsive

Indulgent

Sun Stroked Series

Seaside Seduction

Deep Desire

Private Pleasure

Captured and Claimed Series:

Yours to Take

Yours to Teach

Yours to Keep

Firefighter Heat Series

Fever

Siren

Flash Fire

Playing For Keeps Series

Slow Ride

Wild Ride

Sweet Ride

Breaking the Rules:

Hold Me Down Hard

Pin Me Up Proper

Tie Me Down Tight

Stand Alone Title:

Hands on with the CEO

Torn Between Two Brothers

Holiday Spirit

Unleashed

Knocking on Demon's Door

Web of Desire

ABOUT CATHRYN

New York Times and *USA today* Bestselling author, Cathryn is a wife, mom, sister, daughter, and friend. She loves dogs, sunny weather, anything chocolate (she never says no to a brownie) pizza and red wine. She has two teenagers who keep her busy with their never ending activities, and a husband who is convinced he can turn her into a mixed martial arts fan. Cathryn can never find balance in her life, is always trying to find time to go to the gym, can never keep up with emails, Facebook or Twitter and tries to write page-turning books that her readers will love.

Connect with Cathryn:
Newsletter https://app.mailerlite.com/webforms/landing/c1f8n1
Twitter: https://twitter.com/writercatfox
Facebook: https://www.facebook.com/AuthorCathrynFox?ref=hl
Blog: http://cathrynfox.com/blog/
Goodreads: https://www.goodreads.com/author/show/91799.Cathryn_Fox

Pinterest http://www.pinterest.com/catkalen/